Headaches Can Be
MURDER

Headaches Can Be
MURDER

Marilyn Rausch

and

Mary Donlon

North Star Press of St. Cloud, Inc.
Saint Cloud, Minnesota

Dedication

In loving memory of my parents, Walter and Virginia,
who loved crime stories. MJR

For my home cheering section, Peter, Jessica, and Rachel. MJD

First Edition, September 2012

Printed in the United States of America

Published by
North Star Press of St. Cloud, Inc.
P.O. Box 451
St. Cloud, Minnesota 56302

www.northstarpress.com

Acknowledgements

Without the guidance, support, and encouragement of two writers groups this novel would never have been completed. Our gratitude is extended to the Bob Group—Kathy, Lesley, Karen, and Linda—and the Neva Group—Nico, Mike, Deb, Elise, Jane, Becky, and Kevin.

Our thanks to Romy C Photography for our portraits.

North Star Press has welcomed us and guided us through the process. Their willingness to nurture new authors and promote regional literature is commendable.

We have benefited greatly from our new friends in the North Star Authors Google Group and Sisters in Crime.

Our families and friends have shared in our struggles and rejoiced in our triumphs, offered advice when needed and withheld it when it was not. To them we send our love.

CHAPTER ONE

Iowa, Saturday, November 13

THROUGH TRIAL AND ERROR CHIP COLLINGSWORTH had discovered his cell phone got the best reception from the roof of the tool shed on the Iowa property he had recently purchased. The rickety wooden ladder he found in the shed was missing the bottom two rungs. To get to the prime cell phone location, Chip had to launch himself onto the third rung of the old ladder, gingerly creep to the top, then perch carefully on the edge of the tin roof. The November sun, midway to its zenith, offered no warmth. Procrastinating, he pondered what he would do when ice and snow prevented him from reaching the roof.

Finally he turned on his phone and checked his messages. Four from Lucinda Patterson, his literary agent, and one from his brother Parker.

Tuesday, November 9, 9:05 a.m.
Chip, this is Lucinda. Just a friendly little nudge to remind you your first 50 pages are due tomorrow. Hope sequestering yourself at your little hobby farm has gotten your creative juices flowing.

Wednesday, November 10, 5:31 p.m.
Chip . . . Lucinda. I fully expected to have your submission today. Perhaps it is in cyberspace somewhere between Iowa and New York. I'm giving you the benefit of the doubt here, but the terms of your contract are quite clear. I need those pages pronto.

Thursday, November 11, 9:17 a.m.
No return calls, no emails, no submission . . . I'm steamed, Chip. This is inexcusable. Mystery Ink has been getting nasty. Printing of the

paperback of your first book goes to press tomorrow, and we had agreed to provide an excerpt of book two to insert at the end. What in the hell is going on? I don't care how far away you are. Get me those pages now. Oh, and they better be damn good!

Friday, November 12, 2:23 p.m.
Chip, this is Lucinda Patterson. I'm calling to inform you that you are in breach of contract. You will be contacted shortly by our lawyers. All I can say is that you will be sorry, buddy. Your career is going down the toilet. Goodbye.

Saturday, November 13, 10:31 a.m.
Hey, Chip. I'm waiting to tee off at the club. Can't believe we're still golfing in November, but it's a gorgeous day here in Baltimore. Have you turned into a hayseed yet? Call me. I have some good news.

Chip surveyed his property, the homestead of a defunct farm. When people said that someplace was "in the middle of nowhere," this was the place. The house and outbuildings had been abandoned after the original owner, a bachelor farmer, died, and the fields had been sold to neighboring farmers. All that was left was the buildings and yard. The barn listed to the left, looking as though one well-placed shove could reduce the once-mighty structure to a pile of timber.

A line of tall Norway pines surrounded the farmyard. Beyond that, as far as Chip could see, stretched harvested cornfields.

From the north a black v-shaped flock of Canadian geese came into view. As the birds glided overhead, Chip could hear their loud honks. They, too, seemed to be scolding him for his inertia.

The fields had been lush with waving green stalks of corn on the day he arrived. The sun had been high in the sky. He had gotten in his Volvo the day after the divorce proceedings from his third wife and driven west with no place in mind and no idea of how he would survive financially. Wife number two was suing him for a chunk of his earnings from his book. He stopped in the middle of Iowa at a town named Turners Bend . . . population 932. "I bet my editor would cringe at the lack of an apostrophe in the name," he said to himself as he entered the town. He had run out of gas . . . not gasoline, but the fumes that had been fueling his journey.

Now he was sitting on the roof of a tool shed, being hounded by his agent and verbally assaulted by a bunch of birds. So went life, or at least his life.

Chip found Parker on his contact list and dialed his brother's cell number.

"Hi, little brother, how's your handicap these days?"

"Better than Dad's, and that's all that counts. Hey, I finally got around to reading your book. Not bad. I understand it's a blockbuster, and you're on your way to being the next John Sandford or John Grisham. Your portrayals of Bambi and Erica were pretty thinly veiled, though. I can't believe they haven't put up a fuss."

"Oh, I've heard from Bambi's lawyer, of course. She's sleeping with him now, by the way. Erica could care less. I doubt she has even lowered herself to read it. She's too busy spending her divorce settlement in Paris. So what's the good news you called about?"

"Oh, I was made chief of staff in Neurosurgery, so you can thank me for saving the family name."

"Congrats, I appreciate it. Hey, do you ever see Mary?"

"We have coffee every once in a while at the hospital. She's nursing director of the NICU, and quite happy, I think. Her husband's a pretty decent guy, and she's crazy about those two little boys. I still can't believe you left her for Bambi."

"Let's set the record straight. I didn't leave her. She left me, and it's probably one of the smartest things she ever did. I really screwed up. She was the best thing that happened to me, and I drove her away."

"Hey, don't put yourself down. Sure you made some bad choices, but you've redeemed yourself now and you're sitting on the top of the literary world."

Chip looked at the tool shed roof. He was on top of something, anyway. "Well, I don't imagine I've redeemed myself with Dad."

"Sorry Chip, the course starter's calling my foursome. Take care."

Charles Edgar Collingsworth III, son of Dr. Charles Edgar Collingsworth Jr., the eminent neurosurgeon, and grandson of Dr. Charles Edgar Collingsworth Sr., the world-renowned pioneer of neurosurgery, sat on the roof of a tool shed in the middle of Iowa. His younger brother was now in the place where his family had expected Chip to be.

And Chip, what was he? He was a medical school dropout, who was once married to a smart, hard-working nurse, and who then married a conniving gold-digging cocktail waitress, and subsequently married his prominent Baltimore divorce lawyer. Yes, his own divorce lawyer divorced him! In the end the substantial inheritance from his grandfather was reduced to his Volvo and his laptop.

He had his therapist to thank, or perhaps blame, for him becoming a writer.

"Write down your feelings, Chip. Write about who you want to be. Visualize yourself as a successful, purpose-driven person," Dr. Cooper had said.

"I assume you mean instead of the loser that I am," Chip had replied.

He did write, but not exactly what his therapist had suggested. He wrote *The Cranium Killer*, a whodunit about a serial killer who removed the brains of his victims with surgical precision. Two of the victims were an unscrupulous cocktail waitress and a cold-hearted female attorney. He described their deaths in gory detail, dredging up anatomy lessons from his past. The hero was a brilliant neurosurgeon called in by the police to consult on the crimes. Dr. John Goodman had devoted himself to his profession and had never married, although many young, beautiful women lusted after him. But he was too busy saving lives and tracking down serial killers to return their affections.

One day in a New York bar, Chip sat down next to a tall, striking woman in a gray business suit and stiletto heels—Lucinda Patterson. A few drinks later, he had a literary agent. Two weeks later, she had sold his book to Mystery Ink, a small publisher. Much to his surprise and Lucinda's pleasure, the mystery-reading public was seduced by his lurid descriptions and charmed by the dashing doctor. Lucinda envisioned a multi-book series and signed Chip to a three-book contract. With the publisher's advance, he had updated the plumbing and electricity in his farmhouse.

Chip had set up his laptop, but nothing happened. He had vented his anger at Bambi and Erica by literally dissecting them in his first book. He had assuaged his guilt by creating as his protagonist the perfect doctor his father wanted him to be. He had eradicated his loser status and become a successful author for at least a brief illusionary period of time.

But he had nothing more to write about. He was in hot water again. Lucinda had cleverly written a penalty clause in his contract. He had to produce two more books on a tight timetable or he would lose a bundle of revenue. Dr. Cooper might say he would lose something a lot more important than money—he would lose his newly gained self-respect and purpose and his motivation to be "self-actualized," whatever the hell that meant.

It was cold on the shed roof. The wind nipped his ears, and his nose began to run. He watched tiny flakes float down and land on his jacket, each leaving a wet splotch seconds after touching the nylon shell. He turned around to descend the ladder. He planted his right foot on the top rung. His left foot reached the next rung, and the rotting wood splintered.

He fell to the ground. He heard it. The crack of his skull as it hit the ground. Chip wondered if he was "seeing stars." No. It took him a few seconds to realize they were big, fat snowflakes. An image from *Giants in the Earth* sprang into his mind . . . the farmer who goes out to his barn in a blizzard and isn't found until the snow melts in spring. Would this be how it would end for him? Alone? With no one who gave a rip about him, except for a money-hungry literary agent.

None of his limbs were bent. He had landed flat on this back and hit his head on the frozen mud that surrounded the shed. The wind had been knocked out of him.

He willed himself to breathe. Cautiously he lifted his head and felt the back of his skull. He recalled from his all-too-brief days in medical school that a bump growing out rather than swelling inward was a good sign. He inspected with his hand. Egg-sized bump, no blood, no laceration.

Slowly he rose and made his way into the house, retrieving his cell phone from the ground. He took three Double Strength Tylenol and poured himself a glass of Jack Daniel's. His head was throbbing with growing intensity and his eyes were playing funny tricks on him; images wavered before his eyes.

As he stared at the yellow linoleum floor of his kitchen, it came to him. In a flash of strobbing light, he visualized a frozen body found in the snow, perplexing forensic evidence, and the handsome Dr. Goodman called back into action.

He opened his laptop on the kitchen table and began to write the opening chapter of his second novel. He followed the well-used formula of starting with a dead body. He would end with the solution of the murder. Filling in the space between would be the challenge.

CHAPTER TWO

Brain Freeze, By Charles E. Collingsworth III
Castle Danger, Minnesota

MITCH CALHOUN SAT NAKED AT THE SCARRED PINE DESK, scribbling frantically. His normally tight, neat script was long and sprawling on the ripped out pages from a long forgotten coloring book. The tip of the pen ripped through the frail paper as he underlined his thoughts again and again.

The pen dropped to the floor as he reached up to grip his head, trying to keep it from exploding. A chain of multi-colored lights blinked in his vision, a strobe light show making him nauseous. Unsteady feet carried him into the bathroom. He flicked on the light switch, but the brightness caused another shrieking pain in his skull and he snapped it back off. The faucet handle of the shower creaked as he turned it as hot as it would go; water pipes groaned. The smell of sulfur from the old well added to his queasiness as he leaned against the wall, willing for the blessed heat to come to the water.

When steam fogged up the mirror, he stumbled into the spray, not bothering to close the shower door. Closing his eyes against the scalding sting, he waited for relief that almost always came from the hot water. Instead the pain intensified. He grabbed his head again, pushing in from both sides as if to hold it together. Dropping to his hands and knees, a wave of nausea rose up and he vomited on the floor of the shower. He crawled out of the shower onto the yellowed linoleum.

The strobe lights continued their triangular flashes in his head. Closing his eyes brought no relief. He crawled along the gritty floor on his elbows. Reaching the desk, he attempted to pull himself upright using the chair as a crutch. The chair toppled over and he fell backwards, cracking his head on the barn-board floor. Stars co-mingled with the flashing lights of his vision.

He lay there for a moment, trying to find an inner reserve of strength. *People have to know.* Sitting up slowly, carefully, he reached above his head and pulled down the sheets of the coloring book. He turned over to crawl on his hands and knees once more, gripping the sheets in his hand. He made it to the outside door, reached up to grip the brass knob and tried to stand upright. The pain pushed him down to the floor again. It was a struggle not to pass out.

After the third try, he managed to open the door. A burst of cold air and snow swirled around his wet, naked body, freezing the drops of water to his skin. He winced at the natural light streaming into the darkened cabin. His stomach lurched, and he leaned forward to retch. He fell out the door and landed hard on the frozen stoop.

The ice beneath his body was razor sharp and it ripped into his flesh. Mitch Calhoun did not feel anything, however. The aneurysm had done its job.

"HEY, DOC. WHAT DO WE HAVE HERE?" Detective Mike Frisco looked down at the frozen man on the stoop illuminated by bright spot lights. Snow had been carefully scooped away, but it continued to fall in big, fat flakes from the black sky, threatening to cover up the body once more.

Blue and red lights bounced off the planes of the detective's face. He shivered, hunching his shoulders against the snow that threatened to blow down the collar of his jacket. It was dark, it was cold, and he wanted to be anywhere but here, staring at some bare-assed dead guy. *Why the hell do I live in this tundra again?*

Medical Examiner Sid Jurgenson stood up from his crouch over the body. "Hard to say, Frisco. Looks like it's gonna be awhile before we can even thaw out the body enough to unstick him from the stoop. The guy's a friggin' popsicle. What an idiot. Even on my best drunks I knew better than to wander out into a Minnesota snowstorm without any clothes on."

Frisco shifted on his feet, trying to restore some warmth to his toes.

"So, if this is a case of some drunken bonehead who wandered out and found himself frozen to death, what do you need me for?"

"We don't have a certain cause of death, on account of his being an icicle and all. And we didn't find any booze in the cabin. You need to be involved from the get-go, just in case this turns out to be a homicide."

"Gotcha. Do we have any idea who he is?"

"Joe over there . . ." Sid thumbed in the direction of one of the officers, ". . . found some ID in the cabin. Our victim is Mitch Calhoun. He's outta Maple Grove. Poor bastard's only twenty three." He shook his head. "What a waste."

"Who found the body?"

"Ethel Johnson. She's worked for this sorry excuse of a resort for years. She came over to clean this afternoon, found the door wide open and the shower running. When she tried walking through what she thought was a snow drift at the door, she tripped and fell on our buddy here. Freaked her out but good." He chuckled. "Guess falling on some dead guy's bare backside will do that to you."

"Did she move anything?"

"Nah. She took one look at the dead guy and screamed to high heaven."

Sid turned back towards the cabin in time to see Joe crab-walking around the body with a large aluminum pot, steam rolling out into the cold air. "Excuse me, sirs." When they stepped to the side to let him through, he held out the pot in front of him with brown potholders, trying not to spill the boiling water on his uniform. "Thought this might help get the vic loosened from the pavement."

Sid clapped him on the back, causing a bit of the water to slop over the sides and onto Joe's shoes. "I always said your momma raised a smart boy. Still, I think we're going to need more than warm water on this one." He put his hand to his chin, considering the situation. "Do me a favor, will you? Call Father Mike at St. Agnes and ask if we can borrow one of them tents from the church picnics. You know, one of 'em with the sides that close. Might be able to keep the body from getting any more snow on it and give us a warmer place to work."

Joe ran off to use his cell phone. Sid got on his cell and called his office. "Bud, I need you to run over to Fleet Farm and pick up a couple/three heat lamps they got over there. Bring them on over to the cabins at Marten's resort . . . .Yeah, pronto. And, Bud? Make sure you save the damn receipt, will you? This isn't coming out of my pocket."

He snapped the phone shut and looked at Detective Frisco. "Always feels better when I've got people hopping."

— — — — — —

A FEW HOURS LATER, BETWEEN THE HEAT LAMPS and the warm water, they were able to loosen the body enough to flip it over. Sid knelt down. "That should do it. Here, give me a hand with this bad boy, will you, Frisco?"

Together, they gently pulled at the edges of the body. It came free, but several strips of skin stayed behind.

Joe jumped back. "Holy Mother of God! Look at those chunks of blood frozen around his mouth and nose. What's up with that?"

Sid and Detective Frisco leaned in to take a closer look. The ME spoke first. "Doesn't look like our boy died of exposure, now does it?" Sid took a small pan of warm water and poured it carefully on the patches of skin. Water hissed as it hit the cold concrete. He collected the pieces with tweezers and put them in a plastic evidence bag.

Detective Frisco wrinkled his nose in disgust. "How can you stand this job, Sid?"

Sid shrugged. "Comes with the territory. You just deal with it, you know? Besides, it's the least I can do to return *all* of this boy to his family." He turned to look back at the body that was waiting to be zipped up in the body bag. "Hey. What's that?" He pointed to a taupe-colored glob in the victim's hand.

"Looks like some paper or something. Hey, hand me those tweezers, will you?" The detective started pulling at the paper, but it came out in pieces.

"Better let it be until I get the body back to the lab and thaw it out completely. We sure don't want to destroy any evidence." Sid zipped up the bag and called for the gurney.

He turned back to Detective Frisco. "I've got a bad feeling about this one."

CHAPTER THREE

Turners Bend
Saturday, November 13

THROUGHOUT SATURDAY WORDS FLOWED FROM Chip's injured head and through his fingers, letter after letter, word after word marched across his laptop screen. He wrote the first chapter non-stop, while outside his farmyard silently filled with snow. A victim's frozen body had been discovered in the snow. Re-reading his description of the body elicited an "eew" from Chip. He was pleased. It never ceased to amaze him . . . readers loved blood and guts. The working title came to him in a flash.

Save to new file . . . Brain Freeze.doc. Done.

Chip looked up from the screen and was startled to see that the kitchen was dark, lit only by an eerie greenish glow emanating from his computer. All his senses had been immune to the changes around him in the hours that had passed. He awoke from his writing zone and felt like crap. The effects of the Tylenol had departed, his head pounded, his shoulders ached from hunching over the keyboard and his backside was numb from sitting for hours on the wooden kitchen chair.

The kitchen windows rattled and the dingy, dotted Swiss curtains billowed from the draft. Frost had formed on the inside of the windows, etching icy patterns. The house temperature was bone-chilling. Chip could hear the gravity furnace whirring, but that old octopus in the cellar was losing its battle against the monster blizzard raging outside the house.

Chip went to the back door and flicked on the porch light. Whirling snow obliterated the trees and shed. It eddied and swirled against the black background of the night sky. It was beautiful and frightening at the same time. He stood transfixed. It was his first Midwest whiteout and a meteorological excuse for being late with his submission to Lucinda. A fall from a ladder, a head injury, and now a blizzard—she would buy his excuses. She would know it was a crock, but the woman was driven by greed and *Brain Freeze* would be a moneymaker for her. This storm was saving his sorry ass.

The thermostat was set at seventy-two degrees but read sixty-four. Chip moved it up to eighty and put his terrycloth robe on over his clothes. The thick, white robe had been a complimentary amenity from the Caribbean cruise he and Erica had taken for their honeymoon. The contrast between the robe in its origin and the robe in this time and place made him smile and shake his head. *Poor robe, did it know how comically out of place it was in Turners Bend, Iowa? Was it suffering from culture shock?* His mouth was dry and his stomach growling.

"Now let's see, Bush's Beans or Campbell's Tomato Soup?" Chip went to the refrigerator and sniffed the carton of milk. "Fresh enough for tomato soup, I guess. Talking to myself. That's a sure sign you're cracking up, old boy. Going crazy like the sodbusters cooped up in their prairie homes during the winter."

Warmed up a little and nourished by the soup chased by a swig of whiskey, Chip returned to his computer to send Chapter One to Lucinda.

Sunday, November 14, 1:37 a.m.
Dear Lucinda,
Check the national weather. We are having a frigging blizzard here on the prairie. Phone and Internet service has been spotty. In addition, I had an accident. Just a 12-foot fall from the roof and a concussion, but not to worry, the book is coming along splendidly. Our fans will love this one. See attached.
Chip

SEND. "Pray she buys your malarkey, Chipster."

Chip powered down the laptop and shut the lid. He went to the sink and put some Dawn on a sponge and began to wash his dishes. The wind had been playing the house with an orchestra of sounds, but it suddenly died down and all was still. His ears picked up a new sound . . . first a whining sound and then a scratching that seemed to be coming from the backdoor.

A wild animal? What animals do they have in Iowa? Wolves? Coyotes? Bear? Chip had no idea. No, it really sounded more like a dog. *Wild dog? Rabid dog?* He cautiously knelt down, opened the door a crack and came nose to nose with a golden retriever with frost on its muzzle and pain in its glazed-over brown eyes. The dog whimpered again, and Chip opened the door to let it into the kitchen.

The dog, along with a cloud of snow, fell on to the kitchen floor accompanied by a loud clanging. Attached to a metal collar was a heavy iron chain and at the end the spike that had once anchored the dog to something. Its coat was matted and clumped with frozen snow and ice. It lay motionless except for his heaving chest.

"That's okay, fella, you're safe now." Chip stoked its head trying to say calming, soothing words. "Poor guy." Chip shed his terry robe and draped it over the dog, gently rubbing at the snow and ice. The dog winced. He tried unsuccessfully to remove the collar and chain. The necessary tool might be in the shed, but he wasn't eager to face the elements. It made him feel sick to think of what kind of person would mistreat a dog like this or any animal for that matter. He felt trapped and helpless, aware that he couldn't do anything more for the dog until morning. He laid down on the floor next to the dog and went to sleep, but he was haunted by disturbing dreams of bodies of men and animals in the snow.

At daybreak Chip heard a distant rumbling, and struggling to wake up, he tried to identify the sound . . . *snowplow!* His eyes shot open, and he turned from his position to check the dog's breathing. Less labored, still alive. He grabbed his parka, slipped into his snow boots and ran out the front door heading for the driveway. With each step he sunk into drifts of snow up to his crotch, finding it difficult to stay upright. Part way down the drive he saw the plow approaching and began to wildly wave his arms and shout.

The plow slowed, idled at the end of the drive and turned in, stopping just short of Chip. The driver stuck his head out the window to catch Chip's words.

"Injured stray dog . . . got to get him to a vet."

"Hop in the cab."

As the plow cleared a path to the back door, Chip took the driver's measure. The guy was huge, tall and solid with a reddish beard. He was wearing bib snow pants over a red-and-black wool shirt with thermal underwear visible at the neck and cuffs. No jacket, no hat, no gloves.

Once inside the house, Chip and the plow guy knelt by the dog and removed the robe. The driver ran his hands over the dog, checking each leg and the belly, all the while murmuring reassuring sounds.

"Name's Iver," the driver said.

"The dog?" Chip said, amazed.

The guy smirked. "Naw, I'm Iver. Don't know this hound. Anyways, not a 'he' dog. This is a 'she' dog, a female, a female carrying a litter, if I ain't mistaken. I don't much like folks who treat dogs like this. You need to get her to Doc Swanson pronto. You got a vehicle in that shed?"

"Yes, a Volvo sedan."

Iver stared at Chip and slowly shook his head and rolled his eyes. "Buster, you ain't goin' nowhere in a Volvo today. Take my advice and get yourself a decent half-ton with four-wheel drive if you're gunna live around these parts. Let's load her into the back of my cab, and I'll take the two of you to the vet in town."

Soon the three of them . . . man, dog, and giant . . . were barreling down the highway toward town, snow flying, engine roaring. Chip had never met anyone like Iver, much less conversed with him. For a long time he rode shotgun at a loss for words. Finally he made an attempt.

"Name's Chip. I'm fairly new to Turners Bend," he yelled.

"Yep, heard folks talkin' about you over at the Bun."

"The Bun?"

"The Cinnamon Bun Café. Some are sayin' you're some kind of a writer from out East. Others are suspicious, think you might be an undercover union organizer. Those guys are usually big thugs, so I'd say writer, right?"

He still had a hard time thinking of himself as a writer. It made him uneasy to think about what the people of Turners Bend were saying about him. Did they think he was as alien as he felt himself to be? Were they joking about him or ridiculing him?

"Well, I'm definitely not a union organizer. I'm surprised though that anyone would have even noticed me. I've been keeping to myself. But then I suppose you don't get new residents in this town every day."

A wry smile appeared on Iver's face, and he glanced over at Chip. "We don't get a newcomer every year, much less every day. You're a rare bird."

Chip liked to think of himself as fit and "deceivingly strong," but next to Iver he felt puny. His rimless glasses and longish hair made him feel out of place in Turners Bend. "Rare bird" felt like an all-too-apt description. Wanting to avoid further probing and to change the topic, Chip asked, "This vet in town any good with dogs?"

"Best damn vet in Boone County, even if she is a woman. Born and bred right here in Turners Bend. Dad was a vet before her. Gal knows dogs, cows, horses, and chickens, even cats and birds, I'd guess. She'll do right by your dog."

"She's not my dog. She just came to my door last night."

"That's what you think now. Just wait."

Before Chip could argue the point further, the plow pulled up to a building at the end of Main Street. A small sign read: VETERINARY CLINIC. They entered and Chip surveyed the waiting room. The floor was covered with brown-speckled tiles. Around the walls were blue fiberglass molded chairs. Incongruously, Georgia O'Keefe prints decorated the walls. The phrase "decorator's nightmare" came to Chip's mind.

Iver carried the dog to the exam room, laid her on the table and called out, "Mabel, you got a patient here."

"Hi, Iver. Church is over, so Dr. Swanson'll be down at the Bun. I'll phone her. She should be here in a jiffy," said Mabel, the sturdy-looking woman of indeterminate age with a warm smile who emerged from a room at the back of the clinic. "Don't worry, she'll take good care of your dog," she said with a nod to Chip.

"Got to get back to the plow," said Iver as he departed.

The exam room gleamed with stainless steel . . . exam table, counter tops, instruments. The pungent smell of antiseptics made the hair in

Chip's nose tingle. On the walls were anatomical posters for large animals . . . a cow's GI tract, the skeleton of a horse, a pig's inner ear.

Chip's preconceived notions of an Iowa farm vet were dashed when Dr. Jane Swanson entered the exam room. She looked to be a few years younger than his forty-six years. Her coppery-red hair was pulled back into a long pony tail, and her green eyes sparkled with energy. He was surprised by her size, five-foot-three at the most and probably less than 115 pounds. Her attractiveness stunned him and put him off balance for a few moments.

"I'm Dr. Swanson. Nice to meet you. Let's take a look at your dog." Her handshake was firm and strong.

As she approached the exam table, she saw the chain and spike. Her face turned toward Chip with fire in her eyes, and her mouth clamped tightly. Chip talked rapidly, explaining the circumstances and repeatedly stressing the "not my dog" part of the story. He watched as she lovingly, but thoroughly examined the dog.

"She's had a rough go of it. We'll start an IV with fluids and antibiotics and keep her here so we can watch her closely. I'd say the puppies aren't due for a couple of weeks yet. Let's check her for a microchip."

"A what?"

"Many owners have a small, rice-sized microchip implanted in their dog's shoulder under the skin. I have a scanner that can read the ID number off the chip. The number allows me to access owner identification data."

The vet moved a handheld scanner over the dog's shoulders. "Sorry, no chip. Truthfully though, I would not want to return a dog to anyone who chains it up like this. I'll have my assistant Mabel call you with daily updates. If she pulls through and has the puppies, we'll let you know when you can pick them up."

"Them?" Chip croaked. "But she's *not* my dog."

"We'll see. In the meantime, Mabel will radio Iver in the plow to swing back and take you home. I assume you're the newcomer to Turners Bend."

"Yes, I'm Chip Collingsworth. Thanks for all your help Dr. Swanson. I'm sorry to disturb you on a Sunday."

"Dr. Swanson was my father. Folks here call me Dr. Jane and you're most welcome Mr. Collingsworth."

— — — — — —

BACK IN HIS KITCHEN CHIP MADE A POT OF COFFEE and sat in front of his laptop. He checked his email and found a response from Lucinda. It might be Sunday, but Lucinda was never far from her Blackberry.

Sunday, November 14, 12:32 p.m.
Chip,
Brilliant first chapter. All is forgiven this time, but I expect the full draft completed no later than May 1, so get humping, farm boy. I like the Brain Freeze *title. BTW, Dr. Goodman is in need of some good sex, and don't skimp on the details.*
Lucinda

Chip opened his *Brain Freeze* file. He read the description of the body found in the snow and thought about brain traumas. What could have happened to this guy? His mind switched to the story's location as he dredged up images and details about Duluth and Two Harbors from his memory of summer visits to his Uncle Edward. Ed had owned an iron ore barge company there at one time. He remembered the sensational murders at Glensheen; maybe he could work that into his story.

He couldn't focus. The past twelve hours kept replaying in his head . . . the dog, Iver, the microchip scan, Dr. Jane Swanson . . . especially her. He wrote a list of words to describe Jane: professional, compassionate, clearly competent, stunning. Story ideas about a female character, a woman who would capture Dr. Goodman the way Dr. Jane had entranced him, began to form, then to percolate and finally to appear on the first page of the next chapter of *Brain Freeze*.

Chapter Four

Brain Freeze
Minneapolis, Minnesota

Dr. John Goodman shifted in his seat. Airplane seats were not built with his six-foot-three frame in mind. He set aside the file he was reviewing on the pull-down tray and looked out the window. His mind wandered as his eyes took in the cloud cover below the aircraft.

He had been surprised to hear about another case from his old friend, Mark Tinsdale. He and Mark had been college roommates and had stayed in touch, in spite of the different paths their lives had taken. John had gone on to med school and became a neurosurgeon. Mark had joined the FBI and married his college sweetheart. He had called John in to work on the Cranium Killer case last year, but John had thought that was a one-time thing. Now Mark needed his help again.

John smiled at the memory of Mark's phone call, "We have a new case that I think you'll be interested in. God knows we could use your help. And John? Grab your parka, my friend. You're headed to the North Country."

Mark made it clear that he wouldn't be working with him on this case, however. Another agent, Joe Schwann, would be his contact person. Agent Schwann was based in Minneapolis, which had jurisdiction in Duluth, the location of the crime. Mark didn't go into a lot of detail about the case, but had told him it concerned unusual brain trauma. Since John's specialty was neurosurgery, Mark said that his insight would be invaluable.

John was intrigued. Truth be told, the timing couldn't have been better. He needed a change. The last couple of weeks had been tough. One of his favorite patients, an eight-year-old girl with a dimpled smile, big blue eyes, and, unfortunately, a brain tumor had died the previous Tuesday. In spite of all his expertise, his degrees, his credentials, John was unable to save her. He felt responsible. Everyone lost patients now and then, but sometimes the loss hit him especially hard.

Doctors were always warned not to get emotionally involved with their patients. But, friends and colleagues insisted that it was his compassion that made John so good at his job. But damn if it didn't feel personal sometimes.

On top of losing the little girl, his private life was a train wreck. Tanya, his girlfriend of the last two years had finally given up on him and moved out. John frowned at the memory of their last conversation.

He had been holding her hand, trying to make her understand. "Tanya, we've been through this before. My job has to come first. My patients deserve my full attention. Can't you see that?"

She yanked her hand from his grip. "You know what I think, *Dr. Goodman?* I think you hide behind that job of yours so that you never have to commit to a relationship. What are you so damned afraid of?"

As he sat on the plane en route to Minneapolis, he had time to consider her question. *What am I afraid of exactly?* He *did* care for Tanya. But maybe it wasn't enough. He was beginning to think he wasn't cut out to be in a relationship. Maybe he was just a flawed human being, unwilling to care too much for someone, because it hurt to lose them. Like that little eight-year-old girl with the pixie smile.

The pilot's voice came on over the speakers, "Ladies and gentleman. We have begun our final descent into Minneapolis/St. Paul International airport. The current temperature is a balmy fifteen degrees. It's been our pleasure to fly with you from our origination point of Baltimore/Washington International airport. We hope you have a pleasant stay."

John gathered up his scattered files and drank the remainder of his soda. He closed up the tray and stored his belongings beneath the seat in front of him. After several minutes encased in clouds, the plane broke through. The snow-covered buildings and streets of the Twin Cities appeared out his window as the plane banked to line up with its runway. He took a deep breath and closed his eyes. Landings were never John's favorite.

— — — — —

THE FEMALE MORNING-DRIVE DJ WAS CHEERFUL as she reported doom and gloom on the commute. *"Eastbound lanes of Highway 62 are shutdown at the Cedar*

Avenue/77 exit due to a jackknifed semi-trailer. We suggest you find an alternate route to your destination. . . ."

"Great. Now they tell me." Special Agent Jo Schwann clicked off the radio in disgust. She looked at the clock on the dash. "Today, of all days."

It had been one of those mornings. The old furnace in her 1920s house had petered out last night, and she woke to a chilly fifty-eight degrees. Jo spent forty minutes arranging to have it replaced while she was out of town. No heat for several days would mean frozen pipes in these temperatures.

She loved her house. It was in the Tangletown part of Minneapolis, so called because of the winding streets that took their directional cue from Minnehaha Creek flowing through the area. Jo spent most of her precious free hours restoring the house to its original beauty. It was at times like this, though, that a maintenance-free apartment seemed enticing.

The next snag in her day had appeared when she loaded her luggage into her FBI-issued vehicle, only to find it wouldn't start. Rather than calling a tow truck, she transferred everything to her personal SUV and headed out. Now this.

She tapped her fingers on the steering wheel. She hated to be late for anything. An expert for her next case was waiting for her at the airport.

Looking around at the sea of cars inching along with her, it was hard not to feel a bit claustrophobic. She could see into the red VW Beetle next to her. The driver was talking on his cell phone while eating an Egg McMuffin from McDonalds. Of course, no hands on the steering wheel.

Her mind drifted to last night. Kara, a friend at work, had set her up on a blind date, something Jo had been resisting for months. Jo finally caved. It *had* been a long time since she had been out, though she told herself that the fault lay in the hours and demands of her job—they left little room for a social life.

They arranged to meet at an Irish pub in St. Paul. Her date, Cory, was not at all what she expected. Kara had said that he was a huge hockey fan, played in college in fact. He had gotten tickets to see the Minnesota Wild take on the Anaheim Ducks, and they were going to the game after a quick bite to eat. She expected a tall, outgoing guy with blond hair and blue eyes—the standard Nordic Minnesotan.

Instead, he had a slight build and dark hair, with artsy glasses over brown eyes. When the hostess led her to his table, Cory stood up and knocked over his drink, spilling it on her shoes. "Oh, man. I'm so sorry. Here, let me." He got down on his knees and began wiping her shoes with his napkin. "So clumsy of me."

The night had gone down hill from there. Throughout the meal of fish and chips, Cory was nice, but painfully shy. He wouldn't look her in the eye when he spoke and answers to her questions were mumbled.

After dinner, they walked to the Xcel Energy Center to watch the Wild play. Cory came alive at the game. He drank too many beers, shouted obscenities at the refs and was rude to the people around them. Jo enjoyed hockey as much as the next person raised in Minnesota, but not this time.

When he walked her back to the car, the testosterone-and-beer buzz from the game evidently gave him courage. As she reached into her purse for her car keys, he pulled her tight to him and shoved his tongue in her mouth. When his hands crept down to her butt, she ground the heel of her boot into his foot.

Hopping around on his good foot, he shouted, "Ow! Whatcha do that for? We were getting on so well. Thought you girls with guns liked things a little, um . . . exciting."

She rolled her eyes, clamping her mouth shut to the things she really wanted to say. As she closed her car door, she said instead, "Goodbye, Cory." She crossed blind dates off her mental to-do list.

Jo sighed. Maybe she wasn't meant to find a significant other. Men were either intimidated by what she did for a living or were weirdly fascinated by it. A few months ago, she'd gone out with a guy who continually asked to see her gun. *Ick.*

Her mind landed back in the present. She reached an exit off the backed-up highway and zig-zagged through neighborhoods until she was able to merge onto the interstate heading to the airport. Traffic was slower than normal because of the slippery roads, but at least she was moving.

Jo thought about the case she was about to take on in Duluth. A young man with an aneurysm, but with a twist that brought the FBI onto the scene. She wasn't thrilled about heading up to her old stomping grounds, but her boss thought she was the best agent for the case. On the bright side, she was looking forward to seeing Sid, her father's old friend. He was the ME on the case and had contacted the Bureau when he found out what had caused the burst artery in Mitch Calhoun's head.

Only a few miles from the airport, she passed the exit for the Mall of America on I-494 when a dented green car with Kentucky tags swerved in front of her, causing Jo to react. The SUV's anti-lock brakes shuddered as they tried to gain traction on the snow-packed road. Her heart pounded. A few more feet and she would have slammed into the back end of the guy. She rolled her eyes skyward. "Save me from people who don't know how to drive in snow."

Jo pulled into the short-term parking lot at the airport. She wondered about the neurosurgeon flying in to help out with the case. Her track record with outside experts was spotty. The last one assigned to her had led them on the wrong path. She'd wasted countless hours chasing down a dead-end lead.

Jo glanced down at the picture on the passenger seat. The office had faxed it to her house this morning, along with the flight information of the expert. She had to admit the guy was good-looking. *Not that it mattered.*

JOHN'S FLIGHT ARRIVED A FEW MINUTES EARLY at the Lindberg terminal. He collected his bag from the baggage claim and looked around. Mark had said that Agent Schwann would meet him here.

Waiting for his ride, he sat on one of the rows of connected seats in front of the revolving baggage claim carosels. Amongst all the people hustling in and out of the airport, he noticed a young woman holding a rose. She bit her lip, looking left and right. Tears filled her eyes and she walked over to a gray metal trash can and dropped the rose in. John watched her turn and walk out the automatic doors, into the blustering winds of a January day. *Yeah, love was like that.*

"Dr. Goodman?" John turned his head in time to see a woman hurrying toward him, hand raised. "Excuse me, are you Dr. John Goodman?" John didn't answer for a moment. Mark hadn't told him the agent was a woman, let alone a very attractive redhead with startling green eyes. If he remembered, Mark had said the agent's first name was Joe. But that had been over the phone. Clearly "Joe" was really "Jo."

He got to his feet as she reached him. She stood in front of him, looking up into his face. She enunciated carefully, as if she was talking to a daydreaming teenager. "Excuse me. Are you Dr. John Goodman?"

John looked down at his picture in her hand. Feeling slightly foolish for his reaction to this beautiful woman, he cleared his throat and said, "Um, yes. I'm Dr. Goodman. I presume you are Agent Schwann. Pleased to meet you." He reached out his hand and smiled.

Her handshake was surprisingly firm for such a petite woman—she barely came up to his chin. She looked him up and down, as if taking his measure. John briefly wondered if he met her initial approval. For some reason he didn't understand, it mattered to him.

Jo tilted her head and then smiled. "Welcome to Minnesota, Doctor. I hope you haven't been waiting long. Traffic was crazy and well . . ." Her voice trailed off.

"Not a problem. Just arrived a few minutes ago."

She nodded. "Hope you had a good flight. Please, follow me."

Jo led the way, with John pulling his roller bag behind them. She turned to him on the escalator, "The FBI offices are located here in Minneapolis, but we'll be heading north to Duluth to talk to the ME. I was told you would prefer to view the body in person. The drive will take a couple of hours . . . three if the weather gets worse."

They followed the carpeted hallway past a Caribou Coffee, went up another escalator and walked out automatic doors into a frigid parking lot. The cold made John gasp. He pulled his collar up around his ears. "Jeez. Haven't they ever heard of heat in this state?"

Jo chuckled. "You get used to it. Or at least, you learn to tolerate it. This one's a blast coming in from Canada."

A good healthy shiver made him tense up. "Damn Canadians. This is just not right."

"Wait until you get up north. It's another ten degrees colder up there." Jo grabbed his bag and threw it into the back of her SUV.

They climbed in, and she reached over, snapping on a button to the left of his leg. "Let me introduce you to the invention that has saved the backsides of countless Northerners. The butt warmer."

In a few moments, heat began to circulate through him. He relaxed into the warm leather seat and closed his eyes. "Remind me to send a thank you note to the inventor."

They left the parking garage and headed north. Once they left the Twin Cities area, Interstate 35 was a flat, snowy stretch of road, dominated by semis roaring by, stirring up eddies of snow. Bright sunshine glared off the snow and John reached for the sunglasses he kept in the pocket of his North Face jacket.

John turned in his seat to face Jo. He studied her profile. Daylight coming in through the sunroof lit up her curly hair, making it glow with fire. Jo had pulled it back into a no-nonsense twist, but a few unruly curls had managed to spring loose around her ears. She had long eye lashes, with just a hint of mascara. He cleared his throat. "So, Agent Schwann, tell me about this case. Why is this particular death getting so much attention?"

Jo took her eyes off the Black Bear Casino bus in front of them to glance at John. "A week ago, we got a call from an ME in Duluth. He'd been called on what he thought was going to be a routine case—some drunk kid who wandered out into the cold and died of exposure. Once he got there, he discovered the body was frozen solid. Took him several days to thaw it out." Jo put on her blinker and passed the bus.

"Immediately, he found a few things that told him this was no ordinary case. First, once he was able to straighten the victim's fingers, he found scraps of paper crumpled up in the guy's hand. They were pages torn from a coloring book and had writing all over them."

"What do they say?"

"Most of the writing was illegible, but they did get a few phrases. It said, 'I won't kill' and 'they can't make me' and others to that effect."

"Well, that's certainly weird, but what's all that got to do with needing my help?"

"When the ME performed the autopsy, he found the vic's skull full of blood. It was the work of an aneurysm."

"Again, what does this have to do with me?"

Jo turned her green eyes on John. "The ME found a microchip at the site of the aneurysm."

John's eyes opened wide. "A microchip? I've read several research papers on microchip use in the brains of monkeys, but I hadn't heard that they've been testing them in humans." He thought for a moment, then said, "Shouldn't the Food and Drug Administration be involved, not the FBI? Incidents in which a medical device may have caused or contributed to a death are supposed to be reported to FDA under the Medical Device Reporting program. Seems like this clearly falls under their jurisdiction."

"We're entering the case with the full sanction of the FDA. They recently conducted a series of premarket approval reviews of the device involved. The results were clean." Jo shook her head. "A little *too* clean. And quick. The authorization was pushed through in nearly record time.

"The FDA inspector in charge disappeared immediately after the last review was completed. The investigation into her disappearance revealed that she had recently deposited large sums of cash into her bank account. These deposits corresponded directly with the time period of her audits."

John whistled through his teeth. "Has anyone taken a look at the microchip itself?"

"The ME sent the chip to our offices, and our technology experts have been taking it apart. This was not an ordinary medical gadget. It appears to have functions similar to those used in other artificial intelligence devices. We believe it was a control device."

John snorted. "A control device? You don't think this is some James Bond movie concept where the villainous company purposely creates mind control devices, do you Agent Schwann?"

Jo turned to him, eyes flashing. "James Bond movie concept? Nah, I'd say this is an accepted theory. Don't you think there are plenty of dictator nut-jobs and terrorists who would love to get their hands on microchip technology to control their enemies?"

"I think it's highly unlikely. Think of all the good that could come out of microchip technology. People with brain damage, strokes, Alzheimer's, seizures . . . the possibilities are endless."

"Yes, and the possibilities for abuse are endless as well. That's why there has to be the proper governmental oversight on this . . ."

John interrupted. "I believe in government oversight up to a point. But I've seen first-hand what happens when a group of overzealous bureaucrats get their hands on projects like this. It's a nightmare of red tape. Meanwhile, there are thousands of people who could use the technology right now to vastly improve their lives."

"Government oversight in the medical field is vital. Our vic proves that point."

She has me there. John had been frustrated numerous times over the years when technology that would help a current patient was unavailable due to the long process of FDA approvals. However, the death of Mitch Calhoun spoke volumes.

John looked out the window, thinking about the idea of a microchip for the brain. *Fascinating.* Suddenly, he sat up straight, noticing his surroundings for the first time in a couple of hours. "Hey, that's a beautiful sight, isn't it?"

They had rounded a bend and were looking down over the harbor at the outskirts of Duluth. Several manufacturing plants dotted the edge of an ice-covered bay, pillows of smoke rising from their stacks. Jo pointed out the bridge to Wisconsin that spanned the bay. John said, "I've never been to Lake Superior before. I didn't know it would be so impressive."

They drove through the downtown area, passing restaurants, office buildings, and shops. Kids with University of Minnesota at Duluth jackets hurried along the streets, stepping into coffee shops. They passed the arched gateway leading to the Canal Park area, then continued northward on Highway 61, driving by the beautiful old mansions built with iron ore money perched on the cliffs overlooking Lake Superior.

Jo pointed out the largest mansion to John. It was tucked behind enormous wrought iron fencing. "That's the Glensheen Mansion. It was built by Charles Congdon in the early 1900s. He had his fingers in all kinds of business pies, particularly iron ore. His daughter, Elisabeth inherited the house when he died just ten years after he moved in. She didn't have any biological children, but adopted a daughter. A wild child, to say the least. The daughter got into drugs, the wrong sorts of men, all that. She ended up killing her elderly mother and a nurse in the mansion in the seventies.

"It's open to tours now. 'Course, they don't bring up the murders on the tour, unless someone asks them. They think homicide is bad for business." Jo shrugged her shoulders. "I don't know about that. Seems to me they'd have more tours because of it. People are suckers for ghost stories, you know?"

"You seem to know a lot about this town. Are you from around here?"

She took a moment to respond. When she did, she was looking straight ahead, not at John. "Yes, I am."

He waited a beat for her to add more. When the silence dragged on, he said, "And now you live in Minneapolis and are an agent of the F. B. of I."

Her voice had an edge to it. "That's me. I live in Minneapolis and I'm an FBI agent. Listen, you're not going to be one of those know-it-all experts who asks nosy personal questions, are you?"

John was taken aback at her abruptness. They stared at each other a moment. He wasn't quite sure what note he struck, but it obviously wasn't a good one. John spoke first. "You know, I think we've gotten off on the wrong foot. I'm sorry, I didn't mean to pry. Just making small talk." He looked around. They seemed to have left civilization behind. "Um, are we almost there?"

"Damn it! Missed the turn." She pulled into the next parking lot and did a U-turn. Once they were headed back into town, she spoke up. "Look, I'm the one who should apologize. You asked a perfectly innocent question and I overreacted. Please accept my apologies."

"No problem. I *am* a bit nosy sometimes." He smiled at her and her lips curved upward in response. He found himself trying to think of ways to get a glimpse of that smile again.

CHAPTER FIVE

Turners Bend
Thanksgiving Week

Dᴜʀɪɴɢ ᴛʜᴇ ɴᴇxᴛ ᴡᴇᴇᴋ Cʜɪᴘ ꜰᴇʟʟ ɪɴᴛᴏ ᴀ daily routine attuned to the rhythm and pace of life in Turners Bend. Sandwiched between breakfast at the Bun and an evening beer at the Bend, he worked on *Brain Freeze*. From his vantagepoint as a stranger in town, he keenly observed the events playing out before him, and these observations began to show up in his story in sometimes subtle, and sometimes not so subtle, ways.

The Bun had last been furnished in the sixties with gray linoleum floors and a gray Formica-covered counter. The counter stools and booths were upholstered in dark-red Naugahyde, and the tables were covered with red-and-white-checked plastic tablecloths. Roosters and chickens were printed on the café curtains that covered the bottom half of the front windows. Customers could sit at the tables and still see over the top of the curtains, so as not to miss any action on Main Street.

The café was a beehive of activity every weekday morning. Chip saw the same people, sitting in the same places and eating the same breakfasts morning after morning. This was a routine he had never observed in the Baltimore deli where he got a bagel and schmear to go every morning. No regulars lingered at the deli.

By the end of the week, he had staked out his own place, where he sat alone. It was a small table with a good view of the whole café. He got a few nods and waves, but never an invitation to join another table. It made him feel somewhat like a high school geek, but it did allow him to soak up the local culture and gather color for *Brain Freeze*.

He settled on his breakfast . . . two eggs over-easy, bacon, and wheat toast. On the menu it was called the Bender. He thought it might make him look like he belonged. The bacon was thick-sliced and dotted with pepper. The toast was slathered in butter to which he added homemade strawberry preserves. His cardiologist would have a heart attack if he knew.

Not only the breakfast fare was of interest to him, but also the clientele. Each morning a group of farmers surrounded one of the large tables. The corn had been harvested, and these guys seemed to have time on their hands. They all wore grimy seed caps and plaid flannel shirts and a few actually wore bib overalls. He listened to the clinking of spoons, as sugar and cream were added to cups of steaming black coffee. He was fascinated by one of the oldest-looking farmers, who poured his coffee into his saucer to drink it, another sight he had never witnessed in Baltimore. Conversations started with comments on the weather and proceeded to commodity prices for the day and then on to the fine art of farming. Chip understood little of what was discussed, but he loved their terse sentences and the Scandinavian lilt that reached his ears.

"Water froze up in the trough last night."

"Ja, goin' ta be a cold one this winter. Predicted in the *Almanac*."

"See that new Chalmers over at Bud's place? She's a hellava machine."

"Hear it's got that newfangled GPS system. Foolishness, if you ask me."

"Prices don't get better, he'll be riding that baby right back to the bank."

He wished he had brought along a notebook to record this Midwest language, but then again that might raise even more suspicion about him.

One large booth near the front window was frequented by Turners Bend dignitaries . . . the mayor, the chief of police, the owner of the Feed and Seed and the president of Community Bank and Trust. All were men with too much around their waists and not enough on top of their heads. At times various merchants from along Main Street joined them. Chip picked up tidbits of local doings from this direction, tuning in especially when Chief Walter Fredrickson reported on recent crimes . . . lots of domestics and drunken assaults and an occasional drug bust.

"Hey, Chief, heard Pastor Henderson's boy tried to set up a meth lab in the basement and nearly blew himself to kingdom come."

"Ja, can't wait for next Sunday's sermon. Henderson should send that prodigal son packing. Boy's a bad seed."

"That free-for-all at the Bend last night was a doozie. Some of those boys will never grow up."

His growing interest in all things criminal still surprised him at times. But crime was apparently going to be his genre, and he didn't want to mess with success.

Workers from AgriDynamics, the town's biggest employer, occupied the other large booth. Men from the third shift overlapped with workers for the first shift. They spoke in hushed tones with heads huddled together. Chip could only catch snippets of the conversation.

". . . it's got to stop . . ."

". . . Jesus, I can't afford to lose my job . . ."

". . . the bastard's making a fortune off our backs . . ."

Facial expressions in the group of workers ranged from fear to frustration and from anger to wariness. A head would occasionally pop up with furtive eyes scanning the café's crowd. Chip shifted his chair to catch more of the conversation. Something was going on at AgriDynamics, and it piqued his curiosity. Sinister dealings within a manufacturer could be fuel for his next chapter.

Mabel and Iver sat together at the counter every morning, sometimes joking with each other or with Bernice the waitress and sometimes talking softly in serious, intimate tones.

"You should cut down on the eggs and bacon, Iver. I'm worried about your cholesterol." Mabel placed her hand on Iver's ham-sized arm.

"Don't worry your pretty little head about me, Mabel. It's you we should be fretting about. You work too hard." He reached his arm around her and patted her shoulder.

"If it weren't for my job, I'd be too lonesome. Plus, Jane needs me."

The two would occasionally stop for a few minutes at Chip's table, and they became his first friends in Turners Bend. They were unlike any friends he had ever had, but he was really feeling the need for friends in this town. And strange as it seemed to him, he really liked this "salt of the earth" couple.

"Chip, your dog is a real sweetie," said Mabel as she departed, leaving Iver sitting at the counter. "When Dr. Jane and I are in the office, we let her out, and she follows us around from room to room. I can see she's a real people dog. You got to give her a name, you know. A dog should have a name."

"Well, Mabel, if she's so sweet, why don't you call her 'Honey'?"

"That's perfect. I should have known a writer like you would come up with just the right name. You should be a daddy soon, maybe on Thanksgiving."

Without missing a beat, she continued, "Now about Thanksgiving, you'll come, won't you? Iver, bless his heart, is going to make a deep-fried turkey. Dr. Jane is coming cuz Hal is taking Ingrid and Sven to Disney World. She's bringing the pies. So it's all settled. You come on Thursday about noon. See you then."

Mabel bustled out the door, leaving Chip's head spinning. What in the hell was he going to do with a dog and puppies? Would a deep-fried turkey be like a giant Chicken McNugget? Ingrid and Sven . . . sounded like a comedy team you would hear on the *Prairie Home Companion* radio show. He took his coffee cup and moved to the counter stool next to Iver, hoping for elucidation.

"So, Iver, you and Mabel an item?"

"A what?"

"Do I sense a romance?"

Iver lifted his empty coffee cup, and Bernice gave him a refill.

"Nah, I'm one of those confounded bachelors. She's a widow lady. Her husband, Stan, was a hell of a nice guy. Blew a gasket in his head and died right there in their bed. What about you? You got a lady friend?"

Chip removed his glasses and wiped a butter smear off his lenses with a paper napkin while he gave Iver's questions some thought.

Then he answered, "No, I'm currently a 'confounded' bachelor, too. Say, Mabel just mentioned Ingrid and Sven, are they Dr. Swanson's kids?"

"Yes . . . named after their great-grandparents who came over from the Old Country. They were on the same boat as my grandparents, Astrid and Olaf Ingebretson. Ingrid's a pretty little thing like her mom. She's going to follow in her mother's footsteps and be a vet. Yup, she's got a special way with animals. Don't know what to say about Sven. That boy's a handful, and it's his old man's fault. Jane and Hal been divorced for a long time."

Something inside Chip stirred as he heard this new piece of information. Divorced. Possibly available. He didn't want to sound too eager, but he sure wanted to know more. Or did he? He had vowed to stay away from women. Either they messed up his life or he messed up their lives.

"Does their father live around here?"

"Oh, ja, you can find him over at the Bend most nights, mean son of a bitch when he's drinking and an asshole when he's sober. Thinks he's a big shot because he owns AgriDynamics. Name's Harold H. Swanson III. Uppity name, isn't it?" Chip made a mental note never to use his full name in Turners Bend. Charles Edgar Collingsworth III, impressed people in Baltimore, but in Turners Bend his name would set him apart in a very different way.

Changing topics, Chip asked, "What's going on over there with the workers from AgriDynamics?"

"Rumor has it one of them is going to blow the whistle on old Hal and his shady doings. Hope they do. Guy would sell his own mother down the river. Wouldn't want to put my life on the line to rat on him, though."

Chip and Iver sat together, each quietly sipping their coffee, listening to Bernice softly sing "Cracklin' Rosie," as she polished the stainless steel milk dispenser. Behind the counter Chip spied a copy of *The Cranium Killer*, the back cover facing up. There was the dreadful photograph that Lucinda had insisted on using, one of him holding his eyeglasses and wearing a black turtleneck. He hated that picture, didn't own a black turtleneck and hadn't worn one since high school. Even worse was the front cover, a bloody hand holding a brain. Again, that was Lucinda's idea, and she most definitely called the shots when it came to the jacket graphics. Nevertheless, he was surprised to see the book in Turners Bend and even more surprised to see it behind the café's counter. He wondered if Bernice was reading it. If so, that might account for the strange looks she sometimes gave him.

— — — — — —

BACK AT HIS COMPUTER FOR A DAY OF WRITING, Chip started the next chapter of *Brain Freeze*. He needed to concentrate on the "blown gasket" and microchip in his victim's head, but his mind kept veering off to the beautiful redheaded veterinarian. He had sworn off women, but hearing that she was divorced made him think about her. She was a lot like Mary in many ways, a caring woman with solid values who would most likely know better than to get involved with a guy like him. Anyway, two teenage kids were some serious baggage to avoid. *That was like sticking your knife into the toaster, right?*

Finally he forced himself to stop his spinning and reeling about Dr. Jane and to channel his energy into Dr. Goodman and Jo. Living in their lives was a hell of a lot easier than living in this own. He wished he had not tossed out all his first-year medical schoolbooks. He did not lack for medical resources right within his own family. But, calling his father was out of the question. He avoided talking with him as much as possible. Conversations with Dr. Collingsworth Jr., always spiraled into lectures about Chip's failures, delivered in his father's unmistakable tone of condescension, tinged with disappointment. Chip had spent lots of hours on his analyst's couch talking about his "unresolved father issues." After thousands of dollars, they were still "unresolved."

He called Parker, his father's favored child.

"How's my little bro?"

"Up to my neck in lesions and tumors, as usual."

Yup, he had made the right choice not to be a doctor. "I need some info. If you were to plant a microchip into a brain to control inhibitions, where would you plant it?"

Parker gave a brief laugh. "Well, I'm not in the mind control business, I leave that up to the CIA and KGB. I assume this is for your next novel. Is our hero Dr. Goodman going to loosen the inhibitions of some sexy blonde?"

"No, something more sinister than that, I think, although I'll keep that in mind."

Chip took notes as Parker described various areas of the brain and brain stem and regaled him with his knowledge of recent research in the treatment of various seizure disorders and neurological diseases.

"And aneurysms, where do they most often occur?"

"The Circle of Willis, an arterial circle at the base of the brain."

"Thanks, Parker. I'll give you credit in my acknowledgements."

"Ah, that's sure to impress my colleagues in the American Society of Neurosurgeons. Got to go, Chip, my beeper's going off."

Maybe he was being too sensitive, but he heard it in Parker's parting remark, that bit of sarcasm and their father's tone, the cutting edge that always sliced into Chip's ego. He got the information he needed for his novel, but it grazed his self-image. Dr. Cooper would probably advise him to ignore it . . . "Let it go, Chip," he said to himself.

CHAPTER SIX

Brain Freeze
Duluth, Minnesota

THE ST. LOUIS COUNTY MEDICAL EXAMINER'S office was located within the University of Minnesota at Duluth's School of Medicine. Jo pulled onto the campus and drove down roads narrowed by tall snow banks. Bundled up students trudged along freshly plowed sidewalks, heads bent down to protect their faces from the wind coming off Lake Superior. John wondered if the students recognized each other when they finally saw their faces again in the spring.

The School of Medicine was a no-nonsense, modern building of tan and red brick, running along University Drive. Jo showed her badge to the guard in the station house before entering the parking lot.

As she circled the lot looking for a parking spot, John said, "I forgot to ask. Who manufactured the chip?"

"The serial number on the chip traces back to a corporation called NeuroDynamics, Inc. Ever heard of them?"

John nodded. "I certainly have. The founder of the company, Charles Candleworth, was an old classmate of mine at Johns Hopkins. I ran into him at a neurology conference a couple of years back, and he tried to get me to join his company, working in research. Turned him down flat—I never liked the guy. Always cutting corners in med school. He got caught dealing research papers to other students. Daddy's money hushed it up."

"Well, it looks like Candleworth may be into something considerably more sinister these days." She pulled the SUV into the last spot available in the lot.

"So, tell me about the ME. Is he any good?"

She put the car in park and shut off the engine. "His name's Sid Jurgenson. He's been around forever. A bit of a legend in this part of Minnesota. He's like Brett Favre—says he's going to retire, then changes his mind. Truth is, people here will be sorry at that retirement party. If you'll pardon the expression, he knows where all the bodies are buried."

"Agent Tinsdale says he's quite a character."

Jo chuckled. It was a deep, throaty sound. A wonderful laugh. "That he is. No doubt about it. He's a bit rough around the edges, with a dark sense of humor. Once you get used to that, though, you realize that nothing gets past him."

They entered the doorway and received visitor passes. Their snow covered shoes squeaked on the highly polished floors. Jo led the way to the ME's office.

Behind the reception desk sat a harried looking woman with springy gray hair. Jo and John stood for a moment, waiting for her to notice them. Jo finally cleared her throat. "Excuse, me. We're here to see Sid Jurgenson." The woman peered over her leopard-print reading glasses. She looked them up and down before responding, "And you are . . . ?"

Jo sighed and straightened her shoulders. "I'm Special Agent Jo Schwann of the FBI." She gestured toward John. "And this is Dr. John Goodman. Dr. Jurgenson is expecting us."

The woman reached for the telephone without responding. She punched a button and then spoke into the receiver. "Sid. Some FBI agent and a doc here to see you. Should I send 'em in or tell them to take a seat?"

She nodded and hung up the phone. She tilted her head toward a hallway on the left. "Sid's waiting for you. Go through those double doors over there. He's in the first room on the right." She went back to her paperwork without comment.

When they were out of earshot, John muttered, "She's got the personality of one of those snow banks outside. I'll bet she gets along great with the clientele in here." John looked over at Jo and was rewarded with a smile.

"Wait 'til you meet Sid."

John raised an eyebrow.

Just then, the man in question came through the door. He was the same height as Jo, and bent slightly forward, looking as if he might topple over at any minute. What little hair he had left was pure white and circled a pale, liver-spotted pate. Behind him trotted a golden retriever, nails clicking on the tiled floor. The ME thrust out his hand. "Sid Jurgenson. Glad to meet you! You must be Dr. Goodman." He turned to Jo. "Little Josie Schwann. Good to see you again, girl." He wrapped Jo in a bear hug and looked back at John. "I've known Josie here since she was just a little snippet. Her dad and I were in med school together, way back."

"Good to see you too, Sid. You haven't change a bit. Your wife out there gave us a warm welcome, as always. You would think she'd recognize me."

John coughed. "Your . . . your wife? Um, lovely woman . . ."

Sid clapped him hard on the back, forcing John to step forward to keep his balance. "Yup. That's my Martha. Been my bride for going on forty-eight years. Real dragon lady, isn't she?"

John's eyes widened. "Well, that is . . ."

Sid let out a big belly laugh. "Don't worry. You can't offend me. She's a handful, but she puts up with me and Josie here will tell you that's not easy to do. Don't take offense at her manner. She barely acknowledges knowing *me* sometimes. But, I couldn't run this office without her." He reached down to pat the head of the dog waiting patiently by his side. "And this here's Caddy."

"Caddy, as in golf? Is that your sport?"

"Nah. Never could stand chasing that little bitty ball around all day, calling it a sport. Her full name is Cadaver. Got her when I responded to a call at a farmhouse. There she was, nothing but a pup, cuddled up to the side of her recently deceased master. Been with me ever since. Had to start calling her Caddy, 'cause her real name kinda creeped out the grandkids." He looked down at the dog. "Couldn't run the office without you either, could we, girl?" Caddy barked in response, tail pounding the wall behind her.

"Now that the introductions are over and done with, let's head into the lab and I'll show you what you've come for." He pointed down the hall. "Caddy, office." The dog trotted down the hallway and entered a doorway, hips swaying and tail wagging.

"Beautiful dog you've got there, Dr. Jurgenson."

"Thanks. By the way, name's Sid. You'll find we keep things pretty informal. Here we are." He led them into the autopsy room. Neil Diamond's "Cracklin' Rosie" was blasting from the small, white Bose speakers in the corners of the room.

One of the deputy medical examiners was swaying and singing along as he worked on another autopsy, ". . . now my bay-beeeee."

He was mid-swivel when he noticed the newcomers. A rose flush crept up his neck. He muttered, "Sorry" and clicked off the power button on the sound system. Silence filled the room. Jo hid a smile behind her hand.

Sid spoke, "Always said you had a nice singing voice, Bobby." The blush depended to burgundy and he went back to his work without comment.

John heard some voices in the hallway and then the double doors of the lab swung open, admitting a man in a black wool overcoat. He brushed the snow out of longish black hair, smiling broadly.

"Hey, folks. Sorry I'm late. Just got back from the Cities, visiting the family of the deceased." He reached out a hand to Jo. "Hello, Agent Schwann, good to see you again. Awfully glad Sid thought to call you." He turned to John. "And you must be Dr, Goodman. I'm Detective Mike Frisco. Most people just call me Frisco. Been working this case with Sid here." He rubbed his hands together and blew on them. "Jeez, it's cold out there. So, what did I miss?"

"Not much. Sid was just about to fill us in on his findings."

Jo said, "What did you find out from Calhoun's family?"

"Things just keep getting more and more weird." He pulled out a small notebook and slipped on a pair of reading glasses. "I spoke to his parents. He's been living with them off and on since high school. Seems he's had a hard time holding down a job 'cause he had to take so many sick days on a count of severe depression."

Frisco flipped through a few pages. "Then, about three weeks ago, he came up here to check into some 'cutting edge'—those were his parents' words—medical treatment he'd heard about from an old buddy."

"Any idea who this 'old buddy' was?"

"Nope. Mitch never told them who it was. Anyway, when their son came back, he was a changed man. Over-the top angry. Yelling at them all the time. They said they were actually afraid of him."

"And the depression? Was he cured?"

"That's part of the weirdness. His mom thought he seemed even more depressed. And, he developed these God-awful headaches. He was popping pain meds like they were candy. Then he would sleep for hours."

The detective turned to the last page in his notebook. "Finally had to call the cops one night because he was threatening them with a knife. He slipped out the back door before the cops arrived. His parents didn't know where he'd gone 'til we notified them of their son's death."

Jo shook her head. "Poor people. What a thing to go through. Appreciate the update, Frisco."

The detective turned to the ME. "So, Sid, you tell 'em what happened when you called the manufacturer?"

"I was just getting to that." Sid's bushy, white eyebrows seemed to have a life of their own as he warmed up to the topic. "Cagey bastards. Told me they'd get back to me. Ha! In a pig's eye they'd get back to me. So that's when I called the FDA. The guy I talked to said NeuroDynamics had gotten approval for limited human trials after passing previous reviews with flying colors, all within the last year. That strike you as awfully quick?"

John was shocked. "It certainly does. FDA Level III reviews required for this type of medical device would normally take several years before reaching the human testing phase."

"He also said a final, full-blown audit of the company had taken place two weeks ago. They found the usual minor infractions, wrote up their reports, and shook hands." He snorted. "A load of crap, if you ask me."

Jo spoke. "Were you able to take a look at their official reports?"

"Yeah, they faxed them over a few days ago. The first red flag popped up right away. A doctor from NeuroDynamics is the one who installed the chip into our victim's head. What's the manufacturer doing placing the microchips in heads? Should be an independent doctor.

"Also, according to the documents, the microchip is supposed to be implanted to cure depression. Now, I'm no neurosurgeon, but seems to me it isn't gonna do squat where I found it in Calhoun's brain."

"And, of course, you couldn't ask the lead inspector any follow-up questions because she disappeared right after the review was complete."

"Yup, that pretty much covers it." Sid walked over to a desk in the corner of the room and retrieved a sheaf of papers. "Here, read for yourself."

John accepted the reports from Sid and began to read. He couldn't believe what he was reading. The progress that NeuroDynamics had made in the field of microchips was astounding. He couldn't help but feel admiration for the scientists and medical researchers who had accomplished so much in so little time. "This is incredible."

Sid spoke. "Yeah. Like something out of a science fiction novel, isn't it?"

John shook his head. "I had no idea."

"Now, I can't say as I understood all the technical jargon, but I still think something's off kilter here."

Sid walked over to a stainless steel table. A jar sat in the middle, with a brain floating in fluid. The strong, chemical smells emitting from the container assailed John's nose. "This here's from the body of Mitch Calhoun. When we pulled it out of the skull, it was covered with blood. This boy didn't die a nice, quiet death. It was ugly, and it was excruciating."

He pointed to the cerebral arterial circle. "The rupture took place here, in the Circle of Willis, where the basilar artery joins with one of them pontine arteries."

Jo interrupted. "Do you want to repeat that in English for the medical-term challenged, like me?"

Sid turned to Jo and said. "The circle supplies blood to the brain. Any damage there causes big-time trouble."

She nodded for him to continue.

"Wouldn't have thought too much about it, but then I found that damn microchip." Sid shrugged his shoulders. "'Bout missed it the first couple of times I looked. I was wrapping things up and was about to write up the report, when something reflected the light. And there it was."

"It's amazing that you found it."

"Uh-huh. Pure dumb luck. But it certainly changes things, doesn't it?"

"Can I have those again?" Sid pointed to the papers in John's hands. John handed them back and Sid flipped through them until he found the page he was looking for.

He pointed to a paragraph. "Here, this is what I'm talking about. See? See what I mean? Complete and utter bullshit." Spit flew from Sid's mouth as he spoke.

John re-read the section that Sid had indicated. He was bewildered. "You're right, Sid. There's no way that microchip placed on the Circle of Willis could have controlled depression. But according to the FDA files, that's not where the microchip was implanted."

John took another look at the victim's brain. "The chip couldn't have migrated after surgery, either. The scar tissue around the ruptured area indicates that this was the site of the implant. It would appear either NeuroDynamics falsified their data or the FDA looked the other way." He looked up at Sid. "Why would they put the microchip here? I guess it could have been surgeon error, but that's a hell of a mistake. What were they trying to accomplish?"

Sid said, "Your guess is as good as mine, Doc."

"So, that's when you called the FBI."

"I knew Josie would take this seriously."

John said, "Agent Schwann tells me that the FBI labs have been taking a close look at the chip and they feel that it could be used for some type of mind control. What do you think of that theory?"

Sid scratched his bald pate. "Can't really see it. Again, the location of the chip doesn't support that kind of behavior change."

John leveled his eyes on Jo. "I agree. So, what do we do next?"

"Tomorrow we're going to pay a little visit to NeuroDynamics. It's headquartered in Lake County, Minnesota. Up north from here about forty five miles, just outside of Two Harbors. We don't have enough proof to nail them yet. All we have so far are some half-formed theories and a lot of questions. I intend to get answers."

Frisco's brows knit together. "NeuroDynamics is a big employer. A lot of folks would say it's even raised the standard of living around here. You're gunna catch a whole lotta flak on this one if you're not careful."

Sid snorted and pointed at the brain in front of them. "Well, it sure hasn't done much for this poor bastard's standard of living, now has it?"

CHAPTER SEVEN

Mabel's House
Thanksgiving Day

THANKSGIVING DINNER IN CHIP'S FAMILY had always been a formal catered affair. Both his grandmother and his mother trotted out their finest—Waterford crystal, Limoges and Meissen china, silver pieces purportedly crafted by Paul Revere himself. The food was always excellent, but the atmosphere was stifling. Chip had absented himself since divorce number two.

As he drove up to Mabel's little white bungalow with dark-green shutters, he suspected the contrast with today's meal would be staggering. Plus, he was oddly excited and decided his mission today was to find out more about his new friends, especially Dr. Jane.

With his hostess gift of a box of Whitman's Samplers from the local Walgreens in hand, he walked to the front door and read the handwritten sign: PLEASE COME TO THE BACKDOOR. As he rounded the corner of the house, he saw ice had started to form at the edges of the creek that ran along the back of Mabel's property. Iver was standing in the detached garage tending to what looked like a huge stockpot on a stand. He was sporting a black chefs apron decorated with red and yellow flames; it read: MR. GOOD LOOKIN' IS COOKIN'.

Iver, waving him over, yelled, "Got a fifteen-pounder here. Sure hope you're ready to eat bird. See this here deep fat fryer? All you do is add five gallons of peanut oil, then dunk the bird in the vat, head down. Well, it doesn't exactly have a head, but that end down and the tail end up. In fifty-two minutes the whole thing is done, nice and brown and crispy on the outside and juicy on the inside."

"I would think it would be kind of greasy with all that oil."

"Nah, that's the beauty of this method. Not greasy at all. And I use one of Jane's big needles to inject my secret marinade. Believe me, you never tasted a turkey this dang good before."

"I'm game for a culinary delight, Iver. I'm going to follow my nose to Mabel's kitchen. Bet there's more good eating in there."

On the backdoor was another sign which read: COME IN THE DOOR IS UNLOCKED. Like the front door sign, this one was faded and curled. Apparently Mabel did not lock her house.

Mabel's kitchen was redolent with aromas . . . rosemary and sage, butter and brown sugar, and the yeasty smell of baking dinner rolls. Mabel turned from the avocado green stove. She was wearing a white apron with a pair of big red lips that read KISS THE COOK. So he did.

"Oh, dear, now wasn't that a nice surprise. Make yourself at home. There's beer in the fridge," she said, pointing to the harvest gold refrigerator. "Dr. Jane called. Said she had an emergency. Then she wants to stop by the clinic to get Honey. She thinks her labor's started, so we might just have holiday puppies. Isn't that just wonderful?"

Chip was not at all sure of how "wonderful" this impending birth was going to be. He wondered why he hadn't been more insistent that he was not Honey's owner. He did not care to cope with a litter of puppies. Why had he floated along on the assumptions of other people?

"Mabel, after the puppies are born, then what?"

"We'll keep them for a few days at the clinic, make sure they're nursing okay, give them their first puppy shots and then you can take Honey and the pups home."

"How many do you think there'll be?"

"With a golden, could be six or more, maybe ten if you're lucky."

"Holy Crap . . ." *Lucky?*

Jane came through the door, followed by Iver carrying Honey. She made Honey comfortable in a box lined with a blanket while Iver fetched his beautifully browned turkey from the garage.

Dinner was served in Mabel's tiny dining room. Her table was covered with a paper tablecloth festooned with turkeys and pumpkins. The matching paper napkins were placed on her "good dishes," which she explained had been a bank premium, earned piece by piece twenty years earlier. The four of them held hands as Mabel said grace. Then eating commenced.

Chip felt a sense of belonging that he had never felt at his own family's Thanksgiving table, where he always felt as if he, like the turkey, was going to end up being roasted. The acceptance and genuine warmth these new friends were extending humbled him.

"Saw Chief Fredrickson this morning. Seems they found Owen Hansen beaten to a pulp last night. Had to airlift him to the hospital in Des Moines. Walter thinks Owen was threatening to call the government authorities about some goings on over to the plant," said Iver.

"My God. I figured something was going on from what I've observed at the Bun. Just what is happening over at the plant?" asked Chip.

Iver and Mabel were silent. They shifted their eyes to Jane, who sat grim-faced.

Finally Iver said, "Lots of talk about safety issues and violating government regulations and cooking the books. All I know is that the workers are getting pretty riled up."

Mabel frowned at him.

Jane put down her fork and suddenly turned her ear toward the kitchen, stood and left the table. The four of them gathered around Honey's box staring down at the first little puppy. Dinner was forgotten for the next hour as Jane assisted Honey in the delivery of the next two pups. As each pup was delivered, Mabel placed it near Honey's head. Honey dutifully licked the membrane off each pup.

Chip paced around the kitchen like an expectant father.

"Should Honey be cleaning them that way?" he asked Jane. "Yuck, she's chewing on the umbilical cord."

"That's perfectly normal. She's doing a great job. Usually, birth in a dog can take hours. The average is maybe half an hour between pups."

Two more pups popped out with barely ten minutes between them. Jane took one, turned it upside down and swung it between her legs.

"Is the pup, okay? It looks like a drowned rat." Chip was feeling overwhelmed by the whole birthing process.

"He looked a little slow moving. This is a good way to clean fluid out of a newborn's lungs so he can start breathing. He's fine now."

Two more puppies came out, both strong, active and eager to nurse.

Not much happened for the next fifteen minutes. Jane felt Honey's abdomen. "One more, I believe," reported Jane. "I have to warn you, Chip, the runt may be stillborn."

The last pup was finally expelled and lay motionless on the blanket. Chip knelt beside Jane and picked up the still pup. He cleared the mouth with his pinky finger, blew a puff of air into its face and began to gently massage its body. The pup, limp at first, began to wiggle and mew.

"Oh, my God, look at that. He's breathing and moving," said Chip. He felt a lump forming in the back of his throat and a rush of instant love for this little creature.

Jane turned her gaze to Chip. Her eyes were shining, and she flashed him an angelic smile. "Nice going, Dad. He may just make it. I'm impressed. Ever thought of giving up writing and becoming a vet?"

"I quit medical school. I never intended to be a writer." He shrugged. "I still don't know what I want to be when I grow up. And, I sure as hell never expected to be the owner of a mother dog and eight puppies."

"How'd you know what to do?"

"I don't know. Must be my Boy Scout training kicking into gear after all these years. I got a Lifesaving Badge, and of course, I've had CPR training. I just figured the same principles must work for dogs as they do for humans."

"I wouldn't figure you for a Boy Scout."

"Well, I imagine being a Boy Scout in Baltimore is not the same as being one in Iowa. We just helped little old ladies cross busy streets and sold Christmas wreaths."

DINNER WAS REHEATED AND EATEN WITH GUSTO. The table conversation consisted of a rousing discussion of puppy names from the cute to the goofy to the highly creative.

"I don't see anything wrong with regular dog names like Rover and Rex," offered Iver. "Can't give a golden retriever a silly name."

"I was thinking about the names of famous singers . . . Dolly, Garth, Clint, Madonna, Elvis," suggested Mabel. "Oh, and Cher for one of the girls."

"What about the names of world leaders? Castro, Evita, Putin, Gandhi, Obama."

"Obama would be fine, but Castro? Please, Chip, no dictators or despots." Chip was enjoying the naming process.

Pumpkin pie and coffee were consumed in the afterglow of a good meal and fine friends bound together by the marvel of birth.

—— —— —— —— ——

THE DAY'S ADRENALINE TRUMPED THE TURKEY'S tryptophan. It was 2:00 a.m. and Chip's mind flip-flopped from puppies to Dr. Goodman and from AgriDynamics to NeuroDynamics. His storyline and his life were increasingly difficult to separate, and he had no idea how he got where he was or where he was going with either one. Serendipity propelled him forward. His favorite Maurice Sendak words came to mind, "Let the wild rumpus start."

CHAPTER EIGHT

Brain Freeze
Duluth & Two Harbors, Minnesota

Bʏ ᴛʜᴇ ᴛɪᴍᴇ ᴛʜᴇʏ ʟᴇғᴛ ᴛʜᴇ ME's ᴏғғɪᴄᴇs a few hours later, it was dark and the snow was coming down in fat flakes. It looked like a snow globe outside the windshield of the Highlander.

As Jo pulled out of the parking lot, a loud, insistent ringing emanated from her pocket. She pulled the SUV to the side and fished out her cell phone. "Agent Schwann here." Pause. "Yes, we're just leaving the ME's office now. They found her?" Her eyes widened. "Really? Where?" Pause. "Any withdrawals from the bank account?" She frowned. "Thanks. I'll get back to you." She flipped the phone shut and shoved it back into the recesses of her coat.

John looked at her, waiting for her to fill him in. Jo said, "They've located the lead inspector who conducted the FDA audits. Her body was found in a hotel on the north side of Minneapolis. She died of an apparent drug overdose."

John felt sadness, as he always did when he heard about someone desperate enough to take their own life. *What a waste.* "What did they say about the money?"

Jo responded, "The money's still there. All two hundred grand of it. Oh, and she had just booked a Caribbean cruise, leaving tomorrow. Does it make sense to you that a person sitting on that kind of money and planning that kind of trip would suddenly take her own life?"

"Maybe she felt guilty."

Jo's green eyes were dark. "Or maybe someone decided she was a liability."

John said, "Well, that certainly puts a kink in the whole 'apparent suicide' theory, now doesn't?"

"And heats up our investigation to a whole new level." Jo rubbed her temple. John thought she looked tired. "Damn it. We really needed to talk to that FDA inspector. All the deposits into her account were made in cash, so we can't trace them directly to NeuroDynamics."

"Can't you talk to some of the FDA inspectors who worked with her?"

Jo tucked a stray strand of hair behind her ear. "My co-workers in Minneapolis are following up from their end. All they've learned so far is that the lead agent worked alone most of the time and didn't share much information with the rest of her team."

Jo pulled back onto the road. She just missed being t-boned by a beat-up blue Honda sailing through a stop sign. The driver, a teenage boy wearing a hoodie, flipped her off and drove away. "Damn it! Who taught that kid how to drive on slippery roads?"

John raised an eyebrow. "I'm sure if he knew you carried a gun, he'd have thought twice about giving you the bird."

Jo turned her head to him briefly and gave him a half-smile. "Well, I probably stank at driving in the snow when I was his age, too." She resumed her white-knuckled grip on the steering wheel. Visibility was only a few feet in front of the hood of the SUV.

John brought the subject back to the case. "So, you're going to focus primarily on NeuroDynamics?"

"It's the strongest link we have. After hearing you and Sid talk, I'm convinced this is much more than just a case of human error. My gut tells me we've just scraped the surface of what's going on in this case. You have to admit, a dead FDA agent with a fat bank account and a microchip in the wrong place doesn't look good."

John nodded. "It seems to me, this is turning out to be a case of medical fraud—selling people on the idea of some miracle cure for migraines, depression, or whatever ails you. You still think this is about mind control?"

"Yes, I do. I know we haven't come close to proving it yet, but I keep thinking about that note they found in Calhoun's hand. He referenced being forced to murder someone. I still say we're looking at something more sinister than a scam. That's what we're going to find out."

"So, where we headed now?"

"I think we should call it a day. While you were spending all that time discussing brain and gore with Sid, I booked us a place to stay for the night in Two Harbors. It's only a couple of miles from the headquarters of NeuroDynamics. The hotel was totally booked up for some church group retreat, so they're putting us in a two-bedroom condo on the property. You'll like the resort. It's right on Lake Superior and has its own restaurant."

"Just as long as it has heat, a bed, and a hot shower, I'm all for it. Who knows, maybe we'll get snowed in."

"Don't even joke about that. We've got a job to do. Speaking of which, when you and Sid put your brilliant heads together, did you figure out anything new?"

"Not really. By the way, you were right about Sid. He's impressive. And thorough. I don't think there's anything more we can determine from the body. Unless you can figure out a way to raise the FDA agent from the dead, I think the answers are going to have to come from NeuroDynamics. Have you thought about how we are going to approach them tomorrow?"

She looked away from the snow-covered road for a moment. "I have thought about it. Haven't stopped thinking about it, actually. I don't think we're going to be able to just walk right up to their front door, ring the bell and ask them to hand over all their records. We don't have enough for a warrant right now. After all, they did manage to get FDA approval to implant the chip. We've just got to prove that they used devious methods to obtain the approval—"

John interrupted. "Don't forget that the placement of the chip didn't agree with the reports." He rubbed his chin with the backside of his glove, thinking. "What about gaining entry to their files in a little more underhanded way? My old buddy Dr. Candleworth was desperate to get me onto his staff before. Maybe he'd still be interested in having me come aboard now. Then I could do some snooping."

She crinkled her nose. "I think he'd see right through that. Sid put him on notice when he called to find out more about the microchip in Calhoun's brain. And, since you've become a celebrity of sorts, helping solve that Cranium Killer case last year, the whole world knows that you've worked with the FBI in the past."

She thought for a moment. "*I* could apply for a job there and work undercover. You could tell me what to look for. I could take pictures of anything that looks promising and pass it on to you. I'd have to get a special type of warrant, but I think my boss will be able to push it through legal channels."

"Aren't you forgetting that you are a hometown girl? People might recognize you at NeuroDynamics."

"No one from the area has had much contact with me in years, except for Sid. Besides, I . . . um . . . I changed my last name before I joined the FBI."

John said, "Now that is intriguing. All right, spill it."

Jo smirked. "I don't think so."

"Oh, come on. Let me guess. You once robbed a bank?"

"Yeah, that's it. The FBI loves ex-bank robbers on their payroll."

"Okay then, how about you were married to Brad Pitt and you got tired of all the paparazzi hounding you?"

She burst out laughing, in spite of herself. "That's definitely not it. Do you really think you can charm your way to an answer?"

He shrugged. "Worth a shot." He smiled. "You'll tell me one of these days, though. I have lots of faith in my powers of persuasion."

"I just bet you do."

They drove in silence for the rest of the way to the hotel. It was pitch dark by the time Jo slowed the car to a crawl and turned onto a long, curving driveway surrounded by tall pines and birch trees. At the end of the road, a large two-story hotel was lit up, with wings on either side of the main building spreading out into the woods. She parked the car under the broad overhang, and they walked into the lobby.

While Jo checked them in at the front desk, John walked over to the massive freestanding stone fireplace in the middle of the lobby, with a cozy fire blazing. He pulled off his gloves and held his hands out to the fireplace screen. The warmth crept through his body. When Jo walked over to where he stood, he said, "This feels great. Forget the condo. I'll just bunk here."

Jo held up a key card. "Come on. Would it help if I told you our condo has a fireplace, too?"

"I knew there was something I liked about you. A girl who believes in creature comforts."

"Let's go. We have to drive over to the condo."

—— —— —— —— ——

"I CAN'T BELIEVE WE'RE GETTING SUCH FAST Internet service way out here in the boonies." John clicked away at the keyboard of his laptop. "Hey, listen to this. I followed a link on NeuroDynamics's website to an article Candleworth wrote for one of the major medical journals. He says that they are on the verge of a breakthrough to controling seizures, not just migraines and depression."

She stepped behind John and looked down at his laptop screen. She leaned over, and they quietly read the article.

John had a hard time focusing. When she stood so close to him, he caught a whiff of her perfume. Nothing flowery for this special agent. It was an enticing blend of vanilla and ginger. He inhaled deeply.

She straightened up and crossed her arms across her chest. "Well, would you look at that? That's where the real money is. Military contracts. Now we're talking numbers in the stratosphere."

John whistled. "You're not kidding. The potential for healing soldiers with brain injuries is incredible."

"A big contract like that is ripe for abuse."

John sighed and closed down his laptop. "Enough for now. I'm running on empty. Let's try the restaurant in the hotel."

Jo grinned. "You read my mind. I'm famished."

—— —— —— —— ——

JOHN FINISHED THE LAST BITE OF HIS GRILLED WALLEYE and chased it down with a swallow of chardonnay. He wiped his lips with the napkin and pushed away from the table, stretching his long legs out in front of him. "That was great! Who would've thought lake fish could be so tasty?"

Jo had finished eating her small side salad and half order of manicotti some time ago. Amusement gave way to amazement when he finished an appetizer, a dinner-sized salad, and a large entrée. She shook her head. "What, no room for dessert? Jeez, do you always eat that much? It's a wonder that you don't weigh three hundred pounds!"

"I've been blessed with a fast metabolism and a tall frame. That, and I swim to stay in shape. Wait until you see me put away breakfast."

Jo leaned back into her chair and took a sip from her wineglass. "So, Doctor, how is it that a world-renowned neurosurgeon such as yourself has time to spend with the FBI?"

John looked over at Jo. "I love my job. Most of the time, there's nothing I'd rather be doing." He shrugged. "But even I need a break now and then. Agent Tinsdale is my old college roommate. Occasionally, he calls me up for help on a particular case that falls within my area of expertise. I was able to reschedule some cases and handed off the rest to colleagues. I find working with the FBI rewarding on a different level altogether."

"You know, working this case might mean a lot of down time at first, especially while I find a way into the company. You okay with that?"

His lips curved into a lazy smile and he stretched. "Looking forward to a little down time. Besides, I have faith in you. You'll find info soon enough, and then we'll both be busy."

There was a sudden buzzing from Jo's cell phone that she had placed on the table. She flipped it open and answered it, still thinking about John and all that food. "Hey, Detective Frisco. I was planning on calling you . . . You found what? Oh, my God!"

Jo's face turned pale. John whispered, "What is it?"

She shook her head and continued to listen to the detective. After a minute, she said, "Okay, we'll be right there." She flipped the phone shut.

"What's happened? Bad news?"

Jo swallowed and looked off into space. "It's . . . it's Sid. And his wife. They were found in the medical examiner's offices." She shook her head, as if to clear it of a mental image.

John's eyes widened. "Found? What do you mean, found? Jo, what's going on?"

Tears filled Jo's eyes. She looked at John and said, "They've been murdered."

His body moved of its own accord. John came around to the other side of the table and pulled Jo to her feet. Wrapping her in his arms, he held her close. He could feel Jo trembling in his embrace.

Their waiter stopped by and asked if there was anything he could do to help. Her hands on his chest, Jo pushed away from John. She angrily brushed at the tears in her eyes. She looked at the waiter and shook her head. "We'll take the check, please."

CHAPTER NINE

The Bun
Last Week of November

On the Monday morning after Thanksgiving a pickup truck occupied every parking space on Main Street. Half of them were Fords and half Dodges. The Lutherans owned the Fords, and the Catholics the Dodges. It had nothing to do with religious doctrine and everything to do with the church membership of the town's two auto dealers. The trucks were all half-ton behemoths with loaded beds . . . bales of hay, sacks of feed, deer hunting gear, generators . . . and with snow plow blades on the front. A couple of them were suspended on gigantic tires, screaming Monster Truck Rally. Among them was parked Chip's Volvo, a ninety-eight-pound weakling at a heavyweight wrestling tournament.

Chip sat at his usual table-for-two in the corner where he had a full view of the door and the dining room. It was next to the Bun's unisex restroom. Chip himself had yet to use the cafe's facilities. His mother had instilled in him a fear and dread of public bathrooms, and he avoided them unless absolutely necessary. Male visitors to the restroom gave him a brief nod and females a nervous smile. He was no longer a stranger, but he felt like the patrons viewed him as an oddity.

Iver lumbered into the café and took the vacant seat at Chip's table, just as Bernice hustled by with a carafe of coffee in one hand and a mammoth cinnamon roll in the other. The aromas of cinnamon and vanilla wafted across the table.

"The usual for you two?"

"You know, I think I'll have to succumb to one of those cinnamon rolls instead of my wheat toast this morning," said Chip.

"Make that three," said Iver, laughing as he gave Bernice a wink.

"Hey, Iver, where's Mabel this morning?" asked Chip.

"She's real sick. Thinks it might be that pig flu even though she got all those shots. You'll never get no needle near me. I told her, you get those shots and you're sure to get sick, but the woman won't listen to me."

"That's too bad, Iver. Maybe it's just one of those twenty-four-hour bugs. I guess flu season is upon us. Hope you don't catch it, too."

"Nah, I'm healthy as a horse."

Chip surveyed the crowded tables. "What's going on around here? Why does it look like every farmer in the county is here? And why aren't the AgriDynamics guys here today?"

"Where you been, boy? Haven't you heard what's happening? You know about Owen Hanson being beat up. It's got the AgriDynamics guys skittish. None of them want to get their face rearranged and their ribs poked into their lungs like Owen's, and Owen isn't saying anything, especially with that broken jaw. And then there's Jethro, Oscar Nelson's prize bull. That's what the farmers are all jawing about."

Chip didn't know what to make of that. "What's the story with the bull?"

"Remember that emergency that Doc had on Thanksgiving? It was about Oscar's Holstein bull. Jethro was mighty sick, and then this weekend he bellied up, all twenty-four-hundred pounds of him. Too bad. The fella was the best breeder in Boone County."

This really didn't explain anything to Chip. "So why does a dead bull cause all these farmers to congregate? Surely cows die all the time. Are they holding a wake for him or something?"

Iver peered at him oddly. "It's *how* Jethro died that's got them all worried and speculating. Some said it might be Mad Cow, but Doc Swanson, she said no, isn't anything like Mad Cow and nothing like anything she's ever seen before. It's a mystery, just like in those books you write. She had to put Oscar's whole dang herd in isolation."

"How do you know about the book I wrote?"

"Read it."

Chip was amazed. "You read *The Cranium Killer?*"

"Ja, I had some time on my hands. Not too much snowplowing since that first big blast we had. Chief Fredrickson lent me his copy. Can't say I cared too much for all the details about how the killer cut out the brains of those women. Pretty gross. That story's making some of the women in town a little edgy around you—"

"It's not a memoir," Chip broke in. "Jeez. It's fiction."

Iver was nodding. "Mabel's been assuring them that you're a decent, dog-loving guy."

Bernice arrived with two plates balanced on her arms and a carafe in each hand.

"I nuked those cinnamon rolls a tad for you guys and added a pat of butter just for good measure. Enjoy."

Chip and Iver dug into the fat, cholesterol, and sugar and listened to the conversations around them. Words of worry and agitation took seed, sprouted and grew in numbers as the farmers of Turners Bend faced the threat of an unknown disease among their cows.

"If it ain't Mad Cow, then what in the hell is it?" said the farmer wearing a green John Deere cap.

"Don't know. It's enough to make a fella wonder if isn't one of those bio-terrorist attacks we're always reading about."

"Poor Oscar. I heard when Dr. Jane put his herd into isolation, his ticker just about gave out. This could ruin the old codger, if he doesn't kick the bucket first."

Licking cream cheese frosting off his fingers, Iver said, "With Mabel out sick and Doc busy with this bull business, maybe we should go over to the clinic and see how Honey's doing with your little ones."

—— —— —— —— ——

HONEY LAY CONTENTLY WITH SEVEN LITTLE BODIES nestled at her side each sucking away with vigor. Chip counted the puppies and then got a sick feeling in his gut.

Jane entered and he asked, "Where's my last little guy?"

"Oh, he's in a warmer," she said, pointing across the room. "We're hand feeding him until he's strong enough to fight for a place at his mother's table. I could sure use some help today. Here, I'll show you how to feed him. By the way, we're calling him Runt. I hope you don't mind.

"Chip, Honey should be spayed soon. It's the responsible thing to do. Too many puppies in the country never find homes."

"I'm kind of liking this puppy thing," Chip said as he cradled the little golden pup, "but I know I have to spay her. Promise I'll have you do it soon."

While Iver fussed over the puppies, Chip sat holding Runt and feeding him with a tiny bottle that looked like the kind that children used to feed their baby dolls.

"Which one are you going to take, Iver?" asked Chip.

"I don't have time to take care of a puppy what with the training and all."

"We'll see about that." Chip chuckled to himself.

———

BACK AT HOME THAT AFTERNOON CHIP found a new email from Lucinda.

Monday, November 28, 3:47 p.m.
Chip,
You won't believe this, but I got a call from Howard Glasser. Yes, the movie producer! He's interested in buying the movie rights to The Cranium Killer. *I'm meeting with him in La La Land next week. On the way to Hollywood I'll need to meet with you to go over releases and contracts and my fees. Iowa does have an airport someplace, right? This is BIG and I mean BIG!!!*
Lucinda
P.S. I'm anxious to see all you have written on Brain Freeze, *too.*

———

Chip read through the email three times. Yes, it was big, and he should be whooping around the kitchen and pumping the air like a pro athlete, maybe doing an end zone rap or break dance. But he felt strangely neutral about the movie possibility. He could make some good money, and Lucinda most likely would make a bundle, but being in Turners Bend had changed his outlook on money. He had spent most of his life thinking if he just had a little more money in the bank or just a few more shares of Blue Chip stock then all his problems would be solved. He had not been a believer in the "money isn't everything" motto, but he felt a conversion in the making. A movie could possibly take him away from the peace he had found in Iowa. Even worse, take him away from Jane.

He went to the kitchen window, parted the curtains and looked out at the snow. It was the same snow that had fallen when Jane and Honey and Iver and Mabel had come into his life. He loved that snow. It covered his father's disapproval, and it hid his bitter divorces. It laid down a deep blanket of purity with the promise of new life to come when it melted. It gave him hope, something he hadn't had for a long time.

Then he thought about Lucinda coming to Turners Bend. It gave him no small amount of glee to visualize her trying to order her Skinny Grande Latte at the Bun and coming up against blank stares. This was going to be fun. Well, fun until she found out he was lagging behind in *Brain Freeze*. Lucinda had been accommodating so far, but the woman was a barracuda. She could make him or break him. He was getting used to this feeling of success, and he did not want to blow it, not again, not now.

He started thinking about the story again. He'd had Sid and Martha murdered off, so he better think about what the crime scene should look like. There would have to be lots of blood, of course. He could not bear to write about a dog being killed or dying of grief over his dead owners. He wondered if Caddy could be happy with new owners. Maybe Jane would know. It would be another good excuse for visiting the clinic and feeding Runt.

Parker had been a good resource about brain aneurysms, but now he had to work out more about the microchip. He logged on to the Internet, googled "microchips" and surfed for an hour. One link led to another and then to another and eventually netted him the idea for an intriguing crime.

CHAPTER TEN

Brain Freeze
Duluth, Minnesota

Jo PULLED INTO THE PARKING LOT AT THE UMD medical center for the second time that day. The parking lot was awash in flashing red and blue. Every official vehicle in the county seemed to be crammed into the small lot. She turned off the SUV and sat back, staring through the windshield. When she didn't move or speak for a moment, John gently touched her shoulder and said, "Jo, are you all right?"

Jo blinked. "I'm sorry, did you say something?

"I was wondering how you're holding up. You've known Sid for a long time. This has got to be hard for you."

She hesitated and then nodded. Taking a deep breath, she said, "Let's get this over with."

They walked to the building. Recently fallen snow was trampled by footprints and lined with the narrow tire tracks of emergency equipment. Inside, the once shiny floors were slippery and treacherous from the slush tracked in by boots.

After they were cleared by the police officer protecting the crime scene, they moved towards the ME offices. They were greeted at the door by Detective Frisco. He nodded to Jo and John, his eyes grave.

Jo spoke up. "What's going on, Detective? We left these offices not four hours ago, and Sid and his wife were fine. How could this happen? Here of all places?" Her voice cracked and then she continued. "Where was the security guard?" Reality had not sunk in. *Maybe if I pretend that this is just an ordinary case and the victims are strangers, I can get through this.* She felt light-headed every time she thought about what she would soon witness for herself: the crime scene of someone she cared about.

"The security guard was taken out first. Probably some burnouts trying to score drugs and expensive equipment. A bunch of offices in the building were torn up and vandalized. No one else got hurt. Apparently, Sid, his wife and the security guard were the only ones left in the building."

Jo's eyes opened wide with surprise. "So it was a case of Sid and his wife being at the wrong place at the wrong time?"

"Looks like it. We thought it best to call you in for a couple of reasons. First . . ." He held up a finger. "Because of the case you were working on together. Second . . ." He lifted another finger, "Because you two were some of the last people to see Sid today. We thought you might have noticed something that seemed outta whack before you left."

John shook his head. "Nothing out of the ordinary. We left about an hour after you. By then, the only other people were a couple of the deputy medical examiners, working on unrelated cases. Why on earth would someone think there were any drugs worth stealing in the ME's offices, for chrissakes? It's not like an ME has a stock of medicine to cure his patients of what ails them."

"Yeah, well maybe they came in here not knowing what kind of office it is. Not much, but it's all we've got so far." The detective turned back towards Jo. "We've looked at the surveillance tapes of the lobby. Pisses me off them sons-of-bitches were smart enough to wear ski masks, so we don't have a clue who they are. At least we know there were two of them."

It helped Jo to have a problem to solve. She massaged her temple, thinking. "Have you looked at the tapes from the cameras in Sid's offices yet?"

Frisco raised a brow. "No. The security manager didn't say anything about that. Why would Sid have cameras in his offices?"

"He used them for training purposes and documentation for court cases. They were never meant to record suspicious behavior, so the building security office may not have been aware of them. Maybe we'll get lucky and Sid had them rolling when the bad guys came in. Let's take a look. "

Frisco led them past the desk where Martha had stopped them earlier in the day. A plant had been knocked over, dirt scattered across the sage-green carpet. Jo's gaze was drawn to a woman hunched over behind the desk. "St. Louis County Crime Lab" was emblazoned on the back of her jacket. A blood-covered leg jutted out beside the crime lab technician. The leg was encased in nude panty hose and had a sensible low-healed black pump attached. Jo felt her heart constrict in her chest, and she quickly averted her eyes. She hurried on, following Frisco. Willing herself to not look back.

When they entered the lab, Jo was shocked to see the damage to the previously immaculate room. Not a pane of glass in the cabinets remained intact. Carts were turned over, surgical tools scattered across the floor. Nothing remained of the order Sid had insisted upon for all his years as chief medical examiner. Jo kept her eyes from wandering to the crime lab technician in the corner and from the smears of blood along the floor. At some level, she knew that if she saw Sid's body, she wouldn't be able to work this case. It would be too personal.

John spoke first. "My God. This is unbelievable."

Frisco said, "Watch where you're stepping. We're still working the scene. Agent Schwann, got any idea where Sid would have kept these tapes you're talking about?"

Jo swallowed the bile that had risen in her throat. "Over here, I think. We worked a case together awhile back that Sid recorded for our files." Pointing to the ceiling above the autopsy table, she said, "The camera's up there. It's hard-wired to the recorder."

She stepped carefully over broken glass and walked to a cabinet. "The door has been smashed open, but there are several boxes of office supplies in front, so I guess they didn't notice the recorder." She pushed the boxes aside and reached deep inside the cabinet.

Jo pulled the recorder as far forward as the electrical cords would allow. "Bingo! Looks like it's still on. Let's see what we've got." She pulled out a DVD and handed it to Frisco. "Got a TV/DVD set-up around here?"

Frisco grabbed the disc and said, "Follow me. Let's take it to the security office and pop this sucker into their machines."

John and Jo followed Frisco to the office. Frisco inserted the DVD into the machine and pushed PLAY. Sid's booming voice startled them all. "St. Louis County ME case number 66257, dated January, 25, 2012. Victim: Mitch Calhoun. Young adult male, aged . . ." Sid's voice continued, giving his first impressions of the body. Then Sid himself appeared onscreen. He gave a running commentary as he continued with the autopsy. The DVD was stopped briefly when Sid had completed the autopsy. When it began again, Jo and John recognized themselves onscreen.

Jo wiped a tear that had appeared when she first saw Sid on the screen. She was finding it hard to speak normally. "Sid must have recorded his discussion with Dr. Goodman, to make sure all bases were covered." John nodded.

Frisco skipped forward on the DVD until after Jo and John had left the room onscreen. Sid continued working on the case. The detective muttered, "Must have forgot to turn the thing off."

Continuing to watch the screen, Frisco occasionally fast forwarded when it was clear nothing was relevant. They were rewarded a half hour later when they heard a muffled crash in the background and Sid yelled, "Hey! What's going on out there?"

Sid lurched off-camera. Shouting could be heard and then a groan. Two men appeared on-camera, shoving Sid to the ground. A gaping wound could be seen on Sid's forehead. Blood streamed down his face. The front of his lab coat was smudged with maroon streaks. Jo flinched at the distress she saw on Sid's face. She didn't want to watch anymore; as if turning off the DVD meant that Sid would still be alive. That nothing more would happen to him.

"Wha . . . what have you done? That's my wife out there. You have to let me help her! She's hurt real bad . . ." Sid tried to pull away from the man holding his arm, but he was struck across the jaw with a vicious back-handed blow. He fell to his knees. "What do you want? Don't have anything worth much to you. Here, you can have my wallet."

As Sid reached into his pocket, the other man ripped off the ski mask that had obscured his face. "We're not here for your money, old man. Where is it?" Jo saw the man's face, but it was still hard to see his features, because of the camera angle from above the lab table.

"Where is what? I don't know what you're talking about . . ." The man holding Sid's arm swung again. Sid fell to the floor, unconscious this time. Jo felt a white-hot rage building inside as she watched.

The man without the mask roared, "What the hell are you doing? Now we can't ask him about the chip, can we? Idiot! Do I have to do all the thinking around here?"

The killers rushed off-screen. Several loud crashes and thumps could be heard as they trashed the room. A voice sounded from the distance, "Let's get outta here. There's nothing here. We stay any longer and the cops'll be on our asses. I'm not going back to jail for those bastards."

After they left, Jo could hear deep, raspy breaths for a full three minutes. Then there was nothing left but silence. Jo closed her eyes and a tear leaked out.

Frisco's rough voice filled the small office. "They left him there to die. Like an animal." Jo opened her eyes and saw him clench his fists. "Damn it! Anyone see anything that could help us identify these bastards? I couldn't get a good look at the guy's face, could you?"

Jo was still. Something in the DVD struck her, but she couldn't put her finger on it. "Frisco, back it up a bit, will you? Back to where the guy pulls off his mask."

The detective pushed the reverse search button on the remote. Jo watched intently. When she saw it, she felt her heart speed up with adrenaline. "There! That's it. Pause that."

She pointed to the neck area of the guy without the mask on the screen. "What is that?"

John and Frisco leaned forward, squinting at the screen. John spoke first. "Looks like a tattoo of some kind. A bird, maybe?"

Jo said, "Looks like a crow to me or a raven. It has something in the beak, but I can't make it out."

As Frisco continued to study the still, Jo said, "Frisco, can you get a picture of this frame and check with the local tattoo parlors? Maybe someone will recognize their work. It's a long shot, but maybe we'll get lucky."

Frisco spoke. "I'm on it. By the way, there goes our theory that they were after drugs."

"You're right about that. They ransacked the other offices to make it look like that's what they were after." She crossed her arms. "They killed Sid and his wife over the goddamn microchip that's not even here. It's been at the FBI labs for a couple of days now." Jo kicked at the chair in frustration. "I'd bet my next paycheck that NeuroDynamics sent those two over when Sid called them to ask about the chip he found in Calhoun's head."

Frisco's voice was loud in the small room. "Killing them over a fancy hunk of metal and some wires. Jesus H. Christ!" His eyes zeroed in on Jo. "Tell me you got enough to get a search warrant."

"No. In order to convince a judge to grant a warrant, we would have to prove that these guys were sent here by the manufacturer. We're going to have to go through the back door on this one."

Frisco stared at Jo for a moment and then nodded. "I don't even want to know what you are up to. Just get them."

———————

JO AND THE DETECTIVE SPENT THE NEXT SEVERAL MINUTES reviewing the DVD, looking for missed details. John wandered around the security room, thinking about the ME he had just met, yet admired enormously. *How is it possible to mourn someone you've known for only a few hours?*

In the corner, he spotted a chewed up stuffed squirrel. Startled, he reached down to pick it up. "Detective? What happened to Caddy, Sid's dog?"

Frisco looked away from the TV screen. "When we first arrived, she was locked up in Sid's office. Liked to have killed herself trying to get out, barking to beat the band. Had a helluva time getting her out of the office without her traipsing through the crime scene. Her paws were bloody from trying to scratch her way through the door. She's with one of the agents down the hall, having her paws looked at." He turned back to the screen.

John left the room and headed in the direction Frisco had indicated. He stepped into a small office. The agent in the room nodded a greeting to John. Caddy lifted her head off of her bandaged paws and whimpered softly. Her tail thumped a couple of times on the floor. John crouched down beside her. "Poor girl. You've had quite a traumatic day, haven't you?'

Caddy whined again and licked John's hand. He reached over and scratched her behind the ears. Her amber-colored hair was silky beneath his fingers. She leaned into his hand, tail pounding the linoleum. Her ears perked up at a sound and John felt her tense beneath his hand.

John looked up to see Jo standing in the doorway, looking exhausted. Her voice was hoarse when she spoke. "I think we should head back to the condo. Nothing more we can do here tonight. Frisco and his crew are processing the scene." Jo indicated Caddy with her chin. "How's she doing?"

"She's grieving. I don't know how I know that, but I know it." He looked Jo in the eyes. "She's coming back with us. And I don't give a damn if the resort won't allow pets." His voice left no room for doubt.

Jo opened her mouth as if to object, but then reconsidered. "All right. I'll clear it with Frisco, and then we'll head back to the condo."

CHAPTER ELEVEN

The Bend
Early December

LUCINDA PATTERSON HAD NEVER BEEN west of Philadelphia. After Thanksgiving she flew from New York's JFK to Des Moines International, rented a Beamer and used the GPS app on her Blackberry Smartphone to navigate her way to Turners Bend and the phone's email function to make arrangements with Chip to meet at a local bar. The drive was turning out to be a surreal experience. The miles of desolation made her feel as if she were Sigourney Weaver in a cheesy Armageddon movie. When she pulled off the state highway and drove into what Chip had referred to as "downtown," the set of a '30s movie sprang to mind. She fully expected to see a lanky Jimmy Stewart saunter down the street. *Christ, Lucinda,* she told herself, *this is going above and beyond the call of duty for a client.*

She moved from brilliant sunshine into the Bend's dim, dusty interior, and, lifting her saucer-sized Versace sunglasses, she saw every head turn toward her and all chatter cease. She shook her highlighted blonde hair and with raised chin and a disinterested scowl on her face she made her way to the bar, her high-heeled ankle boots tapping as she crossed the floor. She perched her taut bottom, clad in skin-tight jeans, on a barstool next to the only guy in the place who was wearing a tie and contemplated her drink order.

With sarcasm dripping from her voice, she said to the bartender, "I don't imagine I'm going to get an Appletini here, so I'll have your best scotch on the rocks."

The guy next to her stared into the mirror behind the bar and straightened his tie. She saw him ogling her leopard print silk shirt, unbuttoned enough to reveal a black bra, and her form-fitting, chocolate brown suede jacket.

"Name's Hal Swanson," he said. "I sure hope you're not just passing through Turners Bend."

Lucinda's icy smile matched the diamonds on her tennis bracelet as she lifted her glass to him. "Rest assured, I have no intention of passing through Turners Bend. I plan to turn around and exit this town as soon as possible." She ignored his gaze, finished her scotch and ordered another.

A few minutes later Chip entered the Bend. "Lucinda, sorry I'm late. I see you found your way to a drink. Hi, Joe," Chip said to the bartender, "I'll have a Leinnie."

Chip and Lucinda moved to a table and for the next two hours they labored over the stack of legal documents Lucinda presented. She prided herself on being a tough negotiator.

"Now that a movie contract is on the table, my fee will increase. I need a bigger cut and all my expenses, of course, to travel to California to seal the deal. I could convince Glasser to let you do the screenplay, but honestly, Chip, I think he won't be happy unless we agree to a professional screenwriter. Let's face it, you've had some success with *The Cranium Killer*, but a lot of that is due to my skills and ingenuity."

She sensed that Chip was only vaguely interested in putting up any resistance when he said, "Whatever, Lucinda. In this whole book publishing process so little money has trickled down to me that I doubt I'm going to get rich on this movie deal, especially after you're taken the cream off the top."

"Oh, cry me a river. I'm going to make you into a national success yet. That is unless you go all J.D. Salinger on me and become a recluse in this podunk town."

In the end she persuaded him to consent to her outrageous "finder's fee." As a small concession she decided not to bug him for more chapters of *Brain Freeze*, at least not today.

She noticed Hal remained at the bar listening to the conversation between Chip and herself. He kept his booze, a beer and a bump, coming until he appeared to be well sloshed.

The door opened and a teenage girl entered. She stopped to adjust her eyes to the dim light in the bar and scanned the patrons.

"Oh, hi, Dad," she said to Hal. The girl's voice had a timid, uncertain quality. She glanced warily around the bar and made her way to Lucinda and Chip's table. As she approached, Lucinda was astonished that this young girl with auburn hair and a sweet smile could actually be the daughter of the whiskey-soaked cretin at the bar.

"Excuse me, you're Mr. Collingsworth, aren't you? I recognized your car outside. My mom, I mean Dr. Swanson, would like you to come to the vet clinic as soon as possible." There was a note of urgency in her voice.

Chip quickly stood and shook Lucinda's hand. "I think we're finished. You drive a hard bargain, Lucinda, but I appreciate your fine work on my behalf. Good luck in Hollywood. I'm sure we'll be in touch soon," he said as he followed the teenager out of the bar.

Lucinda started gathering her documents and putting them into her briefcase. Then she saw Hal unsteadily approach with a drink in each hand.

"A gorgeous woman like you can't leave without at least one for the road."

Lucinda hesitated. *Oh hell, I need one more drink to fortify me for that drive out of the boondocks and back to life in real time.*

Hal sat down next to her. He reeked of booze mixed with expensive cologne. She noted the heavy gold bracelet on his right arm and the Rolex watch on his left. The embroidered initials on the cuff of his shirt and the quality of his silk tie did not escape her eye, well practiced in spotting money. "So, your name's Hal, right? Just what do you do in this pathetic little burg?"

"You're looking at the guy who owns this town. Half the people here wouldn't have a job, if it weren't for me. Own AgriDynamics, a wind turbine manufacturer supported lavishly by our dear federal government. We're 'green.' Green like money," he said as he took a swig of his Johnny Walker, dribbling some down the front of his tie.

"That's not all. I've got a little something going on the side. Won't be long and I'll be living the life of leisure and luxury in the tropics, baby.

"See those two hombres over there." Hal pointed to two men seated at a back table, both facing the door. "You might think they're your ordinary run-of-the-mill illegals. Don't let the disguises fool you. They're business associates of mine, and they're making me a very rich man."

Lucinda had no idea what he meant and could have cared less. The two were dressed like farm workers, but she sensed there was something strange about them. As one lifted his can of beer, his denim jacket sleeve fell back to reveal some serious bling, and she noted his hair . . . not cut at a Iowa barbershop, she bet. Not giving it too much more thought, she planned her exit line.

Hal moved his chair closer and began to focus his blurry eyes on her boobs. Lucinda downed her drink and brusquely excused herself. "Sorry, big boy, you're too green for me. Ciao." She flipped her hair, put on her sunglasses and wiggled her hips as she left the Bend.

CHAPTER TWELVE

Brain Freeze
Two Harbors, Minnesota

D R. JOHN GOODMAN AND JO DROVE to the condo in silence, each lost in private thoughts. Once, when he glanced at Jo, he saw the headlights of a car reflecting off the tears on her cheeks. Caddy snored softly in the back seat, exhausted by the day's events.

They arrived back at the condo at three in the morning. Jo muttered good night and wandered into her bedroom, closing the door with a soft *snick* behind her.

For the first time in a long time, John was at a loss for what to do. Too wound up to sleep, he settled himself on the leather couch and propped his feet on the coffee table. Caddy lay stretched out next to him, her head resting on his lap. He rubbed her ears absently, thinking about the last twenty-four hours.

He was tempted to knock on Jo's door. He told himself it was to make sure she was okay, but he knew he was kidding himself. Holding her in his arms again was what he really wanted to do. To comfort her. To feel the length of her against him.

At one point, he had even padded over to her room in his stocking feet, and lifted a hand to rap on her door. But his hand hung in the air. In the end, he walked back to the couch. He rubbed his palm down his face, hearing the rasp of the stubble on his cheeks and chin. Caddy wiggled, breaking into his thoughts.

"Poor old girl. Hey, you must be hungry by now. C'mon. Let's go check out that overpriced bag of dog kibble we picked up at the Gasmart." John walked to the kitchen, the golden retriever following on his heels. Flipping on the light switch, he squinted in the harsh fluorescent glow. He rooted around the cabinets until he located a casserole dish for her food and another for water. Setting the dishes on the floor, he watched Caddy pick at the food.

"Not too hungry, huh? Got a lot on your mind? Me too." He picked up a chunk of the food and held it out to her. She gingerly licked it from his palm. He picked up another piece and offered it to her once more. "What do you think I should do about her?" John indicated Jo's bedroom with his thumb.

Caddy evidently decided she was hungry after all and buried her muzzle in the food bowl, crunching loudly. John chuckled softly. "You're a big help. I come to you for advice and you ignore me." He sighed and walked back to the living room.

John turned at a sound. The room was dark, except for the kitchen light in the next room and the faint glow of the security light outside the condo. Jo stood in the doorway of her room, wearing a long t-shirt. She said nothing, just stood there, studying him. The outline of her legs was clearly visible. His mouth went dry and lust warred with concern.

He swallowed. "Jo, are you doing okay? You should, um, get some sleep. It's been a long, rough day for you." He took a deep breath. "I'm sorry about Sid."

Her voice sounded like gravel. "He helped me out when my dad died. Sometimes, I can't make sense of things. You know?" Her voice broke.

He took a cautious step towards her, afraid of scaring her away. "Yes. I do know. This was a savage thing. A wasteful thing." He took another step.

She walked the last few feet between them and threw herself in his arms. She began to sob. At first, he stood still, worried that no matter what he did, it would be the wrong thing. They had known each other for such a short amount of time, but he already knew her pride, her reserve. John respected that about her. Still, he longed to bring her comfort. He was startled to realize that he hadn't ever felt that way before. About anyone. *I've known her for less than twenty-four hours.*

He wrapped his arms tight around her slim body, his chin resting on the top of her head. She fit perfectly. He closed his eyes and felt her shoulders shake, felt the dampness of her tears soaking into his shirt. Closing his eyes, he whispered, "Shh. It'll be all right. We'll figure this out." He stroked her hair, loving the way the curls wrapped around his fingers.

Her shuddering slowly subsided, and he felt her relax into him. They stood together for several minutes, not moving. He was aware of her warm softness against his chest. His heart pounded a rapid staccato. *Let me do the right thing here.*

John gently pushed her away from him. "I think maybe we'd better get some sleep. Tomorrow—I mean today—is going to be a crazy day." He put a finger under her chin and lifted her head to look into her eyes. "Are you going to be all right?"

She stared into his eyes for a moment and then nodded. "Thanks. I'm not usually like this. So . . . so weepy." She crinkled her nose. "So girly."

"Your secret is safe with me. You've been through a big shock today. I'm glad I was here. Now get some sleep. That's an order, Special Agent Schwann." She smiled at his light teasing and saluted him.

He watched her walk back to her room. Running a hand through his hair, he let out the breath he'd been holding. He whistled softly. "Caddy, here girl. Let's get some sleep too."

━━ ━━ ━━ ━━ ━━

WHEN JO STUMBLED OUT OF BED THE NEXT MORNING, she was surprised by the smell of coffee. She wandered into the kitchen and grabbed a cup for herself. Taking a cautious sip, she closed her eyes in gratitude. The bitterness of the coffee was just what she needed to get going this morning.

She felt well rested, considering she'd only slept five hours. Actually, it was the best night's sleep she had had in quite some time.

A note was propped up next to the coffee maker. In neatly printed block letters, it read: *Doing a few laps at the pool. Join me? J.*

Jo smiled. Carrying the coffee cup with her, she walked into the living room. Pulling her legs up under her she turned on the television remote. She flipped through the channels until she found a local news program.

There was Detective Frisco, giving a summary of the basic facts, looking red-faced and angry. He closed his speech, "This crime was carried out by cowards." He pointed at the camera. "We're gonna find you. Make no mistake about that." Cameras flashed as he walked away from the podium. *Glad he's on my side.* The more she worked with Detective Frisco, the more she respected him. He would work as hard as she in bringing Sid's killers to justice.

Jo clicked off the television. She returned her coffee cup to the kitchen sink and leaned into the cabinet, thinking. Her thoughts kept straying to the smear of Sid's blood she had seen on the floor of his lab. Jo shook her head, clearing away the image. "I have to focus. Can't help Sid if I can't get his killers."

Sitting down at the kitchen table, she pulled a tablet of paper to her and began making notes. Jo possessed an organized mind and it helped to map out a course of action in writing. Starting with the end result of putting those responsible in jail, she backed into every step she would need to take in order to get them there.

After sketching out the process and re-arranging the sequence of events, she was satisfied that she had put together an actionable plan. She snatched her cell phone off the counter and called into the Bureau's offices in Minneapolis.

AN HOUR LATER, JO TURNED HER HEAD WHEN SHE HEARD the key card in the door. John walked in, a t-shirt clinging to his torso and a towel wrapped around his waist. Caddy padded behind him. Jo blushed as she noticed his broad shoulders and flat stomach through the damp shirt. Memories of being held against him last night came rushing back, and she felt a heat rise up in her belly.

"For God's sake, it can't be more than ten degrees outside. What on earth . . . ?" She couldn't seem to form any more words.

"Wonderful morning for a swim. The hotel's got a great pool. I put in a few laps and then jumped into the hot tub afterwards. Warmed me up enough to run back to the condo. Caddy's been keeping me company." He reached down to pet the top of her head. She barked once and thumped her wet tail against Jo's leg.

Jo raised an eyebrow. "So yesterday you couldn't warm up, and today you're traipsing around the snow like a winter hare. Go figure."

He grinned broadly. "I adapt to my surroundings. Hey, let's go grab some breakfast. I'm starving."

"Are you always this annoyingly perky in the morning?"

"Once I've had my morning swim, oh, yeah." He turned on his heel and strode into his bedroom. She heard the shower running.

Jo looked down at Caddy, who had stayed for a morning ear scratch. "Caddy? Tell me the truth, am I in trouble here?"

After a hearty breakfast at a mom-and-pop log cabin restaurant on the way to Gooseberry Falls, they drove back to the condo. Just as Jo put the Toyota in park, her phone buzzed. "Hey Frisco. Saw you on the news this morning. Any new developments?" She listened for a bit, and nodded her head occasionally.

"Yes, I'm sure I want to do this. Let me know when it's set up, will you?" She flipped the phone shut.

When Jo didn't say anything for a moment, John asked, "Anything new?"

Jo shook her head. "No, not really. He had a thought about getting me into NeuroDynamics's headquarters, though." She stared through the windshield for a moment and then turned in her seat to face John. "Just might work. His wife's cousin has the cleaning contract for the building. He's going to try to get me into the three-to-eleven shift. Not exactly what I originally had in mind, but I'd be as good as invisible. The best part is that I'll have access to the building after hours."

John nodded. "I'll hang out here and do some more research on microchip technology and get an idea of what we'll need to prove our case. Then you'll know what to look for." He fidgeted with the zipper of his jacket. "Uh, Jo. Aren't you worried about the legality of any information we find this way? I mean, will it hold up in court?"

"While you were hanging out in the hot tub, I obtained what's commonly referred to as a 'Sneak and Peek' warrant. They're more often used in investigations into the illegal manufacturing of controlled substances, where officers want to confirm the presence of chemicals and to assess the stability of the labs without divulging the investigation. However, it should suit our purposes quite well."

John rubbed the back of his neck. "How does it differ from regular warrants?"

"It gives us a great deal of flexibility, since we don't have to notify NeuroDynamics that we're searching their facilities for seven days. Hence the 'sneak' in the name of the warrant.

"And the 'peek' part?"

"It means we can take a look around and come up with probable cause for a regular warrant. We're going to have to be careful, though. We're not allowed to disturb or physically seize anything while we're checking things out. We'll have some leeway, but there have been a lot of challenges in the courts to these types of warrants, as you can imagine."

John nodded. "And the last thing we want is for these guys to get off on a technicality."

"You got that right. Also, we'll have to watch the clock; if we even come close to the seven-day deadline, we'll file for an extension. It should give us the time we need to find something more solid." She reached for the door handle.

"Sounds like you have this all figured out."

"We're going to nail the bastards." Jo's green eyes narrowed. "Every one of them."

CHAPTER THIRTEEN

Turners Bend
Early December

CHIP RE-READ HIS LAST CHAPTER OF *Brain Freeze.* The discovery of
the "Sneak and Peek" warrant had been a plot saver. Now he could
get Jo into NeuroDynamics and add more suspense. Feeling smug, he
liked the way his story was progressing. He was starting to believe in
himself as a writer.

He sat back and turned his musings to the town of Turners Bend.
It had started to feel like his own, a place unlike Baltimore, and yet so
like home. People on the street and in stores greeted him by name.
Everyone asked about his past and seemed genuinely interested about
where he came from or why he was there. He was included in
conversations in the Bun and the Bend, and residents shared their
thoughts and opinions with him as if he were a long-time friend.

Population 932, or so read the sign at the entrance to town. Chip
had heard residents debate whether the sign had the count from the
1990 census or the 2000 census. They also debated whether that
number had increased or decreased over the past few years. That
wasn't the only point of contention he had observed in the sleepy farm
community. Yet, when an emergency came up or a neighbor needed
help, the town pulled together. Volunteer firefighters and first
responders dropped everything and came running from their homes or
fields or businesses when their pagers beckoned. Turners Bend took
care of its own and yesterday had been an example of just that.

Chip replayed in his head the events that followed his contract
meeting with Lucinda.

— — — — — —

INGRID SPRINTED DOWN THE STREET FROM THE BEND to her mother's
clinic and Chip huffed along behind her. Jane was on the phone.

77

"Chief, Jane here, I got the first responder page and talked with Doc Schultz. I think the best place to land a medi-vac helicopter given the snow is the south parking lot of AgriDynamics. I'll meet you over at Doc's. We've got to get Mabel to the Mayo Clinic ASAP."

"Mom, Mabel's going to be okay, isn't she?"

"She's awfully sick, sweetie, but the Mayo Clinic is one of the best hospitals in the country. They'll find out what's wrong and do their best to help her. You stay here. Honey needs some company, and Runt needs to be bottle-fed. Chip, we could use your help if enough First Responders don't make it in time. Can you come with me?"

Jane was off and running with Chip trailing again. He wondered why he was always bringing up the rear behind Turners Benders. They headed down Main Street, past Harriet's House of Hair, Larson's Hardware, Bill's Barbershop, Grandma's Attic, the antique store only open by appointment, and five empty storefronts. The wide street with its diagonal parking and faux gaslight lamp posts had once been a bustling retail area with a dry goods store, a grocery store, a butcher, a pharmacy and a bakery. The Walmart monster out on the highway had gobbled business up, just as the greedy corporate giant had done in so many small towns across America.

They turned off Main Street and dashed two blocks to a Victorian-style house with a veranda and gingerbread trim. It was badly in need of paint and repair. A crooked sign was hanging from the banister of the porch. It read: Herbert Schultz, MD.

"This is the doctor's office?" Chip felt like he had stepped back about a century in time.

"The parlor is the exam room and the library is the waiting room. Doc and Marion live in the rest of the house. He's been in practice here for sixty years."

Chief Fredrickson pulled up in the town's squad car, and a white hearse came speeding up behind him. A magnetic sign on the door panel read, Turners Bend Ambulance. Two men with First Responder jackets over their overalls jumped out of the vehicle and rolled a gurney out of the back of the hearse. They all rushed into the house.

Chief Fredrickson was clearly in charge. "Get her on that gurney, boys, and be careful. AgriDynamics is moving the cars out of the south parking lot. ETA on the chopper is twenty minutes. Let's move it."

Iver was sitting on a wooden folding chair in the waiting room. His normally ruddy complexion was ashen. "She's real bad, Jane. Doc Schultz doesn't know what it can be. I don't trust anything that don't have wheels on the road, but I got to go with her up to the Mayo. I can't let her be alone. Oh, Lord, I hope that whirlybird doesn't crash and kill us all."

Jane sat next to him, held his big fleshy hand and began to reassure him, "She's going to get top-notch medical care, Iver. She'll be okay. Just stay strong for her."

Chip headed into the exam room. Doc Schultz was leaning on his walker, a stethoscope around his neck. His baggy gray suit was rumpled and his white hair stood out like Einstein's. He handed Mabel's medical chart to the chief and barked instructions to the first responders. "Easy boys, keep that gurney level and strap her in securely. Be sure these medical records get on the helicopter with her."

Chip pulled his cell phone out of his pocket, flipped it open and checked for reception. He accessed his contact list and made a call. "Yes, this is Charles Collingsworth calling for Dr. Jacob Stein." He waited only a few seconds.

"Jake, this is Chip. A friend is on her way to you at Mayo via medi-vac from Turners Bend, Iowa. I'd appreciate it if you could look at her as soon as she arrives, as a favor to me. Here, the local doc can give you a run-down, and thanks, buddy, I owe you one."

"I've got a fifty-seven-year-old female patient complaining of intense headache, dizziness, cramping, visual impairment, profuse sweating, blood pressure 172 over 110, sharp pain in hands and feet. She's cyanotic, definitely blue, but no SOB, no jaundice. No remarkable medical history recently, although she had a nasty case of hepatitis a few years back. He paused. "No, drug use is highly unlikely. Believe me, I know this woman." He listened for a few more minutes and handed the phone back to Chip. "I'll be damned," he said to the assembled group, "Stein is going to run a tox screen. He said it was a wild guess, but he thinks that Mabel may have been poisoned with arsenic or lead or maybe mercury. Her liver might make her especially vulnerable, even in small doses. "

With Iver in the passenger seat, the squad car headed toward the chopper's landing place with its lights flashing and its siren wailing. The ambulance followed close behind. As he watched the taillights disappear, Chip couldn't erase the look he had seen on Iver's face nor his own assessment of Mabel's condition. She was one very sick woman. Their devotion and caring for each other was so palpable that he could almost wrap his hands around it. He was not sure whether or not he had ever experienced a deep and abiding affection like theirs, certainly not one that lasted long. He envied them, and he feared what might happen at the hospital. Although it was a rarity for him, he sent up a little prayer for their health and safety.

As Chip and Jane walked back to her clinic, they saw heads popping out of doors and appearing in windows. "Who is it?" yelled the barber, standing outside next to his red and white striped barber pole.

"Mabel. She's on her way to the Mayo Clinic," reported Jane, news she repeated several more times before they reached her clinic. Chip got the feeling this was not nosiness, but rather genuine concern for a beloved neighbor and friend.

"So, Charles, how do you just happen to know a doctor at the Mayo Clinic?" asked Jane, as she and Chip walked into the empty waiting room.

"Jake was my roommate at Johns Hopkins for my one year in medical school. His father and my father were also classmates. He's now an internist at Mayo. Hell of a nice guy and a damn good doctor. Mabel will have the best. What do you make of that possible poisoning diagnosis?"

"Funny you should ask. I suppose you have heard about Jethro. Well, now another of Oscar's cows is showing symptoms and so is one of Hjalmer Gustafson's bulls. I've sent some blood samples on to the vet school in Iowa City, but I think we might be looking at some kind of poisoning. They called today and asked me to send water samples from each of the farms. But Mabel doesn't live near those farms, so how could they be connected? It's puzzling, isn't it?"

Ingrid was holding Runt when Chip and Jane returned to the clinic. The well-fed pup was sleeping on her lap. He was on his back with his paws in the air, and he snored softly as Ingrid stroked his tummy.

In the dimness of the Bend Chip hadn't noticed the girl's acne. Ingrid's face was in full bloom. She had a pimple on her chin and another one on her nose. She was grim-faced and her eyebrows were scrunched, reflecting her worry. She took a deep breath, as if to steady herself.

"Mom, I didn't have time to tell you before, but Sven wasn't on the bus coming home from school today. While you were gone, Mr. Carlson called from school. Sven wasn't in any of his afternoon classes. I hate it when he does stuff like this. He's such an idiot."

Jane briefly closed her eyes and sighed while rubbing her temples. "Hey, Ingrid, I've told you, your brother's behavior isn't your responsibility. I'll call Chief Fredrickson and ask him to find him and bring him home again. This is just more of his attention-getting stuff."

"Well, if I were you, I'd start with Dad. I have a feeling he's got something to do with this." She returned her attention to Runt, evading eye contact with Jane and Chip.

THE EVENTS OF THAT DAY HAD GIVEN CHIP a throbbing headache. He checked the bathroom mirror to see if his face had a bluish tinge. The face that looked back at him was a pasty winter white. All during the night, blue cows, helicopters turning into birds and fields strewn with dead medical examiners haunted his dreams. He woke at 3:20 a.m. made a pot of coffee, sat down and turned on his computer. No words came to him and the screen eventually timed out and shut down. Floating in his brain was a vague thought about poison, but he couldn't pin it down. Just when it was at the verge of materializing, it eluded him and spun away, escaping into the depths of his celebral cortex.

He had ended up spending the rest of the night surfing the Internet. That's when he found the site that detailed different types of warrants. Now he was off and writing again and in the zone that produced some of his best work.

CHAPTER FOURTEEN

Turners Bend
The Next Day

Oscar Nelson's farm was set way back from the main road. The house, barn and three sheds were clustered together, weathered and weary-looking. The north and west sides were lined with tall, thin jack pines. Viewed from the main road it looked like a deserted island floating in a sea of snow. Chip's Volvo headed toward the house on his way to collect water samples from the cow pasture. With Mabel in the hospital, Sven still missing, and more cows sick, Jane had her hands full. Chip had volunteered to collect water samples from the affected farms. He had convinced her that his field biology class had taught him how to do so. Oscar met him in the yard.

Oscar was short and stocky. He was wearing what Chip had determined was standard farmer garb, a plaid wool shirt under overalls, thermal underwear poking out here and there. On his head was a hat with fur-lined earflaps.

"Jane said you would be coming. She was here yesterday morning. Bertha up and died, just like Jethro, same brown mucous membranes and chocolate-colored blood." Oscar spit chewing tobacco on the ground and wiped his mouth with the back of his hand. "We gotta get a handle on this or I'll lose my whole herd. This could ruin me. A man my age can't just start over again, just too dang old."

"How old would that be, Mr. Nelson, if you don't mind me asking?" Chip was guessing he must be at least seventy from his prune-like face and stooped posture.

"Be eighty-seven this coming July 4th. I'm a Yankee Doodle Dandy. Suppose you're too young to know that song."

"George M. Cohen. I know all the lyrics." He sang, "Grand old nephew of my Uncle Sam, born on the Fourth of July."

Oscar cracked his first and possibly only smile of the day, showing a set of brown-stained teeth. The two trudged out to the cow pasture. Chip had a hard time keeping up with Oscar's pace. In wonderment he was again lagging behind a Turners Bender. He used to think he was in pretty good shape, but he was finding out these Norwegians were genetically "built to last" just like a Dodge Ram truck. He kept his eyes on his boots, sidestepping large cow pies, a couple still fresh and steaming.

Chip had never been in a cow pasture and was totally perplexed by the trough. For one thing, the water in the trough wasn't frozen, although the air temperature had been below freezing for two weeks.

"You can take water from right here," said Oscar. "Bet you never saw a contraption like this before, have you, young fella? This wind turbine pumps the water from that creek over there, through this PVC pipe and into the trough. The turbine also powers an agitator to keep the water from freezing. Pretty slick, huh? Turbine's from right here. Made over at AgriDynamics."

"So there's no well out here. The cows drink creek water . . . but the creek's frozen."

"Just a few inches on the top. The PVC is lying on the creek bed where the water's still flowing. Cows been drinking that water for years and never had a problem before. Can't see how it could be the water."

"Does this creek go by Hjalmer Gustafson's farm?"

"Ja, he's got the same kind of setup I have."

Chip collected six samples of water into sterile tubes, just as Jane had requested, sealing and labeling each. He decided to forego his sample collection at the Gustafson farm since the water source would be the same as here at Oscar's farm. Instead he headed for town hall.

Turners Bend Town Hall was a stone building fronted by tall windows. The brass plaque beside the front door said it was erected by the Works Progress Administration during the 1930s. There was a flagpole in the small patch of front yard with an American flag at the top and the Iowa State flag beneath it. The elements had taken their toll on both of the flags, which were faded and frayed around the edges.

At the front desk a middle-aged woman with a ratted helmet of too-black hair greeted him. "Good morning, Mr. Collingsworth, I'm the city clerk, Flora Fredrickson. How may I help our town writer today?" Chip had seen her at the Bun but they had not been formally introduced. Apparently he was not a complete stranger to her, and she most likely had read *The Cranium Killer*. He steeled himself for more literary criticism.

"It's a pleasure to meet you, Flora. I wonder if you have a county map that would show me the waterways, rivers, creeks, and the like."

"Of course, would you like me to pull up the US Geological Survey's topographic map or would you prefer the aerial photography we use to determine GPS coordinates for chemical application on fields?"

He sensed this was a crucial moment in his relationship with the city clerk. He figured he better not offend her or his name would be mud in town. "You're the expert, Flora. I'd like to follow the path of the creek that flows through Oscar Nelson's farm. I need your advice. Which would you recommend?"

Flora's stern face softened. She reached out her pudgy hand and patted Chip's arm. "Of course, dear, that's what I'm here for. Now if you'll just follow me to the backroom. We'll look at the aerial maps."

Chip followed Flora, watching her ample rump sway and bounce, sway and bounce under her black knit pants.

Flora's red lacquered nails clicked on the keyboard, and she pulled up an aerial map. "That's Beaver Creek. Here is Nelson's farm. The creek flows toward town in this direction." She traced the creek's path with her finger, naming the properties that it passed as it wound its way into town.

"Does it run through Mabel's backyard?"

"Yes, here's Mabel's house. It runs in back of her garage, but how could the creek be related to poor Mabel's illness? She has a well like the rest of us. Folks don't drink out of the creek, even though the water has always been pretty clean."

"Where does it come from west of Nelson's farm?"

"It runs parallel to County Road 15A, out past AgriDynamics and over into Calhoun County."

"Flora, you've been a tremendous help."

"Anytime, Mr. Collingsworth, that's my job." Flora cleared her throat and raised her eyebrows slightly. "You know, there's no finer eligible woman in Turners Bend than Jane Swanson. I've been telling her that it's time to get out there and start dating again, wouldn't you agree?"

Chip was momentarily stunned and stumped for a response. He had expected advice on how to write a crime story not matchmaking. From their first encounter, Chip had been attracted to Jane, but he didn't want to add any fuel to the town's gossip mill. Flora Fredrickson would be just the woman to do that. Plus, he was a three-time loser who had sworn off women for good reason or so he reminded himself.

"I'll have to defer to your good judgement on that score, Flora," he said as he quickly departed.

———————————

AN HOUR LATER, CHIP SHARED HIS FINDINGS WITH JANE. "Beaver Creek must be contaminated with something that's killing the cows. It's possibly the source of Mabel's illness, too. Stein did suspect poisoning. My guess is that it's coming from AgriDynamics. I'm really curious about what's in these water samples." He handed Jane the six water samples he had collected.

"I'll need samples from the creek west of AgriDynamics, too. I don't want to jump to any conclusions until I get the lab report. I'll send the water samples off to Iowa City by UPS. It's going to take a week to ten days to get the results."

Chip turned his attention to his favorite little puppy, Runt, who was being fed by Ingrid. As he watched Ingrid he was struck by her resemblance to Jane. It wasn't just her red hair and green eyes; it was the way she handled the puppy with a mixture of competence and affection. He had a clear image of Jane as a teenager working in this very clinic with her father.

"Honey and her pups will be ready to go home in a day or two," said Jane. "I should spay Honey before she goes home."

"I want her to rest up a little first, then I'll bring her back. I have to confess, Jane, I'm having a hard time thinking about her going under the knife."

"Well, you had better prepare your house for the invasion."

"Here's another confession. I haven't a clue as to what those preparations should be." Excitement and panic mingled in his gut. The thought of eight puppies in a one-bedroom house made his mind reel.

"Ingrid, get Mr. Collingsworth our Puppy Care pamphlet. Really, Chip, it's just like taking care of human babies, but without diapers."

"That's not helping me one bit, Jane."

NOW CHIP SAT AT HIS LAPTOP, TRYING NOT TO THINK about puppies and forcing himself to concentrate on his writing. He recalled his meeting with Flora and hearing the name Calhoun for the county west of Boone. It reminded him that the murders of Mitch Calhoun and Sid, the ME, and his wife, Martha, were still unsolved. He was trying to get a handle on a new character and whether she should be a victim or a villain or both? In some ways she vaguely reminded him of Lucinda. Lucinda, of course, would never be a victim. He supposed he could ask a few of the local book critics. They all wanted to tell him how to write his books. Just yesterday at the Bend the bartender had suggested that he write about a bartender that solves crimes, because "they know all and see all and are a lot smarter than people give them credit for." He tucked that idea away for future reference, and turned his thoughts to the headquarters of NeuroDynamics and the character he decided to name Belinda.

Chapter Fifteen

Brain Freeze
Two Harbors, Minnesota

The NeuroDynamics headquarters was buried deep in the woods, two miles off the highway. It was surrounded by bare birch trees and towering firs. A frozen pond flanked the parking lot to the right. The sprawling, double-story structure looked like a fortress with its dark-gray granite façade. Separate wings contained the various areas of operation.

Jo rolled the cart smoothly down the polished marble floors of the executive wing. The walls were paneled in black walnut, with spotlights in the ceiling above her, highlighting artwork scattered along the hallway. Her shoes were soundless as she stopped at offices here and there, emptying trash cans, running a dust rag over spotless surfaces. Not even her boss at the Bureau would have recognized her—a light brown wig covered her red hair and she had dabbed on a bit of hair color to cover the cinnamon of her brows. Contacts had changed her green eyes to hazel. In the five days since she had started working undercover, her eyes never stopped searching, never stopped reading.

Jo had been correct when she told John that she would be invisible here. In her cleaning services uniform of a white polo shirt and khaki pants, she was a non-entity to the employees. A fixture of the place. Since she worked the later shift, most people had gone home for the day. Jo was free to wander, gathering bits of information.

But nothing worth a damn. Jo gripped the handle of the cart tightly and huffed out a breath in disgust. *I have to find something.* Thus far, she had found a brochure on breast implants in the filing cabinet of the executive assistant, a half-empty fifth of bourbon in the desk of the CIO and some rather disturbing bondage photos on the desktop of the marketing director. Personal demons that had nothing to do with the deaths of Mitch Calhoun and Sid.

She knew *what* she was trying to prove, but wasn't certain what form the evidence would assume. *I hope I recognize it when—and if—I find it.* After talking things over with John, her boss and Frisco, she had several clear objectives. The first was to tie Sid and Martha's killers directly to NeuroDynamics. The second was to prove that the corporation had bribed the FDA official in order to push through their technology in record time without the usual thorough reviews. John and Jo agreed that the third and last objective would be the most difficult to prove. What exactly was the true intention of the technology?

Jo wanted to get into the office of the CEO, Charles Candleworth, but his door was always locked or he was inside, alone. He allowed no one but the owner of the cleaning company to take care of his office. Picking the lock on his door would be a mistake, since there was a security camera pointed directly at his office. *I guess having dirty little secrets makes you a bit paranoid.*

She caught a glimpse of him now and again. John had said that he and Candleworth were about the same age, but Jo found it hard to believe. John was youthful and healthy. This man looked well past his prime. Even if Jo hadn't good reason to suspect him, there was something about the man that she didn't like. His smile never quite reached his eyes and he constantly looked at his watch when one of his staff members talked to him, as if he had more important things on his mind.

Belinda Peterson was the only company executive who worked late, although she usually turned out her office lights by 7:00 p.m. According to the online bios of the NeuroDynamics executive team, Ms. Peterson was chief financial officer. A tall, willowy blonde, she appeared to be about thirty-five. The first few nights that Jo came in to empty the paper shredder in her office, the CFO only nodded absently at Jo's quiet, "Hello."

Tonight, however, the woman was anything but quiet. Heading towards the CFO's office, Jo heard Belinda Peterson shouting into the phone. "I don't care what you want! I'm telling you, this is unacceptable. This company has been bleeding money for far too long, and I'm tired of the board and investors chewing my ass because you can't fix this. Just do it!" She slammed the receiver down on the desk.

She muttered under her breath, "These friggin' headaches are killing me. That goddamn surgeon lied to me. They're worse since they put that chip in my head."

A leaded-crystal vase shattered inches from Jo's head as she stepped into the office. The woman blinked when she noticed Jo. "Oh, sorry. Didn't know anyone was there."

Jo's heartbeat slowed down a few notches. "No problem. I'll clean this up." She bent down and carefully put several large shards of glass in the palm of her hand. She looked up to see the woman massaging her temples with perfectly manicured fingertips, the nails painted a crimson red.

Jo stared at the woman for a moment. *They used the chips on their own people?* Up until this point, she had not been able to search the CFO's office. Belinda was very careful to lock up her office at the end of the night. Jo thought quickly.

"Excuse me, Ms. Peterson, is it? I can clean this mess for you. Why don't you go home and take a couple of Advil for that headache."

Belinda started, as if she had forgotten that anyone was in the room. For a moment, the look on her face was almost feral and then, in an instant, it was normal again. "Oh, yes. Yes, that would be helpful. Just make sure you pull my door shut tight when you leave."

Jo looked down to conceal the excitement on her face. She controlled her voice, "Of course. I'll take care of everything."

She watched while Belinda Peterson packed up her designer briefcase for the night and shut down her computer. She locked the desk drawers. Belinda grabbed the long camel-colored coat hanging on a hook behind the door and was out in the hallway without another word to Jo. The woman's heels clicked on the polished floors and the elevator's *ding* announced its arrival.

Jo unhooked the small whisk broom and dust pan from her cart. She crouched down to sweep up the remaining glass fragments, taking her time in case the CFO returned. After several minutes, she picked up the last piece and wiped down the walls where the water had splashed. The shards and the broken flower stems went into the trash can.

She checked around the corner to see if anyone else was around. Finding no one, she searched the room for security cameras. Satisfied, she pulled on latex gloves and closed the outside window blinds. Walking behind Belinda's desk, she sat in the soft black leather chair and pushed the power button of the desktop. The glow of the computer lit Jo's face, as she focused on the screen.

At the log-on screen, Belinda's user ID came up automatically, but of course, Jo had no idea what the password might be. She picked the desk lock and searched the drawers. Jo hoped that the woman might be careless, but found nothing. Crouching down, she looked under the desk. *Nada.* Jo sat back in the chair and studied the personal effects on top of the desk.

Everything was neat and tidy on the desk. Items were lined up precisely on the surface. There was a paperweight in the shape of the Eiffel Tower on the far right corner, perched on a stack of papers. A smiling Belinda looked out of a picture frame on the opposite corner. Jo presumed the man and two young children in the photo were Belinda's family. They were decked out in ski gear and stood atop a snow-covered slope, squinting into the sun. Jo had a hard time picturing Belinda smiling at anything these days.

She snatched the picture off the desk and flipped it over. Carefully taking the frame apart, she looked at the back of the photo. Written in tight script was: ASPEN, WINTER BREAK, 2010. CARLA, AGED 10 AND THOMAS, AGED 7.

Jo typed both children's names into the computer, in various combinations, to no avail. She put the picture frame back together and returned it to its place on the desk. She sighed, and leaned back in the chair. Out of desperation, she entered "Eiffel Tower". PASSWORD INVALID.

There was a carved wooden nameplate on the desk in the middle. Jo picked it up, admiring the handiwork of the artist. When she flipped it over, she saw a small piece of paper taped to the bottom. Written there was a series of nonsensical numbers and letters. *Thank God for people who can't remember their passwords.* She sat up straight and entered the alpha-numeric sequence on the password line of the computer sign-on screen.

The screen went blank for a moment, and then a welcome screen appeared. Jo did a little victory wiggle in the chair and murmured, "Now we're talking." Pulling up Word documents, she paged down through the titles. Many were inter-office memos between Ms. Peterson, the chief surgeon, and the owner of the company. Jo removed the flash drive that was on a chain around her neck, and began to download the files that looked promising.

As she finished copying the documents, the telephone on Belinda's desk rang. Startled, Jo waited a moment until her heart resumed its normal beat. Taking a deep breath, she searched the spreadsheets. Several files were labeled "GOVERNMENT," "MIDDLE EAST," and "CENTRAL AND SOUTH AMERICA." She downloaded all of these to the flash drive.

Jo looked at her watch. "Time to get out of Dodge." She closed down the desktop, straightened everything to its original position and opened the blinds once again. She pulled the office door closed and headed down the hallway.

At the end of her shift, she returned her cleaning supplies to the storage room. She shrugged into her coat and nodded to the security guard as she left the building. Jo didn't notice when he picked up the phone as she walked to her car.

BY THE TIME JO ARRIVED BACK AT THE CONDO, she was exhausted and hungry. Flipping on the light by the entryway, she leaned against the wall and removed her boots. A soft blue glow emanated from the living room. Jo walked into the room and saw that John had fallen asleep on the couch while watching television. Caddy's head poked up from her spot on the floor in front of John and her tail thumped a few times as a greeting. Jo whispered, "Hello, sweet girl. Did you miss me?" Caddy got to her feet and walked over to Jo, nudging her hand with her muzzle. Jo reached down and rubbed behind her ears. "I missed you, too."

John let out a loud snort and tossed in his sleep, his long legs dangling over the arm of the couch. Smiling, Jo grabbed an extra blanket from the armoire in the living room. She flicked it open and draped it across John's body. Jo watched as a small smile crept across his sleeping face. He looked more like a little boy in that moment than a world-famous neurosurgeon.

She walked into the small kitchen, looking for something to eat. She turned towards the small dining table and saw that John had left a place setting out for her. A note was on the placemat. *Jo. Thought you might be hungry after the long day. There's a sandwich in the fridge for you. Hope you like ham and cheese on rye.* Jo raised an eyebrow. She whispered, "Just when I thought I had you figured out, you do something else to surprise me."

CHAPTER SIXTEEN

Turners Bend
Mid-December

Turners Bend was decked out for the holidays. Garland, wreaths, and lights decorated every storefront on Main Street. The deep woods aroma of freshly cut pine scented the air. The Bun had a Christmas tree where patrons hung mittens, scarves and hats to be sent to homeless shelters in Ames and Des Moines. The Bend hung a silver disco ball in preparation for its New Year's Eve gala. Plywood nativity scenes and inflatable Santas and snowmen were stuck into snow drifts around town. *Krumcakke*, spritz, rosettes, *sandbakkels*, and *lefsa* came pouring out of kitchens around the county to fill the tables at First Lutheran's Christmas Bake Sale. Bathrobes were being gathered for the little shepherds and wisemen who would perform in the annual Christmas pageant at Sacred Heart Catholic Church.

It was a time for homecomings.

Mabel came home after two week at the Mayo clinic, where Dr. Stein had determined she had been suffering from chlorine and nitrite poisoning, most likely from tainted well water. The first week was "touch and go," and Iver only left her side to grab food in the hospital cafeteria. It appeared her kidneys and liver might be shutting down. A brief round of dialysis and Iver's tenderness, along with Stein's considerable skill, reversed the process and began to restore her to health.

Still weak but improving steadily, Iver brought her home. He moved a Glenwood water cooler and big jugs of water into her kitchen. He also quietly moved himself into her house, a move the town's wagging tongues looked on with kindness.

With Mabel on bed rest, Iver became Chip's regular breakfast companion. "I tell you, Chip, we almost lost our girl up there at the

Mayo. Doc Stein said it was life threatening, but he brought her through. He said she's got to recuperate for six months and get her blood tested every month. She's real weak and doesn't have any get-up-and-go. I sure as hell am not going to let her drink any water from that well of hers.

"Say, that Stein is kind of a weird guy. I never saw a guy cover his bald spot with a little black cap before."

Chip snorted the coffee he was drinking. "He's Jewish, Iver. That cap is a yarmulke. It's worn by devote Jewish men."

"You mean like Jesus? No wonder he can bring sick people back from almost being dead."

Chief Fredrickson dragged over an extra chair, as was his habit now, and brought Chip and Iver up to date on the police department's activities.

"I brought Sven home," he reported. "I knew right away where to look for him, but I gave the kid a few days to arrive at an 'attitude adjustment' before I drove out to Hal's deer hunting shack and lugged the cold and hungry kid back to his mother.

"Boy's been a handful ever since Jane divorced Hal. Hal's a piss poor role model, and the kid sure knows how to push Jane's buttons. Told me to go to hell. I told him I'd send him to juvie if he didn't shape up. He tried to tape me with that damn video camera he's always toting around, but I put a stop to that nonsense. Fool kid.

"By the way, Chip, I read that book of yours. I think the police chief could have easily found that serial killer without having to call in a doc to help. You made Chief Katz out to be a bumbling dolt. Next book, give the police some respect. Just my opinion, of course. I suppose handsome doctors sell more books than middle-aged police chiefs."

"I'll take it under advisement, Chief," said Chip, mentally adding another literary review to the growing list of Benders telling him how to write.

HONEY AND HER EIGHT PUPS CAME HOME TO Chip's farmhouse along with an early Christmas gift from Jane and Ingrid . . . a playpen. The puppies ate and played and pooped and pooped and pooped. Then they nestled together in a heap of soft, golden puppy fur and fell asleep for a few hours, only to start the whole process over again. He gave the girls flower names . . . Violet, Pansy, Petunia, and Lily. He named the boys after gods . . . Zeus, Thor, and Jupiter, and then, of course, there was little Runt.

Chip had landline phone service installed in his farmhouse. He found he no longer craved the isolation of his farm. Instead, he had a growing need to communicate and no desire to return to the roof of his shed for decent cell service. He saw the move as a giant step backward in technology and a giant step forward in personal growth and healing. His first call was from California.

"Darling, what's that terrible racket I hear in the background?" Lucinda's voice was strangely deep and melodramatic, like an actress in an old movie. Hollywood was having its effect on her.

"That's just the puppies nipping and yipping."

"Puppies? Did you say puppies?" Now she sounded like a bad imitation of Glenn Close as Cruella de Vil.

"Yes. Say, Lucinda, I'm sorry I'm a little behind on my writing schedule. Things have really been hopping here in Turners Bend." Chip rattled off a tale of dead cows, a poisoned resident, a runaway teen, and eight puppies.

"If there's any trouble in that dreadful place, I suggest you investigate the vile lump of a man I met in that seedy tavern . . . Hal something. I could tell he was up to no good, and there were a couple of goons hanging with him.

"Now about our movie. I'm staying in Hollywood over the holidays. I may have to sleep with Howard Glasser to get this contract finalized, but anything for you, dear. Kiss, kiss to you and your puppies. Tata."

No sooner had he hung up the phone from Lucinda's call, when Jane called. "Chip, the lab results are back from the water samples.

The cows are dying of nitrate poisoning from the water in the creek. I've alerted all the farms along the creek. Mabel doesn't drink water out of the creek, but she must have a faulty well where creek water is seeping in. No one else in town has reported being sick, but I'll warn Doc Schultz to keep an eye out for any additional cases. And, Chip, we're not talking low nitrate levels like we might expect from farm chemical run-off; we're talking dangerous levels of three different nitrates, over 2,100 ppm of KNO_3 alone."

"My chemistry is a little rusty. What is KNO_3?

"Potassium Nitrate, better know as saltpeter. No sexual jokes, please. It's not dangerous in low levels, of course, but it can be converted into nitrites by bacteria and causes symptoms like Mabel's. It's rare, but it happens.

"The lab has sent an alert and request for investigation to the state and federal authorities. They warned me it might be some time before anyone shows up here to do a more exhaustive study. They are short-staffed and the holidays will slow things down, too."

"What about the sample from the creek out west of AgriDynamics?" asked Chip.

Jane did not immediately respond.

"Jane . . ."

"Chip, those samples were clean, but we can't just assume that AgriDynamics is the source."

"Jane, I've got a thought about the possible source of those nitrates. Let me do some online research first. How about having dinner with me? I have to drive over to the pet store in Ames tomorrow for some supplies. Maybe we could get some dinner and talk this over. Do you like Chinese?"

Much to Chip's delight she said, "Yes, as a matter of fact, I love any kind of Asian food."

SPARKED BY LUCINDA'S MENTION OF HAL and the results of the water tests, Chip googled "industrial chemicals" and after an hour of searching link after link, he had a theory to share with Jane. He also had an idea of how to check out his theory and oddly the idea came from *Brain Freeze.*

Chip was getting into the rhythm and discipline of writing for four hours every day. If he could keep on track, he would just make Lucinda's deadline. He was plotting scenes on Post-It Notes, and for lack of a more suitable space, he was putting them on his refrigerator door. The door was plastered with yellow rectangles and the plot was thickening.

Chapter Seventeen

Brain Freeze
Two Harbors, Minnesota

JOHN WOKE EARLY TO THE TANTALIZING SCENTS of bacon and coffee. He sat up and stretched, stiff from being folded on the couch all night. Caddy padded over to him and pulled off the blanket, dragging it behind her to the kitchen. "Okay, I get it. Time for breakfast."

He stood up and reached toward the ceiling, working out the kinks. Wandering out of the living room, he yawned. At the doorway to the kitchen, he paused when he saw Jo. She stood in front of the small stove with a spatula in hand, wearing a white t-shirt and faded jeans. Her feet were bare, with red polish on the toe nails. The morning sun streaming through the kitchen window lit up the curls that flowed freely down her back. He thought it would be a long time before he saw a more lovely sight.

Jo flicked a piece of bacon in Caddy's direction. The retriever snatched it mid-air and swallowed it whole, licking her lips. Jo caught sight of John watching her and smiled. "Hungry?"

When he found he could speak again, he said, "Not everyone can say they've had a special agent of the FBI make them breakfast. Smells delicious."

Jo laughed and turned back towards the stove. She slid the spatula under a slice of French toast, flipping it expertly. "Would you mind setting the table and pouring some coffee?"

He stepped into the kitchen and went to the cabinet next to Jo. Reaching for the cups and plates, he caught the scent of her shampoo. He was grateful his hands were already filled with their dishes. He longed to reach out and wrap one of her curls around his finger.

They bustled around the kitchen, each lost in their own thoughts. Caddy lay next to the table with a rawhide bone, crunching loudly. Jo and John had to step over her each time they moved around the tiny kitchen. John found himself enjoying this quiet, domestic activity. He searched his memory for a similar time with Tanya or any other previous girlfriends and came up empty.

Once they had settled at the table, John ate with his usual gusto. Between bites, he said, "Jo, this is great. How did you learn to cook?"

"Oh, you pick up a thing or two when you have a workaholic father and you are home alone quite a bit. It was either learn to cook or get in trouble with the local boys." Her eyes danced.

John choked on a piece of French toast. Something about the way she said the last line made him forget breakfast for a moment and he felt a stab of jealousy. Not quite meeting her eyes, he said, "And did you . . . I mean, did you get into trouble? With boys I mean?"

She laughed out loud. "Why, Dr. Goodman, are you asking me if I fooled around?" She was clearly enjoying his discomfort.

He raised serious eyes to her taunting ones. "Yes. I guess I am."

"Well, I'm not the type of girl to kiss and tell, so you're just going to have to keep wondering."

He shrugged his shoulders. "One of these days, you're going to spill all your secrets. Hey, speaking of secrets, did you find out anything new yesterday?"

Jo brightened. "Yes! Do you remember the CFO I told you about? Well, turns out she's got a microchip in her head, too. Can you believe it? They are experimenting on their own people."

"You're kidding, right? Why on earth would she allow them to perform surgery on her? Seems like she would be in the know about the risks and short-cuts they've been taking."

"Maybe she doesn't know the whole story. Besides, sounds like she has issues with migraines. She might have been desperate to get rid of them, at any cost."

Jo took a bite of toast and chased it with a swallow of orange juice. "But that's not the only thing I got from eight hours of pushing around the janitor's cart." She got up from the table and picked up the flash drive from the countertop. She walked back over to John and held it up. "I managed to gain access to her desktop."

John raised an eyebrow. "Now I am impressed. You can cook *and* sneak out top secret documents."

"Hurry and finish your breakfast. I got up early this morning and dug through some of the files. Didn't get too far. There are literally hundreds of them and most are pretty mundane. Lots of procedures on reporting cost of goods sold and depreciating assets. Typical bean-counter stuff. However, I did find a few things that look promising."

∎ ∎ ∎ ∎ ∎ ∎

AFTER THEY CLEARED AWAY THE BREAKFAST DISHES, Jo brought the laptop to the table and inserted the flash drive. She pulled up one of the files and said, "This spreadsheet shows several large payments from various banana republic governments. They are all listed as 'prepayment for units.' Suspicious, wouldn't you say?"

She refilled their coffee mugs as John read through the file. He said, "You're right. Just enough to whet our appetite, but it doesn't prove anything. Seems like another piece of the puzzle, though."

Jo sat back down next to John. "I called some of the financial experts in our Minneapolis offices. They are going to track the bank account activities and hopefully come up with more information from their end."

Jo and John spent the better part of the next two hours scanning through all the documents. They eventually came across a memo from the CEO to Ms. Peterson.

Jo pointed at the screen. "Take a look at that. Candleworth sent her a request for payment to people taking part in clinical trials. It makes no mention of what took place during those medical tests, however. They sure were generous with their payments. Ten thousand dollars per person is a lot of money for blood samples and overnight observations. Do you suppose they were paying people to be guinea pigs for the implants?"

"Could be. Is there any mention of who the payees were?"

"Not in this memo. Maybe I can cross reference it to a payment ledger." She opened the spreadsheet software and searched through the titles. Jo clicked on a file named "Trials."

"I'll bet this is it." She scrolled down to payments made on the date of the inter-office memo. Jo sat back in her seat, stunned.

John's eyes scanned the file. He whistled. "My God! There's a payment for twenty thousand dollars to Mitch Calhoun. He was paid for the implant that killed him, all in the name of testing NeuroDynamics's new gadget. I'm all for testing, but . . ." He stood up and began pacing the living room. "This is taking things too far."

He stopped and turned back to Jo. "We've got to put them out of business, Jo. Even if this isn't mind control, it is unethical at best."

Jo's green eyes were troubled. "We need more proof. When we nail him to the wall, he can't wriggle free." She glanced at the clock in the lower right hand corner of the laptop screen. She started. "I've got to go. I'm going to be late for my shift at NeuroDynamics. I've got more digging to do."

John pulled up the sleeve of his sweatshirt to look at the Rolex on his wrist. "I thought your shift didn't start until three. It's only eleven thirty."

"My boss at the cleaning company called while you were asleep. The regular person from the morning shift has to leave early for a family emergency. He asked if I could pick up some of her hours. Keep searching through these files. I'll try to get into the chief surgeon's office today."

John nodded. "Don't know if I'll know what to look for on the CFO's spreadsheets, though. I wasn't exactly a natural in the business class I was required to take in college. I *am* looking forward to taking a look at what you find on the surgeon's computer, though. Then maybe I can start earning my keep around here."

Jo punched him lightly on the arm. "I'm sure you'll more than earn your keep, once we get into the medical details. I almost flunked biology."

As she pulled on her parka, John felt a twinge of regret that their morning together had been cut short and he grew uneasy as Jo took more risks each day. It was as if she was tempting fate.

He said, "Jo, please be careful. These guys are not going to be happy if they find out that you really are cleaning house."

She saluted and headed out into the cold.

CHAPTER EIGHTEEN

Ames, Iowa
December

"NICE CAR," SAID JANE. SHE NESTLED INTO THE RED leather passenger seat of Chip's Volvo C70 coupe and ran her fingers across the light oak inlays on the dash. "Not many of these around central Iowa, I would guess."

"Well, a front-wheel drive convertible isn't very practical for the Midwest, especially during the winter. Iver keeps advising me to get a four-wheel-drive pickup."

"True, but it sure is nice to be riding in luxury for a change." Jane closed her eyes and rested her head against the headrest. Chip punched PLAY on the CD player and Vivaldi's "Spring" softly emanated from the car's twelve speakers.

"This is the first moment's peace I've had since all these poisonings started. So what's your theory, Chip?"

"Flora showed me an aerial map of the county, and I traced Beaver Creek. It runs through the affected farms and along Mabel's property line. It also runs not far from AgriDynamics. I did some research on industrial chemicals. My theory is that AgriDynamics is the source of the toxins, especially since they were not in the water samples west of the plant."

"I don't know how that can be. Hal may be a drunk and a jerk, but he's a smart businessman. He got into the alternative energy trend early with his wind turbine business. He went through all the hoops to qualify as a 'green' corporation. He gets a bundle of federal funds because of it. I can't imagine he'd do anything to risk that."

"What about Owen Hansen, the whistle blower? He supposedly was going to rat on AgriDynamics about something. Something serious enough to get him beat up."

"Oh, my God, I forgot about that incident. I assumed it was about unionization. Hal doesn't want his workers to form a union, and it's been pretty contentious at times. Anyway, Owen didn't work in the plant. He worked in the office. An accountant, I think."

"Maybe AgriDynamics has union or financial problems, but I still wouldn't rule out the plant as the possible source of the nitrates."

Chip and Jane spent the rest of the drive to Ames quietly thinking.

"A penny for your thoughts," he said, breaking their silence.

"I'm digging back into my knowledge of chemistry," said Jane.

"Hope you can come up with something. Chemistry was not one of my strong suits in college. I vaguely remember a D+ in Organic Chem."

Chip, however, had switched from wondering about the chemistry of toxins to thinking about Dr. Jane Swanson, Turners Bend's veterinarian, and a damn attractive woman. Today her hair hung loose instead of in her usual ponytail, and she wore pale lipstick and maybe a little blush. Was this a date? He wasn't sure, and he wasn't sure whether or not he wanted it to be a date. All he really knew was that he was enjoying being in her company.

At the city limits of Ames, Jane said, "By the way, I get a professional discount at Pet City in Ames. You're going to need a lot of puppy food. It's time to wean them and give Honey a break from nursing. Let me warn you, pups are messy eaters at first. You'll have to clean them up after each feeding. Then in about another month, they'll be ready for their new homes."

Chip didn't want to think about finding homes for the puppies. He already knew he couldn't part with Honey or Runt, but that left seven puppies to place in good homes.

After purchasing three, thirty-five-pound bags of Science Diet Lamb and Rice dry puppy food and two cases of canned food, plus some veterinarian supplies for Jane, they headed for the House of Chen restaurant.

They opted for the all-you-can-eat buffet and started with a glass of plum wine and the appetizers: cream cheese wontons, egg rolls, lettuce wraps, shrimp toast, and chicken wings. Next they filled their plates with chicken fried rice, kung pao beef with broccoli, sweet and sour chicken, and egg foo yung. The food was fresh and flavorful, but far from authentic. Not one dish was similar to the food that Chip had savored while visiting Hong Kong, but he kept that opinion to himself and ate with enjoyment of both the food and the company.

Jane poured hot tea into one of the small white cups and sat back in the booth, cradling the cup in her hands. "So, back to your theory about the toxins, even if AgriDynamics is the source, I doubt Hal would look kindly on us marching into AgriDynamics to check his chemicals and take samples. He'd put up a real stink."

"I gathered that. If you don't mind me asking, what's with him? I surmise you two did not have an amicable divorce, and I'm ashamed to say, I know way too much about nasty divorces."

"Hal and I started dating in high school and went off to the University of Iowa together. All of Turners Bend, including the two of us, assumed we would get married. Sven and Ingrid came along and all was fine until Hal started to drink too much. Said he wanted to escape from the stress of work and that he felt trapped in a loveless marriage. He had an affair with a nineteen-year-old receptionist in his office. Like a fool, I said I would forgive him if he went into treatment. They tossed him out of treatment just about the time my father died and the vet practice became my sole responsibility. The day he came home drunk and shoved Ingrid against the wall was the day I kicked him out and filed for divorce."

"When was that?"

"Ingrid was three at the time, so that would have been eleven years ago. To this day Ingrid doesn't want to have much to do with him, but he seems to have some sway over Sven. All in all it's been ugly, but I have custody of the kids, and I find great fulfillment in my practice." She took a sip of tea. "So, now that I've bared my soul, what about you?"

"Married three times, divorced three times. My fault, my fault, and my fault. I'm trying to grow up and get my act together. I'm forty-six, so I'm getting a late start, wouldn't you say?"

"What went wrong in your marriages?"

"Mary, my first wife, and I were very young and immature when we married. She grew up long before I did. She's the one that should have gone to medical school, but she became a RN instead . . . from what I hear a damn good one. After I quit school, our marriage fell apart. I started to spend all my time gambling in Atlantic City. She finally left me. Now she's married to a nice guy and has two kids. We don't have any contact, but my brother sees her at the hospital where they both work. I think I'll always love the memory of the way we were in college."

"And your second wife?"

"Oh, Lord, when I met Bambi—"

"Bambi? Seriously?"

They both laughed. He said, "I was in a downward spiral, drinking, carousing, spending money like I was a rich playboy, which I kind of was. She was a cocktail waitress in a bar I frequented. All tits and ass on the outside, but a gold digger underneath, on the lookout for a guy with a respectable name and a bank account to match. A few lap dances and she had me by the gonads, in more ways than one. Six months after a quickie wedding in Las Vegas, she filed for divorce and walked away with half of my sizable trust fund and a big, satisfied smile on her face. As we left court she whispered 'sucker' in my ear. Have to say I deserved it. Currently she's going after the royalties from my book. My only hope is that she will snag a bigger fish and cut me loose one of these days."

"Dare I ask about wife number three?"

"Ah, that would be my divorce lawyer Erica Slater."

Jane laughed again. "Wow."

"Told you I needed to grow up. Damn smart woman, damn good lawyer. She prevented Bambi from taking my whole trust fund. In court she and Bambi were well-matched. It was quite a circus. Little did I know at the time that I would end up the clown. After the divorce proceedings she pursued me. I really thought she was 'the one,' that I had finally grown up and was ready to settle down and re-join

Baltimore society. No sooner had we married than she turned around, divorced me and took the other half of my trust fund. I still don't know how I missed it."

"Missed what?"

"That she was a lesbian. She said that being married to me confirmed her sexual orientation. She left her law firm and is now spending her time and money in Europe with her former paralegal, a twenty-two-year-old woman."

"Ouch!"

"I ended up with my car and not even a shred of self-respect. Like I said, all three were basically my fault, although I did get a smidgen of revenge against Bambi and Erica."

"How so?"

"I killed them off in *The Cranium Killer*, using the names Brandi and Erin. Had the serial killer removed their brains. Didn't skimp on the details either."

Jane half shrugged. "Well, at least you got something out of the relationships—a plot." Then she changed the topic. "How'd you end up in Turners Bend? No offense, but it's rare for us to get newcomers to the town, and you do seem to be a bit of a fish out of water."

Chip laughed. "And here I thought I was blending in quite nicely. I didn't leave Baltimore with Turners Bend as my destination. It's just where I got tired of running. I decided it would be a good place to hide out, live like a hermit, and write my second book."

"Have you always been a writer?"

Chip laughed again. "No, I stumbled into that gig the same way I stumbled into Turners Bend, but I'm starting to enjoy it. Apparently I may be able to support myself with it, or so says Lucinda Patterson, my literary agent. She's trying to sell the movie rights to my first book."

"Lord, don't mention that to Sven. He wants to be a filmmaker. Have you noticed how he's always videotaping everyone? He's adamant about not being a vet. He won't help out in the clinic or even with our pets at home. He says he doesn't want to go to college and threatens to quit school and go to California or New York. That's one of the battles Hal and I are waging. Hal's encouraging him. I think it's just because he doesn't want to pay his share of college tuition."

Exercising some discretion, Chip did not mention how he had not wanted to follow in his family's footsteps of neurosurgery, the pain it caused, and the rift that now existed between his father and him. He wanted to leave that back in Baltimore.

Chip switched to "Ella Fitzgerald's Greatest Hits" for the drive back to Turners Bend. Jane hummed along to the strains of "Someone to Watch Over Me." They listened to the music companionably and did not talk until they were almost back to town.

"What happens after you finish your book? Will you be moving on or staying in Turners Bend?"

"To be honest, Jane, I don't know. I'm taking it one day at a time right now. I'm seeing where life leads me, as corny as that may sound."

"You've made some friends like Mabel and Iver who would like you to stay. And, I don't know what magic charm you used on Flora Fredrickson, but she was gushing over you yesterday."

"And what about you?"

Jane paused, and Chip held his breath for her response.

"Yes, you've become my friend, too."

Chip tried to remember if he and any of his ex-wives had been friends. Maybe Mary, but definitely not with Bambi or Erica. Both had spit him out as if he were a rotten orange and then tossed him into a juicer until all that was left was pulp.

— — — — —

LATE INTO THE NIGHT CHIP REPLAYED HIS DAY with Jane. She had some of the same qualities that had attracted him to Mary—she was authentic, the real thing. He hadn't touched her once during the trip, but his hands were aching to touch her now, to touch her in the same way that John was aching to touching Jo in *Brain Freeze*. Dr. John Goodman was going to be one lucky bastard. Chip realized he would have to live vicariously through his literary better half for now.

CHAPTER NINETEEN

Brain Freeze
Two Harbors, Minnesota

WHEN JO ENTERED THE BUILDING, SHE DID NOT RECOGNIZE the security guard on duty. He spoke up as she walked past the desk. "Hey. Need to see your ID." His voice was deep and gravely. Something about it stirred a memory, but the more she tried to recall why it sounded familiar, the more elusive it became.

As it was the first time she had been asked to show her badge up close since she started at NeuroDynamics, her heart raced. She controlled her nerves, though, and spoke in an even voice, "Um, sure. No problem. Where's Sam, the guard usually on duty?" She unclipped the badge from her shirt and showed it to the guard. He wrote down her information.

He did not smile at her and his eyes showed no emotion. His face was ruddy, and dotted with pock marks. His uniform looked new and still had fold marks from the packaging. The collar of his shirt was tightly buttoned and his nametag read KURT. "Out sick." He slid the badge back across the desk towards Jo.

Jo snatched it up and reattached it to her pocket. "Thanks." She walked down the hallway and tried to calm her breathing. Something did not feel right.

JO QUICKLY WORKED THROUGH THE OFFICES and soon forgot about the unsettling encounter with the new security guard. She wanted to have plenty of free time to wander through the surgical wing of the building. When she entered the chief surgeon's office to straighten up, she wedged a paper clip into the latch of the door, so that the lock wouldn't catch when he closed his office for the day.

It was dark outside when the last of the surgical staff left. Jo looked up and down the hallways, and quietly slipped into the office. The office was dark, but the fluorescent lights from the hallway revealed a tastefully decorated space. There was an over-sized cherry desk with a leather upholstered chair and two matching visitor chairs. One wall was covered with diplomas and awards. A ficus tree in a heavy Mediterranean pot stood next to the floor-to-ceiling window that ran the entire length of the room. A faint scent of cigar smoke lingered in the room. Jo wrinkled her nose. "It's always the doctors that don't follow their own advice," she muttered.

Jo slipped on gloves and removed the paper clip from the door latch, quietly closing the door behind her. She closed all the blinds and turned on the desk lamp. The laptop was gone. The chief surgeon must have taken it home. "Damn." She sat down in the leather chair and pulled at the drawer handle on the right hand side of the desk. The drawer would not budge. Next, she tried the middle drawer. It slid open without resistance.

The open drawer contained a tray of pens and pencils, a stethoscope and a set of keys. With the middle drawer still open, she reached once more for the lower right drawer. This time is pulled open easily. The locking mechanism operated through the middle drawer. She'd seen this before. Satisfied, she began flipping through the files with her index finger. Yanking out the files revealed that they were personnel medical documents. Jo tore off a piece of note paper from a pad on the desk and wrote down the names of the staff and their contact information.

She found nothing of value in the other desk drawers, except the doctor's supply of cigars. She snatched up the keys she found and looked around the office. Beneath the wall of diplomas stood a cherry cabinet that matched the desk. Jo walked over, clicked on the pen light she kept in her pocket and inserted a key. The drawer creaked as she pulled it open, loud in the silence of the room.

The top drawer contained patient files. Inserting the pen light between her teeth and aiming its narrow beam into the cabinet, she flipped through the tabs quickly, looking first for the file on Mitch Calhoun. It was missing. She looked through all the files, to make sure it had not been misfiled. It was definitely not in the cabinet.

Jo did find the file for Belinda Peterson, however. She pulled it out of the cabinet and brought it over to the desk. Just as she was about to read it, she heard a noise outside the door. She slid the file beneath her shirt and turned off the desk lamp. Jo crept over to the door and opened it just a crack. When she didn't see anyone, she opened the door further and poked her head into the hallway. No one there.

Jo retrieved the file from her shirt and flipped the light back on. Pulling out her cell phone, she took pictures of all pages that looked relevant. She went back to the cabinet and grabbed a handful of files. Fifteen minutes later, she felt that she had copies of anything remotely helpful and then returned everything as she had found it. Jo rolled her supply cart towards the elevator.

— — — — —

THE REST OF HER SHIFT FINALLY ENDED AND SHE PACKED UP her things for home. The security guard was not at the desk when she left the building.

She put up her hood when she stepped out into the frigid night. The cold stole the breath from her mouth and her nostrils threatened to freeze shut. The full moon reflecting off the snow gave Jo's surroundings a blue other-worldly cast.

Her teeth were chattering by the time she reached the Highlander. As she held up the remote to unlock the car, she heard the squeak of boots running behind her. Startled, she turned around.

"Hey. Forgot something." She came face to face with the guard who had stopped her at the beginning of her shift. The moonlight exaggerated the pock marks on his cheeks, and she could smell tobacco on his breath. He held out her insulated lunch bag. "Found this in the locker room when I was makin' the rounds."

Jo took the bag from his hands. "Uh, thanks. You were in the ladies' locker room? Isn't that a bit . . . inappropriate?" Her heart was pounding. She wished she hadn't left her gun at the condo. She felt naked without it.

He leaned against the side of her SUV. His smile was wolfish and his eyes glittered. "You never know what you're gonna find. Take care now on that ride back to your condo." He turned on his heel and walked back to the building.

"How do you know I live in a condo?" Jo whispered as she watched him go.

Jo unlocked her car door and climbed in. She locked the doors behind her. Her hand shook as she inserted the key and started the engine. Digging her cell phone out of her pocket, she took a deep breath and then released it slowly. She dialed. "John. Just wanted to let you know I'm on my way back."

— — — — —

Jo waited for the engine to heat up. A shiver that wasn't entirely due to the outside temperatures rippled down her body. Looking out the windshield, she saw snowflakes sparkle like glitter in the vees of white created by the powerful security lights in the parking lot.

Clicking on the seat warmer, she spoke aloud. "It's not like I've never dealt with creeps like him before. Worse, in fact." She shook her head, disgusted with herself for getting worked up about the security guard. "Jeez, trained at Quantico and in the field for six years. Acting like a rookie with first-day jitters."

She was comforted by the fact that John was expecting her back at the condo soon. Jo was surprised to find that she couldn't wait to see him again. They had fallen into a comfortable routine. She was eager to share her day— and the files she had filched—with him.

Thinking about John made her forget for a moment about the security guard, and she relaxed into the warmed gray leather seats. She closed her eyes. Alone in her car, she could face the growing attraction she felt for the doctor. Sure, he was smart. One didn't become a world famous neurosurgeon without being brilliant.

But there was more to it than that. He was caring and considerate. She was beginning to trust him in ways she didn't think possible. John had a wonderful sense of humor, and she found herself making jokes, just to hear that deep laughter of his.

Of course, she couldn't help finding him attractive. He was strong, tall and lean, with a swimmer's body that would catch any woman's eye. More and more often, she found herself watching him, wondering what it would be like to have those lips on hers, hearing his deep voice close to her ear.

She sat up straight. "Damnit! That's it!" Her heart thudded as she finally figured out why the security guard's voice sounded familiar. Jo's hands gripped the steering wheel until her knuckles turned white. She was filled with a rage she didn't know she possessed. Jo looked toward the headquarters' entrance. As if on cue, Kurt walked out, the wind pulling the heavy door out of his hand and knocking it against the wall. His shoulders scrunched up to his ears and he pulled on black leather gloves as he walked.

Jo scooted down in her seat, so that he wouldn't see her. She quickly turned off the Highlander. Peering over the dash, she watched him trudge through the parking lot. He didn't look in her direction, and climbed into the cab of a red Ford F-150. He started up the truck and took off, the back end of the pickup fishtailing as he headed towards the exit.

Jo waited a moment, then pulled out of the parking lot and followed him. "Calm down, Jo. Being pissed off is not going to help you catch this guy." She took a deep breath. But every time she tried to tamp down her anger, Kurt's voice replayed in her head. She heard him say over and over again, "We're not here for your money, old man. Where is it?" *One of the bastards that killed Sid.*

Jo trailed the truck, down the two-lane road that led to the highway. She stayed far enough back. She couldn't risk having him spot her in his rear-view mirror. When Kurt turned south, she likewise turned right. They drove through downtown Two Harbors and headed towards Duluth. The roads had been plowed earlier in the day, but the billowing snow was accumulating once again.

Following the truck, Jo thought about all the times that Sid had been there for her, all the ways he had helped her through her grief, and her anger. *I owe him.* Her jaw clenched as she watched one of his killer's drive in front of her.

The taillights abruptly glowed a bright red. "Why the hell is he stopping?" She didn't have a choice. She had to slow down. The pickup idled for a couple of minutes and then Kurt spun it around on the slippery road and faced her. Her eyes widened as the snowplow mounted on the front of Kurt's truck headed straight for her Highlander, picking up speed.

She came to a complete stop, put the car in reverse, trying to get out of his way. Looking over her shoulder, she backed up. When she glanced back at the advancing truck, she saw that Kurt was almost on top of her. He smiled then. She could see his face clearly above the snowplow. *He's enjoying this!* Jo's heart raced. *I won't die this way.*

Slam! As the truck hit the front of Jo's SUV, her body jerked with the impact of the deployed airbag. Dust-like particles of powder puffed into her face, causing her eyes to burn. The airbag deflated at once, as the gas escaped through the vents in the fabric. Impatiently swiping a hand across tearing eyes, she floored the accelerator. She tried to get away from him, but Kurt kept the front of the truck on the bumper of her vehicle. He pushed her backwards, ever backwards.

A bright light appeared in her rear-view mirror. A large utility truck was coming up behind her. The horn blared. She was going to be crushed between the two trucks as they rushed at each other. Her voice began as a whisper, "Oh, my God. Ohmigod! OHMIGOD!" Jo reacted without thought. She cranked the steering wheel hard. Time seemed to stretch out forever as the Highlander spun away from Kurt's truck and skittered across the snow-covered highway, the rollover warning signal beeping loudly in her ears. The anti-lock brakes shuddered beneath her right foot as she came to a stop on the shoulder at the opposite side of the road.

She heard the scream of the utility truck's brakes when the driver tried to stop. He struck Kurt's pick-up head on. The crunch of metal on metal was deafening. Jo rushed out the door, running to where the two vehicles had collided. The driver of the other truck was slumped over the wheel. Jo checked for a pulse. Nothing.

Sprinting over to Kurt's truck, she pried open the passenger door. Residue from the deployed airbags hung in the air. She ripped the airbag away from his body. He was in bad shape. There was a gaping wound on his forehead and blood covered his face, flowing freely. The front end of the truck had been compressed at impact and Kurt's legs were crushed under the dashboard. His eyes widened as Jo leaned over him, and he smiled a terrible, bloody smile. He coughed out, "You'll . . . never catch 'em. They'll just . . . move." His eyes went blank and the security guard was still.

Jo grabbed his shoulders and shook him. She shouted, "Who helped you kill the medical examiner?" His head flopped loosely to the side.

Wind whipped Jo's curls about her face as she watched the life leave his body. She reached out a tentative hand and crooked her finger in the collar of his shirt. Tugging it open, the tattoo of a crow on his neck was clear.

When she pulled her hand away, there was a smear of his blood on her finger. She shivered and wiped it off on his shirt. Her hand shook as she reached into her coat pocket and flipped open her cell phone. "Frisco. Yeah, it's me, Agent Schwann. Found one of Sid's killers. You might want to send someone from the ME's office with a couple of body bags. Tow trucks, too."

CHAPTER TWENTY

Turners Bend
January

By MID-JANUARY TURNERS BEND was in hibernation. An ice storm followed by fourteen inches of new snow had paralyzed the county. Snowbirds had flown the coop to Florida and Arizona or left in their Winnebago trailer homes. High school basketball games were the highlight of the week for most residents, and everyone crawled out of their caves to cheer on the Prairie Dogs despite their dismal one and seven season to date. Dreams of reaching the state basketball tournament were melting a lot faster than the ice and snow.

Iver sometimes plowed for ten hours a day. Then did it the next day when it snowed again. He plowed out Chip's road and always stopped in for a cup of coffee. He would pull one of the kitchen chairs over to the playpen to watch the puppies, delighting in their antics.

"Look at that Zeus. Isn't he just the biggest little bully? Pansy can just take so much, and then she nips him, but that don't seem to faze him one darn bit."

"What do you think, Iver. Which one do you want?" This was the week that Chip was determined to find homes for the puppies.

"Not for me, but I'm thinking about one for Mabel. She's been kinda blue, not being able to work and being cooped up in that house. I reckon that little Petunia is about the sweetest one. I've been thinking she'd be the one for Mabel."

"I think you're right about that. Petunia is ideal for Mabel, but I've been thinking Thor should be your dog. He's going to be the biggest and strongest of the lot. Thor was the Viking god of thunder, you know. I can see him riding in the passenger seat next to you in the plow and on your road grader in the summer. You'd make a magnificent pair, and no one would ever mess with the two of you."

Iver didn't say anything, but Chip saw a smile that told him he had just placed two of the puppies. He was learning that with some "city slicker" showmanship he was going to be able to find good homes for the rest of the puppies.

Iver's smile turned tentative. He cleared his throat and turned his eyes away from Chip. "I been wondering if I could show you another gift I been thinking on giving Mabel." He put his hand in the pocket of his overalls and pulled out a small red velvet box.

Chip opened the box and let out a long low whistle. "Why you sly old dog." Nestled in the box was a half-carat, emerald-cut diamond set in a yellow gold band. "Congratulations, buddy. She's a fine woman."

"When we almost lost her up at the Mayo, I knew I had to stick around and take care of her, 'cause I don't want to be without her. But, I don't know if she wants to put up with me. I'm no prize." He picked up Petunia and kissed the top of her head.

"Tell you what, Iver, you bring her Petunia and give her that ring, and I guarantee you'll be hearing wedding bells before the snow melts."

Iver hesitated. "There's one more thing. I'd be mighty grateful if you'd be my best man."

Chip was blown away. "Iver, that's such an honor. I don't know what to say . . . except, yes, I sure will."

─── ─── ─── ─── ───

THE NEXT MORNING CHIP GOT TWO CUPS OF COFFEE and two cinnamon rolls to-go from the Bun and trotted over to Town Hall to beguile Flora, his next prospective puppy parent, with 500 calories of baked goodness.

"Hi, lovely lady. I was hoping I could join you for a coffee break this morning."

"Just the man I wanted to see. I understand you had a date with Dr. Jane. I wouldn't dream of sticking my nose in your business, but I thought you might want my advice about how to impress her." In her bright-red sweater and matching lipstick Flora looked like an overly ripe cherry.

"You know how I value your expertise, Flora. In fact, did I tell you I named my girl puppies after you? They all have flower names."

"Oh, my. I don't know what to say." Flora patted her hair.

"There's one in particular, her name is Pansy, and I think of you every time I watch her. Why don't you come by and take a look at her? I know you won't be able to resist her." Warming to the role of dog salesman, Chip put his hand over his heart.

"I think I might just do that. And, you know, my granddaughter in Des Moines is having a birthday coming up. Is there another little flower for her?" She put her hand over her own heart.

"I think every little girl should have a puppy named Violet, don't you?"

Hook, line and sinker . . . two fish with one rod and reel.

— — — — —

FOUR DOWN AND THREE TO GO. This was easier than Chip thought it would be. He was wondering if he hadn't missed his calling. His next stop was the firehouse. Zeke and Porky, two volunteer firefighters, were polishing the hook and ladder. Zeke was over six feet, tall and slender as a broom handle. In sharp contrast, Porky was just over five feet and rotund.

"Hi, guys. How are Turners Bend's finest today?"

"Busy as we want to be," replied Zeke. "Want some lunch? Porky makes a mean chili."

"That'd be great." Zeke was right. Porky's chili made Chip's nose run and eyes water. He identified garlic and onion and possibly cinnamon and nutmeg, as well as hot peppers and chili powder and possibly chocolate. "Wow, what have you got in here?"

Zeke laughed and ran his hand over his shaved head. "I used to have hair before I ate Porky's chili."

Porky was a retired hog farmer—thus his nickname. He was too old and too overweight to fight fires, but his culinary skills were an asset to the department. He pushed his 285 pounds up from a chair and refilled Chip's bowl. "Secret family recipe of twenty-nine herbs and spices." He laughed and his belly bounced like a department store Santa Claus.

"You guys ever think about getting a firehouse dog?" Chip launched into his sales pitch.

"You mean like one of those dalmatians?"

"Well, I hear they're temperamental. I was thinking more of a fine golden retriever, maybe a pup to train as a rescue dog."

A friendly argument followed in which Zeke and Porky battled over which one of them would be a better trainer. In the end Chip succeeded in placing both Jupiter and Zeus, one for each man.

He was down to Lily, the last little girl. Chip had heard that Ingrid's fifteenth birthday was around the corner. He would give Lily to Ingrid as a gift, and voila all the puppies would be gone.

Chip was pleased with himself until the puppies started to depart. As each puppy left for its new home, Chip, Honey, and Runt suffered. He fought back tears when he realized that Violet was going to Des Moines, a place where he may never see her again. Honey seemed to fret, as if she had misplaced her babies, and Runt continually sought Chip's lap in loneliness for his brothers and sisters. They were a pathetic threesome for days, as they moped and wandered from room to room.

The phone rang.

"How's the puppy-daddy?" Lucinda was back to her New York accent.

"I'm going to have Honey spayed. She and I couldn't go through this again. It was just too hard to give our puppies away."

"God, Chip, I think you've gone soft in the head. They're dogs for Pete's sake. Now, down to business. I hated to leave Rodeo Drive, but a girl has to work. Howie paid us a nice sum for the movie rights. He has to find a screenwriter, director and financing before anything happens, but in the meantime we've got money in the bank. After I pay the expenses for my time in Hollywood and take my fees, I'll send you the rest."

"If there's any left, that is."

"Don't be snide, Collingsworth. Just forget about puppies and get going on *Brain Freeze*. Must I remind you that your deadline is fast approaching? Bye."

Chip was not good with deadlines. Things always seemed to get in the way of finishing anything on time. Today he was more interested in what was happening in Turners Bend than he was in meeting Lucinda's demands. Jane had voiced her frustration at the slow response from state and federal authorities, and there didn't seem to be much the locals could do but to send out warnings about the creek water. He was trying to fit all the pieces together . . . the poisonings, the plant, Hal, Owen's beating . . . and he had a nagging feeling that he was missing something, something more sinister than illegal dumping of toxic materials.

CHAPTER TWENTY-ONE

The Bend
Mid-February

THE BEND WAS THE ONLY DRINKING ESTABLISHMENT in Turners Bend. The "B" in its neon sign had run out of gas. Chip never failed to view it as a prophetic omen . . . THE _ END. Business at the Bend was inversely related to the weather, the worse the weather the bigger the crowd at the bar. There was some crossover between the morning regulars at the Bun and the evening regulars at the Bend, but there was an additional element of rough-looking, tough-talking young males. They drank heavily, cussed with every third word and used their fists when their limited vocabularies failed to communicate their points of view.

The day before Valentine's Day, the Bend hosted Iver's bachelor party. It consisted of lots of backslapping and teasing and a few bawdy jokes, but no strippers, no lap dancers and no naked girls popping out of cakes. Thus, it was shaping up to be unlike any bachelor party Chip had attended in Baltimore. He didn't know what Benders expected from the best man, but he felt he should make a toast.

Without an available microphone, Chip was unsure how to get the crowd's attention. He stood on a chair and clinked two beer bottles together.

"Hey, Joe, pull the plug on that jukebox so we can hear this dude," said a guy in a leather vest and cowboy hat. Eventually the room quieted.

"Tomorrow Iver is going to become the luckiest guy in Turners Bend. Don't know how, but he managed to snag the best available woman in town. I think we would all agree that Mabel is the grand prize. She must want someone to plow her driveway pretty damn bad."

When the hooting ceased, Chip continued. "On the other hand, Mabel is smart enough to know a good thing when it comes along.

He's a diamond in the rough, and underneath those overalls is a heart of gold. I'm proud to call him my friend. Let's hoist our glasses to Iver and Mabel. The next round's on me."

In a rich baritone Oscar Nelson started "For He's a Jolly Good Fellow" and the others joined in, as Iver stood red-faced and grinning.

One guy who did not sing along was Hal Swanson. He sat bleary-eyed at the bar, drinking the establishment's best single-malt scotch, Johnny Walker Black Label. Chip took measure of the man, an ex-high school football player gone soft and puffy with buttons straining his silvery silk shirt. His face was red and splotchy and his nose pitted . . . sign of a veteran drinker. A lexicon of adjectives came to Chip's mind . . . sleazy, slimy, pseudo-suave, self-possessed, ruthless, conniving, but also smart.

Chip put his plan into action. "I'm buying this round. What are you drinking, Hal?" Chip took the barstool next to him. Hal's whitened teeth sparkled like in a TV toothpaste ad.

"I'm a man who never turns down a free drink. Make it a double, Joe."

"I need to do some research for my next book. Do you have any openings at AgriDynamics? I want to get some first-hand experience in a manufacturing company."

Hal swigged half of his drink, sloshing some over the side of the glass.

Chip continued. "My agent is giving me pressure to get moving on this book. You met her a few weeks ago. Tall, flashy dame. What she doesn't take in commissions and fees, my ex-wives do."

"Hey, I remember that bitch, and I sure as hell know about ex-wives that give you crap and rob you blind. All I've got is a weekend opening in the warehouse. It's on the third shift, but you can have it, if you want."

"I'll give it a try for a few weeks, just to get a feel for it." They shook hands, and Chip walked away from the bar, congratulating himself and rubbing his hand on the side of his pants, as if it had come away greasy from the shake. The third shift on a weekend would be the perfect time to nose around AgriDynamics, look for toxins and see what other illegal activities might be going on.

ON VALENTINE'S DAY, IVER AND MABEL were married at First Lutheran. Mabel wore a light-blue suit with a matching pillbox hat, trimmed with a wisp of veiling. Jane, her attendant, worn a mid-length navy-blue dress with long sleeves and a scooped neck low enough to show a peek of cleavage. Chip had never seen her in a dress before. Her curves delighted him as he stood next to Iver during the brief ceremony. The scent of roses was intoxicating, sweet and cloying. It was a heady experience for him, and his hormones began to surge.

Mabel recited her vows in a strong, determined voice. She smiled sweetly at Iver as he stumbled his way through his vows, Pastor Henderson having to slowly repeat segments for him. Isabelle Johnson, the church's oldest soprano, warbled her way through "O Perfect Love," just a bit off key and with overdone dynamics.

When Isabelle got to *"Grant them the joy which brightens earthly sorrow; grant them the peace which calms all earthly strife,"* Chip looked over and saw a single tear overflow Jane's lower eyelid and roll down her cheek. Seeing Jane's sentimental side was a new revelation for Chip. Her softer side only served to loosen the control he was attempting to rein in on his own emotions.

Iver and Mabel kissed chastely and turned to the congregation. Pastor Henderson's booming voice ended the ceremony. "Now for the first time as husband and wife, I present to you Mr. and Mrs. Iver Ingebretson." The pianist pounded out a jaunty version of "Oh, Happy Day" as the bride and groom marched down the aisle.

THE AROMA OF ROASTED MEAT PERMEATED the fellowship hall. "Smells good," said Chip, as he and Jane stood in the buffet line at the reception.

"The women of First know how to put on a good spread, but it's the same for every wedding I've ever attended here . . . roast beef and gravy, mashed potatoes, corn and coleslaw . . . the menu never varies."

"I meant to tell you earlier, Jane. You look terrific." *Jeez. Way to sound like Mickey Rooney talking to Judy Garland in some corny Andy Hardy movie.*

"You don't look too bad yourself. I don't think I've ever seen you in a suit, and I know I've never seen Iver in one. Poor guy, I bet he can't wait to shed it, and his collar is so tight it looks like his head is going to pop off."

They both laughed, and Chip put his hand on Jane's lower back as they moved along in the buffet line. He bent down and whispered in her ear, "At least there's cake for dessert." And there was a cake, a dark-chocolate fudge cake with thick cream-cheese frosting, crowned with a plastic bride and groom, a couple that couldn't look more unlike Mabel and Iver.

Mabel threw her bouquet of pink roses and baby's breath to a cluster of unmarried women. She aimed for Jane, but it sailed over her head and was caught by Isabelle Johnson. Isabelle was delighted. At age seventy-six she was still hoping to snag one of Turners Bend's bachelor farmers. Chip saw several of those bachelors make a hasty exit to the parking lot.

CHIP THOUGHT THAT GOING UNDERCOVER AT AGRIDYNAMICS was as good of an idea as Jo going undercover at NeuroDynamics, although he didn't expect it to be as dangerous. Dr. Goodman was sure a lot smoother with Jo than he was with Jane. What was it about her that turned him into a blithering fool? He wanted to be the tall, handsome, worldly Dr. Goodman, but instead he teeter-tottered between a greasy Don Juan and a clueless Beaver Cleaver. He always felt unbalanced in her presence. Why wasn't his love life imitating his art?

CHAPTER TWENTY-TWO

Brain Freeze
Two Harbors, Minnesota

CADDY'S BARK ANNOUNCED THE ARRIVAL OF JO'S SUV. John opened the door to the condo and stood in the doorway, waiting for her. The cold air stung his cheeks, but the tension across his back and neck eased when he saw her. She climbed the steps and looked up at him with tired eyes. John reached for her hand and pulled her into the condo. He unzipped her coat and removed her hat and gloves. She stood like a young child, waiting to be cared for.

"Jo, what happened? When you called, you said you were on your way back to the condo. That was two and a half hours ago." His words took on a sharp edge. "Why didn't you answer your cell?"

She looked away from him and shrugged. Yanking the wig off her head, she set it on the table and ran her fingers through her hair. "I got a little hung up."

His brows came together. He reached for her arm, turning her towards him once again. "Hung up? Jesus, Jo. I was worried."

She raised her eyes to his. "You're not my babysitter, John. You don't have to worry about me. I'm a big girl, remember?"

John felt his cheeks grow warm with anger. "Yeah, I know. A big girl with a badge and a gun. Well, get used to it. I'm going to worry about you. Now, tell me what's going on."

Jo looked at the floor and shivered. Her voice was subdued. "I was in a small accident."

"Accident?" John strode to the door and looked out the side window at the SUV. He whirled around. "The front grill is a mess. What the hell happened?"

"After I talked to you, I planned on leaving, just like I said. While I waited for the car to warm up, I saw the security guard head out the door, and I decided to follow him."

John walked back over to Jo. "What made you do that?"

When she didn't answer, he prompted her, "Jo . . ."

Jo sighed. When she spoke, her voice sounded weary. "I think he's been following me."

He struggled to keep his fears tamped down. "Maybe you should start from the beginning. C'mon, let's get you by the fire to warm up."

John settled her on the raised stone hearth. He turned down the lights in the condo, so that only the fire lit up the living room. The seasoned logs behind her crackled and popped. Wrapping a blanket around her, he rubbed her arms quickly, trying to warm her. Keeping busy to calm down. Caddy settled at her feet, her head leaning against Jo's leg.

John finally sat on the couch across from her. "Now, tell me what this is all about."

Jo gripped the edges of the blanket and held them under her chin. "I managed to take some pictures of the files in the chief surgeon's office."

"Well, maybe now we can figure out exactly what they are doing."

"I hope so, but while I was going through the files, I heard a noise outside of the office. At first, I thought I imagined it. But then, when I was leaving, the guard told me to take care driving back to the condo. John, how'd he know I'm staying in a condo?"

He searched his mind for a reasonable explanation; anything but the possibility that Jo was in danger. "Lucky guess, maybe? Look, you've been cautious. Don't you think that if they were on to you, they would have made their move by now?"

She shook her head, her curls falling into her face. "The more I thought about what he said, the more pissed off I got. After I finished talking to you, I kept thinking about the guy. I finally realized that his voice was familiar. Then I remembered why."

Jo turned to John once more, the firelight causing shadows to dance across her features. Her eyes were hard pieces of emerald in the dim light. "He was one of the killers on the tape at Sid's office. I'm sure of it."

John sucked in a breath and let it out slowly. He closed his eyes briefly. "That's why you followed him."

Jo filled him in on the chase and the deadly crash. She told him about the tattoo.

There was a pain in John's stomach that grew larger with each word. *Jesus Christ, what a mess . . .* He could no longer pretend that Jo's life wasn't in jeopardy. John ran a hand through his hair, making the shorter hairs stand on end. "Damn it. This is getting way out of hand. You and I could both end up like Sid."

He stood up and began to pace. "They're on to you now. They're going to know you were in the accident. Your cover is blown. This has to end. Take what we've got to your boss and let's get the hell out of here. Let someone else take the risk." He felt helpless and frustrated. He knew what she did for a living, and he knew she was highly trained. None of that meant he liked it.

Jo let the blanket slide down her back. She stood up, squaring her shoulders. "No, John. The accident occurred in Frisco's jurisdiction. He took my statement and knows I need more time. He says he can keep the victims' names and my part in the accident out of the papers for a day, maybe two at the most. There were no witnesses. For now, it was a tragic accident on a snowy night, but I was never there.

"I've thought about this on the drive back. I want to see this through to the end. NeuroDynamics can't win. I'm all right. I'm going to call my boss and give him an update."

John gathered her in his arms. He needed to reassure himself that she was here and she was safe. Jo resisted at first, then wrapped her arms around his waist. Her voice was muffled against his sweater. He could feel her warm breath through the fabric. "I was scared, John. More frightened than I've ever been. I thought, 'This is it. I'm going to die on this snowy road, alone.' All I could think of was the life I hadn't yet lived.

"After I'd escaped the accident, I was beyond relieved. Until I realized because of my survival, two others died. I know Kurt was a murderer and he probably deserved what he got, but that trucker didn't. He was just in the wrong place. I couldn't do anything to stop it. Do you know how that feels?"

An image of the young patient who had died before he came to Minnesota popped into his head. And the countless other deaths that he couldn't stop. He held her tighter. "Yeah, I know how that feels."

They stood together. He heard the sizzle of overheated sap from a log in the fireplace. He tucked his finger under her chin and forced her to look up at him. "I don't know if you're fearless or reckless. Maybe a bit of both. When I think of what might have happened . . ."

John's finger trailed along her jaw line. She quivered at his touch. He could hear the huskiness of his own voice when he said, "Are you still cold?"

Her voice was low, "No, not anymore." She reached a hand behind his head and pulled him down to her lips. Her kiss was an almost savage assault on his mouth, as if she wanted to prove to them both that she had survived.

What am I getting into here? John wanted this to happen. Hell, he had wanted it practically from the first moment he met her. But this would be more than just a casual relationship. She was giving him a gift by trusting him, and he felt humbled by it. Then the thought vanished, and he kissed her with an intensity that matched hers.

She ground her hips against him. Raising his head in surprise, he gasped. He walked her to the couch and then settled her on his lap. Lowering his mouth to the hollow beneath her throat, he caught the scent of vanilla. The vibration of her moan was on his lips. He buried his hands in her hair, feeling its silkiness, the curls wrapping themselves around his fingers.

Jo reached up and grasped his hand, putting it to her left breast. His thumb teased the erect nipple through the thin fabric of her shirt. Her breath was coming in small, shallow pants. "I want to take this off." She tugged at the hem of her shirt.

"No, let me." He pushed her hands aside and lifted the shirt over her head, tossing it to the floor. Unhooking her lacey bra, he slid it down her arms. Her full breasts glowed in the firelight. A prayer escaped from him, "God, you're beautiful."

Jo ran a hand through his hair and guided his head down to her chest. He gently pushed her off his lap and onto the couch. Partly lying across her, he sucked on her nipple. He teased it with his teeth, until she arched her back, moaning deeply. Jo reached down to his crotch. His body jerked in response. It was difficult to draw a deep breath. She whispered, "Take off your clothes. I want to touch you, to see you."

John eased himself off her and tugged the sweater over his head. He slowly unbuttoned the shirt beneath, wanting this to last. Her eyes glittered in the dim light. Sitting up, she watched as he unbuckled his belt. She roughly shoved his hands aside and said, "My turn."

Jo stood up and kissed his chest. Her hands trailed along his flat stomach. Fingertips traced the whorls of hair above his belt line. He inhaled sharply when she ran the tip of her tongue across his nipple and then blew on it, the wetness reacting to the cool air. The pleasure of her touch was almost painful.

Hooking a finger in his belt loop, she pulled him toward her bedroom. "Come with me." He went along willingly, already missing the feel of her hands on him. Aching to touch her again.

Caddy stood up, ready to follow them into the bedroom. John gently pushed her aside and closed the door on her. "Sorry, old girl. I think I can handle this by myself."

CHAPTER TWENTY-THREE

Wednesday, March 8, 2:13 p.m.

Chip,
 Atta boy! Have you been practicing with that No-where-ville vet? Keep it up (no pun intended). Your readers want sex, sex, and more sex. They aren't getting it at home, so you've got to give it to them full blast in your book. What about a shower or tub scene for Jo and John? Soap and sex are so delicious! The two of them have to go at it passionately, with a capital 'P'. . . nibbles, licking, sucking right through to multiple orgasms. Show how those Iowa bulls do it! Or I'll personally castrate you!

Lucinda

CHAPTER TWENTY-FOUR

Brain Freeze
Two Harbors, Minnesota

Jo WAITED UNTIL JOHN HAD CLOSED THE DOOR and she had his full attention. She shimmied out of her jeans, taking her time. Panties soon followed, and she kicked them off the end of her toe.

John stood still, his eyes roving freely over her body. She felt feverish, as he seemed to take in every inch of her. She hadn't felt this vulnerable for a long time and she was surprised to find that she wasn't afraid to trust him.

In a slightly strangled voice, he said, "You're incredible."

Feeling anything but incredible after the night she'd had, she wrinkled her nose. "I need a shower, to wash away tonight. Come with me?" Without waiting for an answer, she turned on her heel and walked to the master bath.

She turned around just in time to see him quickly stepping out of his jeans. Her eyes widened as she looked him over. Years of swimming had given him a powerful body. His shoulders were broad, tapering down to a narrow waist. His legs were long and strong. She smiled to herself when she saw how aroused he was.

"C'mon, Doctor. You look like you could use some, um, soap yourself."

His response was more growl than words. He stepped behind her as she reached behind the shower curtain to turn on the water. John grabbed her hips and pulled her to him.

There was an insistent ache between her legs. She turned around to kiss him deeply on the mouth. He groaned as she caressed him, hands exploring.

John's breath was hot in her ear. "I think we'd better get into that shower. I'm looking forward to soaping you up."

The shower stall was wide and deep, with a bench built into the wall. Steam swirled around them. Jo snatched the bar of soap and began to lather up her hands. She motioned for John to turn around and then rubbed the soap across his shoulders, down his back, caressing his buttocks. His hands braced himself against the wall, as if he needed help standing upright. He turned his head towards her, water streaming down his face.

"You are a terrible tease."

"I'm glad you noticed." Her hands moved down his hard thighs and calves. After soaping up her hands again, she gently turned him around and started rubbing his chest. She took her time moving down to his stomach and then stroked his inner thigh. His reaction was almost violent. He wrapped his hand tightly around hers and held it still.

"Stop. Just give me a second." He closed his eyes, as if mentally counting. When he opened his eyes again, he said, "Give me that soap. It's *my* turn." She shivered at his words, anticipating his hands gliding across her flesh.

His hands were strong and slippery. When his thumb brushed across her nipple, her body vibrated in response. She roughly grabbed his hand and shoved it between her thighs. Closing her eyes, she whimpered, "Touch me."

His fingers explored her wetness. Jo's breath came in quick, shallow pants.

She opened her eyes to look at him. "I want to feel you inside me. Here, sit on the bench."

When he sat down, she straddled him. John gripped her hips and slowly she slid down on the length of him. He released a deep groan. Water pounded her back as she moved up and down, up and down. The bench dug into her knees on either side of his thighs. She held onto his shoulders as they moved together. Jo felt her breasts bounce with the rhythm of their lovemaking. Her eyes locked onto his.

Just as she thought she couldn't wait another moment, he closed his eyes at last and shuddered, calling out her name. She felt him jerk inside her, and a moan escaped her lips. She felt the pulse of her orgasm squeeze around him. She closed her eyes and dropped her forehead to his shoulder. "My God."

— — — — — —

AN HOUR LATER, JO LAY IN THE CIRCLE OF HIS ARMS on the queen-sized bed in her room. She could hear his heart beat strong and steady as she rested her head on his chest.

Moonlight streamed through the windows. It had been a long time since she felt this safe. "John?"

"Hmm?"

"Do you remember our conversation a while ago about my name change?"

She felt him shift. "Yes."

She sat up, wrapping the sheet around her torso. "I'd like to tell you about it."

John propped himself up on his elbow, giving her his full attention.

She took a deep breath. "You remember that Sid mentioned he went to med school with my father?"

John nodded.

"My father was a big shot doctor in Duluth for years. Had the biggest OB/GYN office in St. Louis County. When I was seventeen, he was accused of inappropriately touching one his patients. She took him to court. He was found not guilty, but his practice fell apart soon after. No one trusted him anymore. The whispering behind his back followed him everywhere. He closed his office one night and stuck a gun in his mouth." The pain of that long ago night still caused her heart to constrict.

John reached out to clasp her hand that had crumpled up the sheet. "That's terrible. I'm so sorry. Is that why you left the area and settled in the Twin Cities?"

Her curls fell forward as she nodded. "My mother died of breast cancer when I was young, so it was just me and my dad for all those years. When he killed himself, there was nothing left for me here. I changed my last name to my mother's maiden name, packed up my stuff and headed south. I was accepted at the U of M, finished my coursework and then was recruited by the FBI right out of college. And I haven't looked back. Until now."

John was silent for a moment. When he spoke again, his voice was gentle. "I'm glad you told me."

She bit her lower lip, not meeting his eyes. "You still want to be involved with me?"

"What if I told you something about myself that I've never told anyone else?"

"You don't have to do that . . ."

His eyes met hers in the dim light of the room. He cleared his throat. "During my first year of training to be a neurosurgeon, I shadowed Dr. Michaelson, an elderly but brilliant doctor. A pioneer in the field. He took me under his wing and favored me above all the other students. Looking back, I'm not sure why. I was just this dumb, cocky kid, fresh out of med school, no different than the rest."

John began to fidget with the blanket. "One night, Dr. Michaelson came into work drunk. I mean, plastered. I was horrified. Pretty tough to see a man I practically worshipped fall off his pedestal." He swallowed.

"An emergency case came through the doors, a head injury from a wicked car accident. It should have been Dr. Michaelson's case, but by then he was passed out in the lounge. I . . . I took the case. Thought I could fix the poor woman's head injuries. I couldn't do a damn thing for her and she died. A more experienced surgeon might have saved her." Jo could see the pain that still lingered in John's eyes at the memory.

"Did you get into trouble?"

"No. When Dr. Michaelson woke up, he found out that I tried to cover-up for him and took all the blame. The only reason he didn't lose his license was because of his reputation. He was 'encouraged' to take early retirement."

Jo looked at him. "And you blamed yourself?"

"Yes. I know that my mentor shouldn't have been drinking, but in the end, it was my arrogance that killed the patient. I took a six-month leave of absence after that to get my head back together. I'd like to think I came back a more humble man."

Jo leaned forward and pulled him into her arms. They were both silent as Jo felt his heartbeat once more. Sharing her story with him had released the weight she had carried for too long and for that, she was grateful.

She thought about his story and was touched by his honesty. Somehow, in the space of a few hours, he had become more real to her than anyone she had ever known.

CHAPTER TWENTY-FIVE

Turners Bend
Mid-March

Mᴀʀᴄʜ ᴄᴀᴍᴇ ʀᴏᴀʀɪɴɢ ɪɴ ᴡɪᴛʜ ᴡɪᴄᴋᴇᴅ ᴡɪɴᴅs that growled and snarled in a good imitation of a lion. Locals reassured Chip that its entrance foretold a lamb-like departure, but the end of the month was a long time to wait for a release from winter's fangs and claws. Chip surfed the Internet, reading about cures for SAD, Seasonal Affective Disorder.

He sat in his kitchen, staring at his computer screen and feeling depleted. After writing Jo and John's sex scenes, he was blocked. The ringing phone made him jump. He looked at the caller ID and hesitated, unsure whether or not he was in the right mood to talk with Lucinda. He braced himself and picked up the phone.

"Hi, Lucinda. How's my literary agent extraordinaire?"

"Cut the crap. You're giving me a migraine, and I don't have a microchip in my brain like poor Belinda in *Brain Freeze*." Chip held the phone away from his ear. Lucinda was at her bitchiest. "It's friggin' March 15 and you're two months from your deadline. I get two sex-filled chapters from you and now squat. "

"Sorry, Lucinda, things have been hectic around here, and I've been really busy."

"I don't care how many bovines go belly up or if it's the Queen of France getting married, you need to be writing. Sounds to me like woman problems. Oh, God, that's it, isn't it? I'll bet you anything that vet is derailing you."

"Where are my royalties?" said Chip, thinking a change of topic might be the best defense.

"Lord, save me from two-bit hack writers. I'll have the accounting department cut deposit your earnings to date in your Bank

America account. *The Cranium Killer* continues to sell well, but don't expect a lot of cash to trickle down to you, and you are going to earn squat from *Brain Freeze* if you don't get humping. Goodbye."

Honey ambled over, sat and put her head in Chip's lap. She always seemed to know when he needed canine love. "Sweet girl, what did I ever do without you?" He rubbed her ears, and she thumped her tail on the kitchen floor.

The last two weekends at AgriDynamics had been hard on Chip. To say that he was not used to hard work was an understatement. Being a caddy at his father's country club had been the extent of his experience with any work requiring physical stamina. The back strain was killing him and worse yet, he hadn't gotten near to where any chemicals were stored. The only strange thing he had noted was that every night about 2:00 a.m., a truck loaded with barrels left the plant and returned with the same barrels in the back an hour later. He wanted to know what was in those barrels. What the heck, maybe he would just ask next weekend.

Over the past two weeks he had been spending time with Jane, but never alone. She had begun to join him at the Bun most mornings. They chatted about puppy training, her practice, Sven and Ingrid, his new book, town gossip, the coming of spring. They took her kids out for pizza and a Twilight movie one night and had Sunday dinner with Mabel and Iver. He kept his hands to himself. They were just friends he reminded himself each time that he returned home from seeing her. He found her scarf in his car and kept it. It smelled of her coconut-scented shampoo.

"Iver and Mabel are quite the lovebirds, aren't they?" Jane said one morning. She and Chip were sharing a cinnamon roll at the Bun. "I caught him nuzzling her in the kitchen yesterday when we were there for dinner. Kind of sweet. I'm happy for them."

"Makes you believe in second chances, doesn't it?"

"You know what they say, 'once burned, twice shy'. I don't know if I really could handle a second time around."

"Well, I guess I had my second chance twice, so I've run out of chances." Chip was trying to make a joke, but Jane didn't laugh.

She held her coffee mug in both hands and stared out the café's front window. After a few moments she turned her pensive face into an overly bright smile and picked up the check. "On me today, Chip. I've got to get out to check Oscar's herd this morning and then over to the firehouse to deworm Zeus and Jupiter. See what a fun life I have?"

As Jane left to pay the bill, he realized Lucinda had a point. He had writer's inertia. He couldn't seem to concentrate. His mind was either scheming on how to snoop around ArgiDynamics or drifting off to think about Jane, how she looked at the wedding, how he wanted to see more of that cleavage, smell her hair, kiss her long slender neck.

THE CREW THAT WORKED THE 11:00 P.M. TO 7:00 A.M. shift at AgriDynamics was a surly bunch of guys. The weekend workers on that shift were part-timers who had to work a second job to make ends meet. In the warehouse they plodded through the packing of turbine parts being shipped around the country. The shift boss barked out orders. Occasionally grumbling could be heard, but most of the time the men toted the parts and loaded the crates without much comment and with robotic precision.

Break time was at 3:00 a.m. The break room consisted of a few tables and chairs, a microwave oven, a small refrigerator, and two vending machines . . . one with soft drinks and the other with candy and chips.

Chip surveyed the choices and opted for a diet cola and a Nut Goodie candy bar. He had become hooked on the maple-flavored filling and peanuts covered with chocolate, even though they looked like something you would find in a cow pasture. He took a chair next to a guy with the name "Hank" embroidered on the pocket of his navy blue work shirt.

"Hey, Hank, whatever happened to Owen Hansen, that guy that got beat up?" said Chip as he munched on his none-too-nutritious lunch.

"Heard he left town, took his family and moved to Des Moines and working in a Kum and Go. Guess he learned the hard way it's best to keep your mouth shut around here."

"Thanks for the heads up. I sure wouldn't want to get the shit kicked out of me like that."

Hank turned his attention to his baloney sandwich and grabbed the sports section of the crumpled newspaper on the table. Underneath was a book, a dog-eared copy of *The Cranium Killer*. He wondered if the same copy of his book floated all around town or if he was actually generating some sales in Turners Bend.

Chip saw this conversation wasn't getting him anywhere, and he sure didn't want to hear another critique of his book. So, he changed his tack. "I'd like to stay around long enough to get the job of driving that truck that pulls out of here every night with those barrels."

Hank looked up from his paper and scanned the room as if to see if anyone else was paying attention and had overheard Chip's remark. He lowered his voice. "Take my advice. Nobody wants that job. If you value your skin, you'll forget you ever saw that truck or those barrels or lots of other goings on around here. Just keep your head down and don't ask any questions."

"Thanks, I'll do that. Hey, any high school basketball scores in that paper?" It hadn't taken Chip long to learn that high school and college basketball were the most often discussed topics during the winter in Iowa. Men, who apparently couldn't remember their mate's name and referred to her as "the wife," could tell you the name, number and stats for every high school player in the county.

"Yes, the Prairie Dogs beat the Wolverines 65 to 59 last night. Course the Wolverines' center, Jason Krautbauer, is only five-foot-eleven. But, he's a sophomore and still growing. His brother, Justin, is a freshman over at Iowa State, and he's six-foot-three."

Later in the shift, Chip got an unexpected break in his investigation.

"Hey, new guy, we need another bale of straw to fill this crate. The bales are in the storeroom next to the break room. Haul one in here," said the shift boss.

Chip walked into the storeroom and pulled the chain of the overhead fluorescent light. The room contained several bales of straw, and along one wall were a dozen or so barrels, similar to the ones he had seen on the truck. He took his cell phone from his pocket and snapped photos of the labels on the barrels.

Driving home in the early morning light, Chip's body was tired and aching but his mind was alive and all his neurons were firing. He fed Honey and Runt and let them out in the yard to roam in the tiny patch where some snow had finally melted. He brewed a pot of double strength coffee and made four slices of toast with peanut butter and homemade rhubarb jam, a gift from Mabel. He downloaded the photos from his phone and printed them to get a better look at the labels.

Two hours later, he had completed his online research of the chemicals and how they were used in manufacturing. He also searched for information on how wind turbines were made but found little on that topic. The EPA site, however, did contain guidelines and regulations about the use of "green" chemicals. He sensed he was getting somewhere, but he was too tired to put it all together.

To appease his Prada-wearing devil of an agent, he emailed Lucinda a chapter he had written the previous day, let the dogs into the house and fell into his bed without removing his clothes. Honey jumped up on the bed beside him, and Runt whined until Chip lifted him up onto the bed. Dust-laden air blowing from the furnace mingled with the stink of wet dogs. Chip mused about his past life when he slept between satin sheets and caressed a woman dressed in only French perfume. Oddly, this seemed an improvement.

Soon all three were asleep.

CHAPTER TWENTY-SIX

Brain Freeze
Two Harbors, Minnesota

JOHN SLID HIS ARM OUT FROM BENEATH Jo, careful not to wake her. In the pale morning light, he watched her turn over in her sleep, coppery-red hair cascading across his pillow. She let out a soft sigh. He reached to move a curl that had strayed to her cheek. The tension from last night had been erased from her face, replaced by a look of utter peace.

He eased out of bed and quietly slipped on his jeans and a tattered Johns Hopkins sweatshirt. Opening the bedroom door slowly, he was greeted by Caddy. Evidently she had forgiven him for shutting her out of the room last night because she licked his hand and her tail wagged furiously.

He whispered, "Would you like to go out? What time is it, anyway?" He looked at his wrist, but realized he had left his watch on the nightstand. Stepping over to the window, he pulled the blinds up and peered outside. The sky to the east was taking on a pink hue.

John let Caddy out the door, cold air rushing in. He shivered. "Come right back. Don't make me come out there to find you."

He started the coffee maker in the kitchen and brought the laptop to the table, turning it on. Grabbing Jo's camera from the counter, he downloaded the pictures she had taken of the pages from NeuroDynamics's medical files. The clarity of the pictures was good enough in most cases to read the details. Clicking through the picture files, he stopped at the one labeled *Peterson, Belinda*. The first several pages contained basic post-surgery notes, such as blood pressure, pulse, and weight. Next, he read the notes that had been transcribed from the doctor's voice recordings. *Patient shows promising signs of adaptation to microchip and injection. Early work with subject indicates willingness to abandon inhibitions, including committing petty crimes.*

"Good God, what are they doing?" John switched back and forth between the files. "This makes no sense."

140

Caddy scratched at the door. John did his best to remove the clumps of snow from her paws and fur. She followed him into the kitchen, where he filled her bowls with kibble and water. He poured himself a cup of coffee and sat back down to work.

Several cups of coffee later, he had more questions than answers. His cell phone lay on the stack of notes he'd been scribbling.

He sat back, and stretched, stiff from hunching over the computer. He looked over to see Jo standing in the doorway, watching him. She was wearing his shirt from last night and her tousled hair flowed around her shoulders. John felt his stomach flip at the sight of her, and he smiled. "Good morning. You look well rested."

Her returning smile was wide. "Amazing what great sex will do for a night's sleep." She walked over to the table and leaned over to pick up his mug. He had a view of her breasts as the shirt fell open. Feeling his heartbeat speed up, he lost his train of thought.

Jo took a sip of coffee and closed her eyes. "Mmmm. You're up early. I didn't hear you get out of bed." She looked at the computer screen and his notes. "I see you've made good use of the time. Find anything?"

"Just a hell of a lot more unknowns. By the way, if you expect me to have a real conversation with you this morning about the case, you'd better button that shirt. You are very distracting."

Her green eyes slanted as she slowly buttoned up the shirt. "All right. But I enjoy distracting you." Jo kissed him on the cheek, grabbed his mug and refilled it. She pulled up a chair next to him. "So, tell me about these questions you have. Maybe between the two of us, we'll work out some direction."

John brought his mind back, slightly disappointed that they weren't heading into the bedroom once more. He opened the file on Belinda Peterson first. "See this? It says the microchip was implanted in the same location as it was for Mitch Calhoun. Now, unlike his implant, this one makes sense. According to the documents signed by Ms. Peterson, the object was to reduce migraines by controlling the swelling of the blood vessels. The chip was placed on the Circle of Willis, which is a sort of an air traffic control tower at the base of the brain to direct the flow of blood. Controlling the swelling there would help control the swelling in the rest of the blood vessels."

"Okay, I follow you so far. What's the issue?"

"If your theory of mind control is correct, then I don't understand why they would place the microchip on that ring of arteries. The only thing the chip could accomplish at that location is to control the flow of the blood. It could be used to inflict excruciating pain, making the victim pliable enough to do as they were told. However, this form of torture would only be effective for a very short period of time, as death would be a rapid result."

"So, where would a microchip have to be placed in order to control behavior?"

John rubbed his palm across his cheek and felt the rough stubble. "There are a few options, but they're all deep within the brain itself. Surgery of that sort would have to be done by a highly specialized neurosurgeon and would involve more major surgery than indicated here, and with months of rehabilitation." He leaned back in his chair and laced his fingers behind his head. "I don't see how they could have pulled that off without the patient's knowledge."

Jo stood up and paced. "I hear what you're saying. But, John, they're figuring out how to control people. Between the note we found in Mitch Calhoun's hand and the changes his parents noted in his behavior up to the time of his death, my gut tells me we're on to something here."

John cleared his throat. "Yeah, well, I think I've found some evidence of mind control in these files, too."

Jo stopped pacing and walked back to the table. She waited, then prompted, "And . . ."

He clicked through several pages until he found what he was looking for. "These notes indicate that Ms. Peterson was being tested in regards to her willingness to do anything she was told, including commit petty crimes. Now you and I both know that it's difficult to make someone do anything they find morally repugnant, such as murder, unless they're predisposed that way. But what if they've found a way to suppress a person's morals, to make them forget that murder is wrong?" He shook his head, looking at the glowing screen in front of him.

Jo pointed at the computer. "There's nothing else that might lead us in the right direction?"

"Not really. There are some cryptic reference to 'injections at the site.' The files don't indicate what's being injected, however. They only refer to something called NC-15. And, by the way, the release form that Belinda Peterson signed says nothing about it."

"And you have no idea what this NC-15 could be."

"None at all. I spent half the morning trying to figure it out. I called several of my research and development buddies, trying to get some answers. I also checked with the FDA. They have no record of it in their review files. Absolutely no one has heard of NC-15. Same thing with Internet searches. Closest I came was a reference to a color of women's makeup." John smirked. "Somehow, I don't think they are injecting cosmetics into people's brains."

"So, where does that leave us?"

"I'd assume that this substance, whatever it is, was created by NeuroDynamics and without FDA knowledge or approval. I have to tell you, I'd love to find out exactly what it is and what it does."

Jo began pacing again. Caddy rubbed her head against Jo, begging for attention. "Good morning, girl. Sorry I didn't greet you earlier. What was I thinking?" She scratched Caddy's ears and stared off at nothing, as if thinking through what he had discovered.

She gave Caddy's head a final pat. "Well, then. We're just going to have to find a way to get more information. I'll go back into NeuroDynamics and find out about this NC-15."

John felt his chest tighten. "Is that wise? If your adventure last night with the guard is any indication, they're on to you. Going in there now would be like crawling into the proverbial lion's den. Shouldn't we just send in the FDA to investigate the new substance?"

"You said yourself, we have no idea what it is. Just some obscure reference in a file. I think we need to get some more detail. *Then* we call the FDA."

John thought for a moment. "What if we tried a different tactic? Why don't we contact Belinda Peterson and tell her what we know. She can get more information from the inside than we can."

"Pretty dicey, don't you think? What if she's in on it and tells Candleworth?"

"I'd be willing to bet that she has no idea about that little injection she received and how they are playing games with her head. You saw the file. Imagine her reaction to seeing it."

"And you're sure she doesn't know about this NC-15?"

"Nothing about it in the release she signed."

Jo tapped her chin, and didn't respond immediately. She seemed to be weighing all the options. John knew he had convinced her when she looked up and said, "All right. I'll give Clark Benson, my boss back in Minneapolis, a call and catch him up. If he agrees, we'll contact Ms. Peterson."

"While you are doing that, I'm going to go for a swim. Reading about what those bastards are doing in the name of 'medical research' put some serious stress kinks in my shoulders. Be back soon."

CHAPTER TWENTY-SEVEN

Turners Bend
April

Eᴀʀʟʏ ꜱᴘʀɪɴɢ ᴄᴀᴍᴇ ᴛᴏ Tᴜʀɴᴇʀꜱ Bᴇɴᴅ. The snow was almost gone. Only piles of snirt, that strange combination of snow and dirt, were left along the roadsides. Iver traded his snowplow for his road grader, as his road maintenance duties switched from winter to spring. The Feed and Seed was abuzz with farmers buying seed and homeowners buying fertilizer and starter plants. The Winnebagos rolled back into town. The retirees and senior citizens had returned. The air smelled green and loamy.

During Holy Week the Bun served hot cross buns and hard cooked eggs dyed pink and purple and green.

"God, these hot cross buns are good," Chip said to Jane. "Here have one." He lowered his voice. "I'm anxious to show you something I can't really discuss here. Do you have time to come out to my house today?"

"Sure, I could stop by after supper. I'll bring some dewormer for Runt."

Chip laughed. "Ah, that's a hostess gift I have never received before."

"Okay, I'll bring a bottle of wine along with the dewormer. How's that?"

"It's a date."

———

Cʜɪᴘ ʟᴏᴏᴋᴇᴅ ɪɴ ʜɪꜱ ᴄʟᴏꜱᴇᴛ. Wᴀꜱ ɪᴛ ᴀ ᴅᴀᴛᴇ? A bottle of wine might indicate that it was. If so, what should he wear? He opted for a button-down collar dress shirt and a cashmere sweater vest with his best jeans. He splashed on some Polo. He was excited, both to share what he had discovered about AgriDynamics and to be alone with Jane.

When Jane arrived he knew he had made the right decision. She was also wearing jeans but not her usual sweatshirt. Her top tonight was a black, close-fitting shirt with a deep v-neck. Her hair was down and she had added dangly silver and turquoise earrings. The unmistakable scent of Chanel entered the kitchen with her. Smiling, she held up two bags, one in each hand.

"Chardonnay or dewormer? Take your pick."

"That's a tough one, but I think I'll start with the Chardonnay and save the dewormer for another day." Chip opened the wine, poured two glasses and gave one to Jane.

"Sorry about the Arby's glasses. I haven't invested in any glassware yet. Here's to the loveliest vet in Iowa." He lifted his glass and let his eyes wander to her breasts. She clinked glasses with him, and added her own toast.

"Here's to Iowa's best mystery writer. I read *The Cranium Killer*, and it's great fun. Maybe you could write one where a vet solves the crime. What's the next one called? "

"*Brain Freeze*, unless the editor decides to change it. Sorry, no vet in the story, but Dr. Goodman returns if you're interested in handsome neurosurgeons."

"Oh, I suppose your female readers will be pleased." Jane tugged down her shirt.

Chip was imagining removing that shirt. An awkward moment passed. He took a gulp of wine. In his past life, this was the time he would have made his move, planted a kiss on her exposed neck, and lightly placed his hand on one of those tempting breasts. But, that was then, and this was Jane. That was when he was a "player" living the fast life in a world of money, booze, gambling, and women with questionable morals. This was Jane, a caring, competent, decent vet and mother in Iowa, a "real woman," as far from a plastic Barbie doll or a country club princess as any woman could be. She was a woman out of his class in the best possible ways.

"At the Bun you mentioned something you wanted to show me." Jane sounded a bit uncomfortable, as if she had sensed his interest in her breasts.

"Oh, yes. Here, look at what I have on my computer."

Jane stood behind Chip, placed her hands on his shoulders and bent over to view his laptop as Chip showed her the photos of the labels, the informational sites on the chemicals and the EPA site.

"These are not eco-friendly chemicals, not EPA-approved. Look at all the nitrates they contain." He showed her the label listings and warnings. "I'm pretty sure these are like the barrels I see leaving the warehouse late at night."

"But why would Hal use them?"

"Here look at these cost comparisons. There's a pretty drastic difference in these chemicals, especially in the degreasers and solvents, and their ecological counterparts. He may be doing it to cut costs."

"It still doesn't make total sense to me. Why would he dump them in Beaver Creek, if that's what he's doing? Wouldn't those chemicals be used up in the manufacturing process?"

"Yes, and that's where I'm stumped. Something else must be put in those barrels when they are empty and that's what's getting dumped late at night. First we have to confirm the dumping, and then we have to determine exactly what is being dumped and why. My guess is that it's another cost-cutting measure. Disposal of hazardous waste has to be very expensive."

"For some reason I always thought Hal was an honest businessman, even though he was totally dishonest with me about his extra-marital affairs. Maybe I was wrong. If this is driven by money, I would guess we're talking more than cutting a few dollars.

"I wish the state authorities would get a move on and give us some assistance. Seems they breathe down our necks when we don't want them, like the time they cited Gus Jorgenson's swine operation with a huge fine for very minor infractions and almost put him out of business. Then when we really need them, they're too busy."

Chip shut down his laptop and poured them each another glass of wine.

"Make yourself comfortable in the living room, and I'll make us some microwave popcorn. I'm a master chef with the microwave."

Chip put his iPod into the Bose speakers and selected a Gershwin track, turning it down low. *"Embrace me, you sweet embraceable you,"* crooned a sensual voice. He left to make a bag of Pop Secret. When he returned to the living room, Jane had removed her shoes and propped her feet up on the scarred coffee table that Chip had purchased at a thrift store. He sat beside her and placed his arm along the back of the sofa behind her head. *"Just one look at you, my heart goes tipsy in me . . ."*

Jane took a sip of wine and placed her tumbler on the table. She laid her head on Chip's arm and closed her eyes. "This is divinely peaceful."

Chip bent his head and lightly kissed each of her eyelids. He waited for a response, then heard a deep sigh.

"Mmm, nice," said Jane.

It was all the encouragement that Chip needed. He moved down to plant another kiss on her nose and then another on her lips. He kept each a light, brief, butterfly kiss. She placed her hands on the sides of his face and lightly kissed him on the mouth, then followed with a deeper, longer kiss. Many kisses.

As she arched her body, Chip worked his way down with his mouth and tongue and hands. He kissed her neck and felt her hardening nipples. Together they discarded items of clothing and discovered and explored soft and wet places, hard and hot places. Her black shirt and nude demi-bra and his blue vest and shirt were hastily removed and tossed on the floor, until they were skin to skin. Jane leaned back on the coach and opened herself for Chip. He entered tentatively. She wrapped her legs around him, her hips rocking, inviting deeper and deeper thrusts, until they were at last sated.

They moved from the couch to Chip's bed where they rested in each other's arms until the adventure started again with the same excruciating pleasure seeking.

———

CHIP WOKE TO SEE THE SUN BREAKING THROUGH the rain clouds. For the first time this spring, he heard the cheerful chirping of birds. He brought the bed sheet to his nose and sniffed the sensual mixture of Chanel, Polo, and sex. Jane had left before dawn in order to wake her kids and get them off to school. Damn, he had vowed to let John and Jo go at it and to keep himself free from any romantic entanglements. He had messed up three times and sworn off any further romances. So much for making vows he was doomed to break. He finished the song, *"Don't be a naughty baby, come to Papa, come to Papa do, my sweet embraceable you."*

CHAPTER TWENTY-EIGHT

Turners Bend
April

H EAVY APRIL RAINS HAD BEEN KEEPING THE farmers out of the fields. Jane saw them as she entered the Bun, their eyes focused out the windows, their pent-up energy chomping at the bit, ready to mount their tractors and ride across their acres. Maybe today's sun would bring the dry spell they needed. They sat silently stirring their coffee round and round. More sugar, more cream, *clink, clink, clink.*

Jane made it home that morning just minutes before 7:00 a.m., the time she usually woke Sven and Ingrid for school. Now a little over an hour later she moved through the crowded café and headed for Chip's still empty table, the table for two in the far corner of the Bun. She could have easily joined the Fredricksons and their cronies in their booth or taken the vacant chair at the farmers' table, but she needed to be alone, to think, to sort out her conflicting feelings for a few moments before Chip arrived. Mornings after first sex were fraught with both uncertainty and residual passion. Jane had a dose of each, plus embarrassment. Here she was, a mother of teenage children, a vet, a middle-aged woman, someone who should know better than to get involved with a guy who had been married and divorced three times. She resolved to stop her foolish behavior and nip this relationship in the bud before it went any further. And yet, there was something about him that was so alluring, so tempting. What was it?

Chip entered the café, spotted her and ambled toward the table with a boyish grin on his face. He looked so happy, she thought. So cute with his slightly messed, curly hair and his rimless eye glasses. He lacked the physical signs of hard labor that she saw in most of Turners Bend's farmers and factory workers. He didn't have a potbelly or a receding hairline like the town's merchants and businessmen. She guessed he probably played tennis in school, not big enough for football, too short for basketball. Chip Collingsworth was about as unlike her ex-husband as a guy could be.

"Hey," he said, as he took the chair across from her.

"Hey, yourself."

He reached to cover her hand with his, but she pulled hers away and nodded over to the booth where Chief Fredrickson, Flora, and other city officials were sitting. "Last night was . . ." she hesitated, searching for the right word.

"You were amazing last night, pretty lady."

She felt heat rise from her neck and flood into her face. Her resolve was weakening, taking a direct hit.

Chip gazed into her eyes and lowered his voice. He nodded his head toward the counter. "I was thinking about clearing that lunch counter over there, and going for an encore."

"If I remember correctly, you had an encore last night." And, a wonderful encore it was, she recalled.

"*Ah, yes, I remember it well.*" He sang in a bad imitation of Maurice Chevalier. "I guess it will have to be called a reprise then. So when?"

She took a deep breath. This was where she had to put the brakes on this relationship. "I have a vet practice to take care of, and you have a book to write and a weekend sleuthing job. And truthfully, Chip, I'm not sure this is such a good idea. Maybe it was the wine. Maybe it was that I had gone too long without. I don't know. I have baggage. You have baggage. Let's just slow down."

"Can I at least walk you to your office?"

She heard hurt and disappointment in his voice. Doubt began to creep in on little paws. He really was damn attractive, awfully sweet. "Sure, let's head out," she said.

FLORA WASN'T MISSING ANY OF THE LOOKS between Jane and Chip. Her gaze followed them as they left the Bun together. As they walked passed the front window, she noticed they were holding hands.

"I do believe our Jane has a new beau," she said to her husband.

"Now, Flora, don't go meddling. Just let nature takes it course," said the chief.

"By the looks of it, nature has already taken its course, my dear." Flora was smugly pleased with herself. She prided herself on her matchmaking, and this one was coming along nicely. The aura she sensed around Chip and Jane, that after-sex glow, was a dead give-away.

—— —— —— ——

NATURE ALMOST TOOK ITS COURSE AGAIN IN JANE'S CLINIC. The privacy of the office induced passionate kissing and groping.

"So much for slowing down. Chip, we've got to concentrate on our jobs and on what could be happening out at AgriDynamics," Jane said as she straightened her clothes and hair.

His cupped hands reached for her breasts. She pushed him away.

"You really are a boob man, aren't you? Now try to focus on something other than my chest. What's our plan of action?"

He smiled and wiggled his eyebrows.

"No, our plan about the poisonings, you lech," she said, shaking her head, suppressing a smile. "What can we do without getting in trouble with the law or government agencies?"

"This weekend I'm going to get a look at the manufacturing process. I'll sneak into the plant and look around for those barrels."

"Okay, I'm going to stake-out in the plant parking lot and follow the truck. I want to confirm that the barrels are being dumped into the creek. What time of night does the truck leave the warehouse?"

"It's usually about 2:00 a.m., but I don't want you to do that. It's too dangerous."

"I can take care of myself, thank you very much." She felt an instantaneous flare of indignation and heard the edge in her own voice. He would find out that she could be a tigress in more ways than one. He had no right to tell her what she could or could not do. Hal had been "protective" in that horrid dominating, demeaning way; and she would not tolerate men treating her like that any more.

"Okay, okay, so now we have a plan for Saturday night. Sunday afternoon is open to compare notes, if you're free," he said. He stood back from her a little.

"Sven and Ingrid will be with Hal's family for their grandmother's birthday. We can meet at my place, say at 1:00 p.m. This is a time to report on what we find. Nothing else, okay?" Her intent was to convey a "no sex" message, but did she truly want to put an end to this delicious sex? Her head and her heart were telling her two different things, but her hormones were screaming loud and clear.

CHIP COULDN'T DECIDE IF HE SHOULD CONTINUE pursuing Jane or stay away from the flames for fear of getting burned. And, what did she want? Her words said one thing, but her kisses said another. She was running hot and cold on him, one moment leading him on, the next pushing him away. He had no idea where they were headed.

He had trouble getting to the task of working on the next chapter of *Brain Freeze*. And now, he had to figure out where John and Jo were headed. *Should Dr. Goodman really fall for this sassy FBI agent or should it be another one of the debonair doctor's flings?*

CHAPTER TWENTY-NINE

Brain Freeze
Two Harbors & Duluth, Minnesota

JOHN ENTERED THE CONDO AND SHED HIS PARKA. Caddy greeted him as a long lost friend and stood on back legs while he rubbed at her ears. Her tail swung back and forth with pure canine joy. "Nothing like forty laps in the pool to get the brain firing again, eh, girl?" John had taken a break from the files, hoping the exercise would jar something loose in his brain. The answers still hadn't come to him, but his energy had been recharged.

Jo stood up from her spot at the table and walked over to him. She smiled at John and ran her fingers through his still wet, slightly frozen hair. She wrinkled her nose. "Ugh. You smell like chlorine."

John pointed to the notes scattered across the table. "Come up with any good schemes?"

"Getting there. I . . ." Jo's cell phone rumbled across the tabletop, and she reached for it.

"Hey, Frisco, get any hits on the names I gave you yet?" She pulled a pad of paper toward her and took notes, listening intently. At one point, her eyes widened. "Cause of death?" More notes. "No, no. I'll be right there." She clicked the phone shut.

"New developments?"

She turned to face John. "Frisco followed up on the microchip patients I found in the surgeon's files. His people are still tracking down some of them, but Kurt, the security guard from the accident last night was on the list. Last name was Manning. The tattoo on his neck matches the one from the DVD of Sid's murder. He was definitely one of the guys."

"Any leads on the other killer?"

Jo rubbed her face with her hands. "No. They're still working on it. Wish we would have found out about Manning sooner. Would've been nice to question him and find his partner."

Jo's eyes looked tired and her shoulders slumped. "I haven't told you the worst part. Remember Thomas Falco from the files? Frisco recognized that name right away."

"Why's that?"

"Because Thomas Falco fatally shot his wife and teenage son last night, before he died."

The calming effects of John's swim evaporated quickly. It infuriated him that medical technology was being used to destroy lives. He said, "Jesus. Let me guess. He turned the gun on himself."

"No, not a mark on him. The ME says it was another aneurysm and that he found a microchip in the same spot as the others. Frisco is meeting us for the autopsy review."

FRISCO MET THEM AT THE DOOR OF THE MEDICAL BUILDING. No one remarked on the strangeness of being back at the coroner's lab without Sid. Jo felt a shiver when she entered the room. The office showed no sign of the chaos and murders that had taken place the prior week. It was back to business as usual.

Except the music was gone. Bobby Henke, the acting ME, no longer sang along with Neil Diamond. The whoosh of air through the ventilation system was the only background sound in the room. Jo briefly wondered if Bobby was the one who had performed the autopsies on Sid and his wife. *Poor man.* She had thought watching the murder on the DVD was horrible enough, but she couldn't imagine what it must have been like for Bobby probing the lifeless bodies of his former boss and Martha.

Jo glanced toward the corner where Sid had been discovered. She found it hard *not* to look. It was as if the absence of a body made it possible for Sid to still be alive. She sighed and squared her shoulders.

"So, Doc, did you find anything else? Frisco said it was an aneurysm, like Mitch Calhoun's case."

Bobby looked up from the body of Thomas Falco. Eyes gazed out of thick glasses, giving him the perpetual appearance of a startled owl. Unlike Sid, his voice was timid and strangely high-pitched. "Same thing. By all appearances, could almost be the same brain. Same spot on the Circle of

Willis." He shook his head. "Even though I knew to look for it, I almost missed that little bitty microchip."

Detective Frisco pulled Jo away from the table, while John and Bobby talked more about the victim.

"Agent Schwann, I'm getting quite a pile-up of dead bodies in my county. People are calling for my head on a friggin' platter. How did you come by those names?"

"I found them in files from the chief surgeon's office in NeuroDynamics. Looks like they're all guinea pigs for testing. Dr. Goodman thinks that the microchips cause the aneurysms. It was like they were implanted to take out the test cases when their assigned tasks either failed or were completed."

"Holy shit! But how the hell—and why—are they controlling people?"

"That's what we still have to figure out.

We're getting close, Frisco. I know it. John and I are going to talk to the CFO today. We're hoping she'll help put the final pieces together."

Frisco grabbed her arm. "Is that a good idea? What makes you think she won't take Candleworth's side?"

"John thinks he can convince her with the evidence we have so far. Seems like they've been using her head as their personal playground, too."

Frisco said, "Just remember, keep your eyes open. If she so much as reaches for her telephone when you tell her what you've been up to, you get some back-up. These guys aren't messing around. Hell, if Two Harbors was in my jurisdiction, I'd be there myself."

"I don't think it will come to that . . ."

Frisco continued as if she hadn't spoken. "Normally, I'd contact the sheriff up there, but word's out that he's been awfully cozy with Candleworth. Likes the perks that come with having a big-ass company in his county." Frisco shook his head. "Fucking sell-out. Never liked him anyway."

"I called my boss in Minneapolis. He's aware of what's going on and is sending up some additional agents. Now that we've established a connection between Sid's killers and NeuroDynamics, the investigation can proceed much quicker. We shouldn't have any trouble getting a warrant now." She put her hands on her hips. "This has got to end, Frisco. We owe it to Sid and the others."

"Got some fire power with you?"

She patted the slight bulge of her coat pocket. "Got it covered."

The detective nodded. "Be careful."

"You can count on it." She indicated the lab with her chin. "Weird being back here without the old man, isn't it?"

The corners of Frisco's mouth turned down. "Weird doesn't begin to cover it."

JO AND JOHN DROVE NORTHEAST ALONG THE LAKESHORE on Highway 61, towards the home of NeuroDynamics's CFO. The all-weather tires squeaked on the snow-covered roads, a sure sign of frigid cold. The skies were a brilliant blue, but the sun was at its farthest point and did little to warm the day.

Not taking her eyes off the road, Jo said, "Do you think we can convince Ms. Peterson to help us?"

"There's obviously a chance that she won't believe us. I know we've uncovered enough of NeuroDynamics's blatant criminal acts so that the FBI will discover the full truth with or without her help." John paused, then said, "But at the very least, I want to be the one to tell her what they've done to her. She deserves to hear it from someone who can explain it all to her. If she agrees to help us, it's icing on the cake, as far as I'm concerned."

Jo thought for a moment about the compassionate man sitting next to her. He wanted to bring down Candleworth and his organization, but he never stopped thinking about the welfare of the individuals who were little more than pawns. If she was honest with herself, it was one of the main reasons she was falling in love with him. He cared about the victims as much as she did.

She reached out a hand to John and they rode the rest of the way to Belinda Peterson's house in silence.

Just south of the turn-off for Split Rock Light House, they found the house number on a weathered post on the lake side of the highway. The unpaved driveway disappeared into the woods, and they wound their way down until they reached a honey-colored wood log home, with a green shingled roof. Jo parked the Highlander behind a blue sedan, and they got out of the SUV. She heard the chatter of crows as they walked up the sidewalk.

Jo rang the doorbell and shivered in the cold while they waited for someone to answer. After a minute without an answer, John pounded on the door. Finally, they heard the click of the deadbolt being turned and the door opened, revealing a gaunt-looking Belinda Peterson.

She shielded her eyes from the bright sunshine and said, "What do you want? Can't you read?" She pointed to a small sign pasted to the sidelight next to the door. It read: NO SOLICITORS.

When Belinda started to close the door, Jo stuck her booted foot in the opening, afraid that they wouldn't be given a chance to explain. She felt the pain radiate up her leg as the door struck, but ignored it and said, "We're not here to sell you anything. We just want to talk to you. It's important."

Her eyes widened when she took a closer look at Jo. "Hey, aren't you the cleaning lady from the office?" She pointed to John. "And who's this?" Confusion mingled with indignation on her face.

Jo said, "I'm sorry to have deceived you. I'm not part of the cleaning crew at NeuroDynamics. I am Special Agent Jo Schwann, with the FBI, and I've been working undercover in your company." She pulled out her credentials.

Belinda scrunched up her features as she glanced at Jo's badge. "I don't understand. This must be some kind of mistake. What does the FBI want with me?"

Jo said, "May we come inside?"

Belinda cut her eyes toward John. "And who's this? Another FBI agent?"

John spoke up. "No, ma'am. My name is Dr. John Goodman. I'm assisting Agent Schwann with the investigation into your company. Please, may we come in and explain everything?"

Jo held her breath, willing Belinda to let them enter.

The CFO kept her hand on the door and Jo watched the indecision cross her features. Belinda finally stepped aside to let them in.

Jo waited for her eyes to adjust to the dimly lit house. All the shades had been drawn and only a sliver of sunshine escaped around the edges of the windows. She and John followed Belinda into a spacious family room.

There was a blazing fire in the gas log fireplace at the far end of the room and Belinda asked them to be seated on the leather couch in front of it. She eased down in a chair next to them, curling her feet up beneath her.

To Jo, the woman no longer resembled the commanding CFO she had first met in her office only a few days earlier. She wore a tattered bathrobe and her hair was pulled back in a messy ponytail. Her face was free of makeup and the firelight accentuated the dark circles under her eyes.

Belinda reached for a bottle of ibuprofen on the end table next to her and swallowed three pills without a drink of water. Jo glanced at John. His brows came together and he said, "Ms. Peterson, are you all right?"

She waved off his question with her hand and said, "Just a bad headache." John's frown deepened, and Jo thought he would say something more, but he just shook his head. *He's biding his time, waiting to help her. He knows we have to gain her trust first.*

Belinda rubbed at her temples. "So, tell me. What is this all about?"

Jo leaned forward. "About two weeks ago, the FBI received a call from the medical examiner's office in Duluth. They had discovered a NeuroDynamics microchip in the brain of recently deceased young man, by the name of Mitch Calhoun. Does that name sound familiar to you?"

Belinda frowned. "Yes, he was one of our test patients. But you aren't insinuating that the microchip caused his death, are you? Dr. Candleworth, the CEO of my company told us about his death and said that he died of natural causes."

John sent a fleeting look at Jo and then spoke. "You were told a lie. Mr. Calhoun died of an aneurysm that resulted from the microchip. And he's not the only one. Thomas Falco died yesterday. I saw the brains of both men and I saw the damage the microchips inflicted."

"You must be mistaken . . ."

"I have copies of the ME's reports here with me. May I turn on the lamp and show them to you?"

He flicked on the table lamp and pulled a stack of papers from his bag. He retrieved several pages and showed them to her.

Belinda quickly read through the reports, and then looked up in shock. "No, no that can't be. There must be some kind of mistake. *I* have one of the microchips. Are you saying they're defective?"

Jo said, "Not exactly. Functionally, it appears that they are operating exactly the way they are intended. However, it is the *intent* that we are concerned about. Were you aware that you were also injected with some substance called NC-15 when you received the microchip?"

Belinda crossed her arms. "No, I don't believe you. That microchip was put in my head to relieve migraines. Dr. Candleworth would never do such a thing. He's a good man. You're making this all up just to scare me." She stood up. "I think you should leave now."

John spoke quickly. "Believe me, I wish this weren't true. But it is. Here is a copy of your medical file. It proves that you received the injection and that they have been testing your ability to be controlled ever since."

Belinda plopped back onto her chair as if her legs could no longer support the weight of what she had been told. Her face was chalk white as she said, "Control? Let me see that." She snatched the papers out of John's hands.

Jo watched as the horror spread across Belinda Peterson's face. Belinda released a cry of pain and read aloud from the report. "*Early work with subject indicates willingness to abandon inhibitions, including committing petty crimes.* What have they done to me?"

John said, "It appears that this NC-15 has some kind of mind control properties. Do you know anything about it?"

Belinda's eyes filled with tears. "No, I've never heard of this substance. This is a nightmare. What can I do?"

Jo spoke rapidly, seizing the opportunity to gain Belinda's help. "You can get us inside information." She reached out and placed a hand on her knee. "Will you help us?"

The tears spilled down Belinda's cheeks as she said, "Tell me what to do."

CHAPTER THIRTY

AgriDynamics

The AgriDynamics plant was about seven miles west of town. The sprawling complex covered several acres. It looked like a commercial airplane hangar but with loading docks. Cranes loaded crates containing disassembled wind turbines onto flat beds and semis from an independent trucking firm hauled them away. Three wind turbines on the property supplied power.

Chip was working what he hoped would be his final weekend. He was assigned to help Hank pack crates. Hank was tall and thin with a perpetual haggard look that resulted from his struggle to support a wife and four kids on the earnings from two low-paying jobs.

"Where are these babies headed, Hank?"

"We used to ship most of our turbines to wind farms out west, California, Idaho, even Mexico. Now our business is mostly in the Midwest. This load is going up to Minnesota."

"Looks to me like Swanson is sitting on a gold mine here. Probably pulling in big bucks, I would bet."

"Used to."

"Not anymore? Why's that?"

"Hal isn't keeping up with Japan and China. Their innovations and new technologies are blowing us away. He once was real hands-on and interested in moving the company forward. Now it seems he's only interested in the bottom line and the bottle.

"Herman over on the manufacturing end is a real engineer, got a degree and all. To hear him talk, we'll be out of business in five years. He says we're making Stone Age turbines."

"It's almost lunch break, but I've got to take a leak now. See you in the break room." Chip headed in the direction of the restroom but

161

kept on going down a long corridor that led to the manufacturing side of the plant. He inched open a heavy metal door, slipped in and stood in the shadows along the wall.

Acrid fumes burned his eyes and nose. He took out his camera phone and began to take photos of the workers in their booties, gloves, and facemasks. The lunch bell rang.

"Clean up those spills and dump that solvent in the barrel before you go to lunch," said the supervisor who was dressed in a full HAZMAT suit. He turned and spotted Chip. "Hey, what in the hell are you doing in here without protective gear? This epoxy resin is dangerous. Get your ass out of here."

Chip exited with the workers. Outside the area they deposited their protective wear into another barrel.

With an eerie feeling, Chip scanned the plant one more time. He thought he saw someone on the glass-enclosed catwalk above the workers, but then dismissed it as a shadow.

—— —— —— —— ——

JANE SAT IN HER TRUCK NURSING THE STRONG bitter coffee in her thermal travel mug. Her eyes were on the doors of the truck bays but her mind was elsewhere. Lust was doing battle with reality. Was she really falling for this guy? He would probably finish his book and head back to Baltimore or maybe out to Hollywood. Then where would she be? She had her kids and her profession. That was more than enough. Chip just didn't fit in her life, even if he was starting to fit into the community. Sure, the sex was good. No . . . the sex was great. But she couldn't let it cloud her judgement. Tomorrow she would break it off with him, end it before it caused her more heartbreak than she could endure again.

Mental turmoil almost caused her to miss the truck as it exited the warehouse and headed down the state road. With her headlights off she followed at a safe distance, using the truck's taillights as her guide. It turned off the main road and headed down the rutted dirt road that led to the town's landfill. She pulled over and shifted into park, letting the engine idle.

The driver stepped out of the cab. In the hazy glow of the moon, his astronaut-like HAZMAT suit was mesmerizing. He unloaded the barrels and began to dump their contents.

She put the truck in reverse and slowly backed up onto the main road, turned on her headlights and pushed the speedometer up to eighty miles per hour, heading for home. She had little doubt that Chip's speculations were being confirmed. A thick fog was clouding the road ahead, and her mind was as murky as her vision. *Now what,* she pondered. *Now what?*

AT THE END OF HIS SHIFT CHIP TOLD THE warehouse supervisor that he would not be returning. He had learned all he needed to know and his camera phone had the proof.

He arrived home at 7:30 a.m., fell into bed with his clothes on and set the alarm for noon. That would give him enough time to shower, google 'epoxy resins' and get to Jane's by 1:00 p.m. Sunday would be his day of rest from *Brain Freeze.*

Five hours later Chip dressed in clean jeans and an open-necked white shirt with the tails out. He packed up his laptop, jumped into the Volvo and drove to Jane's hobby farm southeast of town. About a half a mile from her place he spotted her running along the road. He pulled over along side her.

"Hi, want a lift the rest of the way?"

"No thanks. Go ahead. I want to finish my run."

Disappointment began to creep into Chip's mind. Jane was obviously not primping for this afternoon. She was dressed in baggy gray sweats and her hair was pulled through the back of a green John Deere cap. Maybe a shower together was what she had in mind, but he doubted it. Maybe she was just becoming comfortable with him, which would please him to no end, but he doubted that, too. He had a gnawing feeling that their relationship was already reaching a rough patch.

In her kitchen Jane grabbed a bottle of water from the refrigerator. "I've got bottled water, Diet Coke or I could make a pot of coffee. What would you like?

Chip was longing for a beer, but opted for Coke.

"What happened last night at the plant? Did you get into the manufacturing area?"

"Yes, and it was quite a sight. Looked like Chernobyl in there. Apparently a highly toxic epoxy resin is used as an adhesive and an equally toxic solvent is used for cleaning up. Then everything, including the disposable gloves and masks worn by the workers, is dumped into barrels. I got a few pictures and loaded them on my laptop. Take a look."

Jane clicked through the photos. "That HAZMAT suit the supervisor is wearing is the same type of suit the truck driver was wearing. Scary to think that the production workers aren't taking an equal amount of protection, isn't it?"

"Did the driver dump the barrels into Beaver Creek?"

"No, he dumped the stuff in the town landfill. But the creek is near enough that hazardous materials could run off into it."

"It's pretty clear to me, Jane. Hal is using non-EPA approved chemicals, failing to properly dispose of hazardous wastes and polluting Beaver Creek, endangering the livestock and people of Turners Bend. On top of that, he is taking federal funds for running a green operation that supplies alternative energy. When Owen Hansen threatened to expose him, he must have sent some goons to stop him. This is criminal. The authorities have to be brought in, and he needs to be shut down."

Jane paced back and forth in her kitchen. She sighed and shook her head.

"Chip, we can't do this. I want to talk to Hal. Get him to promise to stop this. If we inform the authorities, someone else could get hurt. Shutting down AgriDynamics would be devastating. Haven't you noticed it's the biggest employer in Boone County? The economy is bad enough already and family farms are dying—the town would shrivel up and die. I don't want that on my conscience."

"Come on, Jane, the guy's a drunk. He's gone down a slippery path. Do you think he is going to listen to his ex-wife? He deserves to be put behind bars."

Jane stopped her pacing. She stood still and quiet for a moment. A chill entered the room and sent warning signals up and down Chip's spine.

"Chip, he is the father of my children. He is a native son of this town. I will not have him exposed in this manner. You're an outsider here. You just can't bop into town and turn us upside down. Go write your crime stories and stay out of our business. And stay out of my life, too. Do you hear me? Get out of my house, and get out of my life."

Stunned at her vehemence, Chip moved toward her with outstretched arms. "Calm down, Jane. You're getting carried away, saying things you don't mean."

"I'm sorry, Chip. I don't want to be angry with you. Please go and let me think about this. I need time. I need space." Her anger had turned to pleading. Chip gave her a brief hug and left.

FOR THE NEXT TWO DAYS, CHIP COULDN'T SLEEP, he couldn't eat, and he sure couldn't write. He wrestled with his feelings for Jane and the moral dilemma that he found himself in concerning AgriDynamics. He didn't go to the Bun. He wanted to go to the Bend, but feared he might run into Hal. He didn't check his email or answer his phone. Honey sensed something was wrong and followed him around the house. Runt, however, didn't have his mother's sensitivities. He wanted to play and kept bringing his sock toy to Chip for a game. "Sorry, boy, I'm not in the mood for any games. Go lay down." Finally, Runt gave up and flopped over, instantly falling asleep, and Chip lifted him into his playpen.

He put Honey in the Volvo and headed out for a long drive. He rolled down the back windows, and Honey stuck her head out the window to catch the breeze. She closed her eyes and her nose twitched as the wind blew back her silky ears.

CHAPTER THIRTY-ONE

Turners Bend
Late April

THE RAINS OF EARLY APRIL HAD CEASED AND WITH May approaching planting season was underway. All around Boone County fields were being plowed. In the distance droning engines could be heard as tractors plowed up the rich, black soil. From the road the giant insects ate their way across the landscape. Green John Deeres, yellow Caterpillars, red Massey Fergusons and blue New Hollands churned the earth into deep furrows from sunup to sundown.

Until he came to Iowa, Chip had never experienced the intoxicating smell of soil. He had never imagined what a calming effect it would have on him. He powered down his car window and drove at a slow steady speed, savoring the mossy, musky, piquant aroma. He thought about what Jane had said about the community of Turners Bend and its people, the people who in just six months had become so dear to him. He came to the conclusion that he would have to let Jane deal with Hal and AgriDynamics in her own way.

After two hours he turned toward home. He pulled the Volvo into the garage, let Honey out and walked toward the backdoor. As he approached, he saw the broken window, shards of glass on the porch. The door stood ajar. He did not see any vehicles or hear any noises, so he cautiously pushed the door open with his foot and peered into the kitchen expecting the place to be ransacked. At first nothing seemed to be disturbed. He entered and began to explore. His laptop was gone from the kitchen table. In the living room the only things missing were his iPod and Bose speakers. Then it hit him. The playpen was empty. Where was Runt? He called for him, searching everywhere, every room, every closet, under the bed. No Runt. He ran outside and began to call and whistle, searching around his property. What kind of people would take his puppy? Or did he somehow escape and run out the open door?

Chip returned to the house and phoned the police station. The dispatcher relayed his call to Chief Fredrickson.

"Chief, this is Chip Collingsworth. I've had a break-in at my place. Some of my electronics are missing, and Runt is gone. Broke in the backdoor. Don't know why. If the fool would have tried the knob, he would have found I hadn't locked it."

"Sit tight, Chip, Jim and I will be out in about fifteen minutes. In the meantime, don't touch anything."

Fredrickson and Deputy Jim Anderson arrived a few minutes later with the lights flashing on the squad car. Chip saw Walter groan and roll his eyes as he exited from the passenger side.

"Jim's still a rookie, likes to use those lights anytime he gets a chance. Did you find Runt?"

"No, after we're finished here, I'll start driving around looking for him. He's got a microchip, so if anyone finds him, I sure hope they take him to Jane."

"Let's have a look inside."

Jim painstakingly filled out a report on the missing items and took photos of the door, the kitchen and the living room. Fredrickson snooped around.

"Did you check the fridge for anything missing, Chip?"

"No, I didn't look there. Why would I?

"I got a hunch."

Chip opened the refrigerator. "I had a six-pack of Bud Light in here, and it's gone." He opened the freezer compartment. "Oh, and my bucket of ice cream is gone, too. What kind of thieves take beer and ice cream, for Christ sakes?"

"Kids. Electronics, beer, and ice cream—must be kids. You use that laptop for your mystery writing?"

"Yes, but I always back-up everything on a flash drive, plus my agent has a copy of all the chapters I've written to date. I also have my email contact list backed up on another flash drive, so I can retrieve all that."

"Anything of importance that's not backed-up?"

Chip thought about all the research on chemicals and epoxy resins he had done in the past week and the photos. All the photos were gone. "I may have lost some research and some photos."

"That music system of yours worth much?" Walter now occupied one of the kitchen chairs. He had removed one of his boots and was massaging his foot.

"Pretty expensive. The Bose speakers are top-of-the-line. You going to dust for prints?"

"Well, I expect Jim would love to do that, but we don't have a CSI in these parts. We'd have to send them off to the Iowa BCI. No teenagers in Turners Bend with criminal records, so it's unlikely we would get a match anyway. Stuff will turn up. Kids will brag about it at school and someone will turn them in."

"I thought the pastor's kid had a meth lab charge."

Walter hesitated. "Well, we kind of let that go. First offense, pastor's kid, the explosion scared the crap out of him. He never got as far as cooking any meth. I just gave him a good talking to and made him pick up litter along the state road.

"Jim, I think we're finished here. We'll be in touch, Chip. I'll put out an alert for Runt. I know you're fond of that little mutt."

The squad pulled out of the yard with its lights flashing and sped down the road as if it were in wild pursuit of a felon. Chip called Jane.

"Jane, my house was robbed this afternoon, and Runt's gone. The door was left ajar. He probably just ran out the door. I'm heading out to search for him, but if you get an inquiry about a stray dog I'd appreciate a call."

"Oh, my God, Chip. How long has he been gone?"

"Could be two or three hours or so."

"Okay, I'm on my way. I'll search east of your property and you search west."

JANE AND CHIP SEARCHED UNTIL IT WAS TOO DARK to continue. No puppy. Runt had been missing at least nine hours at this point. They returned to Chip's house and ate cheese sandwiches and had a cup of coffee. Honey sat at attention next to Chip, her gaze fixed on his face as if expecting him to produce Runt of any minute.

"I'd offer you a beer, but they took my beer. Want something stronger?"

"No, I better get home. Sven and Ingrid will be home soon."

Honey shifted her head and twitched her tail. Then she went to the door and began to whine. Chip let her outside, and she raced behind the shed. A few seconds later she returned with a very dirty Runt frolicking behind her.

Jane scooped up the puppy and began to examine him.

"He's muddy and covered with burrs, but otherwise I'd say that he just had a little canine adventure. He needs a bath and a good meal. I bet he'll sleep soundly tonight." She kissed Runt on the head, then she kissed Chip on the cheek and was gone.

With no laptop, Chip was relieved of this writing routine for the evening. He pulled off the burrs, put Runt in the tub for a bath and fed him. The puppy was soon asleep. Losing his electronics was disturbing, but losing Runt would have been disastrous. As he stroked Runt's little body its warmth shot straight to his heart. His affection for the miscreant surprised him. Sappy as it seemed, Runt was his baby.

He hadn't reminded Jane about what the thieves might find on his computer. He'd wait and see what happened. As he lay in bed, he thought about that kiss. Not exactly make-up sex, but it was a start, a good sign. The phone rang, startling him from his musing.

With weariness evident in her voice, Jane said, "Chip, Sven skipped out on his grandmother's birthday party. Ingrid said he left with Leif Henderson in Leif's car, and when they returned they smelled like beer."

CHAPTER THIRTY-TWO

Monday, May 1, 10:30 a.m.

Lucinda,

My house was robbed yesterday and my computer is gone. I'm sending this from Flora's computer at City Hall. I have Brain Freeze *backed up and you have all but my most recent chapter, but I'm going to need a 30-day extension on my deadline. Sorry, but I'm sure you understand that the circumstances are beyond my control.*

Chip

Monday, May 1, 11:00 a.m.

Chip,

Like hell. They must sell computers somewhere in fly-over country. Get yourself a new one pronto, cowboy. I'll give you until May 15, NO LONGER. But, you have to get started blogging ASAP. The paperback edition of TCK hits the shelves next week. Check your contract! Mystery Ink put some ditzy junior editor named Sha'desha on BF. She thinks you have written me into BF as Belinda. I let her know I am certainly not the victim type, and even without a migraine headache, I'm bitchier than Belinda. Then I had her taken off the project. How can someone with a stupid apostrophe in her damn name be a copy editor?? BTW, who is Flora? I thought the horse doctor's name was Jane. Stay away from the dames and keep writing.

Lucinda

Chip deleted Lucinda's reply. "I tell you, Flora, my literary agent is a pain in the ass. Pardon my French."

"I heard about the robbery. Most people in Turners Bend don't lock their house or car doors. We trust our neighbors. When something like this happens, makes me wonder what the world is coming to." Flora brushed dog hair off of Chip's suede jacket.

"Chief thinks it's kids and that I'll get my stuff back. Guess I'll have to drive into Ames to get a new computer."

"Maybe Jane would enjoy another trip to Ames with you." Flora turned her face away from Chip to hide her sly smile.

"Right now Jane probably wouldn't walk across Main Street with me."

"You lovebirds have a spat? I thought things were pretty cozy between the two of you."

Chip ran his hand through his hair, which was in need of a trim. "So did I. I don't have a very good track record with women. I always seem to make a mess of relationships."

"If I were you, I'd start by sending her two dozen long-stem roses and an apology note and ask for a date."

"I don't know what to apologize for."

"Doesn't matter, just say you're sorry. I know just the florist to do it. I'll take care of everything for you, including a dinner reservation in Ames. Just trust me." Flora picked up the phone and set her plan in motion.

"YOU KNOW, CHIP, I HAVE NEVER RECEIVED SO MANY roses at one time. There must have been three dozen. They're gorgeous, but you really didn't have to do that. How did you know that yellow roses were my favorite?" Jane was settled in the Volvo for a second trip to Ames.

Chip gulped. "Three dozen, huh? Lucky guess on the color."

"About the apology, I should be the one apologizing to you. I thought I could reason with Hal, but I failed."

"What happened?"

"Oh, the usual ranting and raving and name calling, followed by some threats. He denied everything, said it was just another of my attempts to stick it to him, told me to butt out or . . . ." Jane's voice trailed off, and she looked out the passenger window.

"Or what, Jane?"

"Or my boyfriend might end up like Owen Hansen."

"Am I that boyfriend?" He tried not to sound too eager, but failed.

Jane let out a humorless laugh. "Now, let me see, which of my many boyfriends could he have been talking about? Yes, I assume he was referring to you."

"Seems that is good news-bad news for me. I'm your boyfriend, good news. I might get beaten to a pulp, bad news. So, now what do we do?"

"I don't know. That was Plan A, and I have no idea what Plan B should be."

Jane reached over and put her hand on Chip's thigh. He placed his hand on top of hers, and they stayed that way until they turned into Best Buy.

CHIP SPENT TWO HOURS GOING THROUGH set-up protocols on his new laptop and another hour recreating the partial chapter of *Brain Freeze* that he had lost. His evening with Jane had ended with a long, lingering kiss. He thought he might have to send roses to Flora, too. The woman may be a nosy matchmaker, but she knew her stuff. The goodnight kiss alone was worth three dozen roses and an expensive dinner.

CHAPTER THIRTY-THREE

Brain Freeze
Two Harbors, Minnesota

JOHN COMPLETED A TURN AT ONE END OF THE POOL and clicked the lap counter function on his wrist watch. He reached forward with a powerful stroke of his arm and pulled himself through the water. After more than two decades of swimming, first competitively and then finally, for sheer pleasure, the rhythm of the strokes was second nature.

Although he did not consider himself to be an introvert, there was something about the solitude of swimming that John craved. It was different than working out in a gym, where inevitably a sweaty guy on the treadmill next to him spent his entire workout shouting into a cell phone. In the pool, there was a wonderful absence of distractions. It was a world unto itself.

Additionally, he had read several medical studies that supported his belief that swimming increased the blood flow to the brain, which explained why John often found simple solutions to complex problems or conceived of new ideas in the middle of a lap. Today, he began his laps with thoughts of the case and what he hoped Belinda Peterson might discover.

Neither he nor Jo had slept well the night before. They lingered at Belinda Peterson's house for several hours the previous evening, going over the evidence they had accumulated thus far. By the end of their visit, Belinda seemed to have a clear idea of what they were looking for. The plan called for her to spend the following day—today—looking for specific information on NC-15. Jo stressed to Belinda that she needed to be cautious. What they were looking for was important, but not worth the risk of being discovered. God only knew what Candleworth would do to the CFO if she were found out. She looked shell-shocked by the time they left.

He and Jo had a light dinner and then headed to bed early. Their love making was slow and sweet, and when they drifted off to sleep, John wrapped his arms around Jo. Around two o'clock in the morning, he was wide awake.

He tossed a few times in Jo's bed and then finally got up to watch TV, clicking through the channels to quiet his thoughts. He had not mentioned it to Jo, but he too was worried about Belinda. Not only about the risks she would take, but the headaches that obviously plagued her. John couldn't help but think about the damage he had seen in some of the other victims' brains. A prayer escaped from his lips, offered up to spare Belinda Peterson the agony that went through Mitch Calhoun's head.

A little later, Jo had walked out into the living room, followed by Caddy. Jo sat next to John and dropped her head to his shoulder. The dog curled up on the other side of him and put a heavy paw on his lap. Without saying a word, they watched *Casablanca*. Something about watching the drama of another time period had relaxed them and all three finally dropped off to sleep again.

Now, a third of the way through his swimming routine, his thoughts meandered to his feelings about Jo. He had never known a woman like her before. She was intelligent, but impulsive. Bossy, sure, but she listened to his opinions. She was fierce and stubborn. Their personalities were as different as they were similar. Jo made love to him with abandon, and just thinking about the expression on her face when she climaxed made his heart race. But there was more to it than that.

She took life head on. Grabbed it by the throat and showed no mercy. He admired her for it, but part of him wondered if he could live with the knowledge that her job was dangerous and that she was frequently in harm's way.

Of course, living with a neurosurgeon's schedule and demands was no picnic either. His years of dating had left a trail of disappointed lovers, all who complained that his work always came first. He didn't want life with Jo to be that way.

As he clicked off another lap, he thought, "What the hell do I want to happen? Like I'm going to pack up and move to Minneapolis to be with a special agent of the FBI."

Powerful kicks, laden with frustration, drove him onward. *Idiot. I don't even know how she feels about me. I could be just another lover to her.* But if he was being honest with himself, he didn't really believe it. Jo was not the type of woman to hop from bed to bed.

Getting ready to make another turn, his thoughts were interrupted when he noticed a shadow cast into the pool. Reaching for the edge, he pulled himself upright and pulled off his goggles. Squinting into the bright florescent lights overhead, he saw that the shadow belonged to Jo. Her curls escaped from the confines of her ponytail, springy in the humidity of the pool enclosure. The fact that he had just been thinking of her and what the future might hold for them made him feel as if he had conjured her. *Speak of the devil.*

John felt the warmth of her greeting smile all the way down to the pit of his stomach. He had the urge to reach out and pull her into the pool with him, winter coat and all. Before he acted on the impulse, he shook his head to erase any further thoughts of what he would like to do to her in the water. He cleared his throat, "Good morning. Any word from our co-conspirator yet?"

Jo snatched his towel from a lounge chair and handed it to him as he hoisted himself onto the deck. She unzipped her coat and crouched down next to him. "Wish I had time to join you. Looks inviting." Putting her hands on either side of his head, she turned his face toward her, and gave him a long, lingering kiss. His body reacted immediately and he dropped the towel in his lap, before she could see the evidence of his desire. He felt his face grow warm with embarrassment.

She looked down and smiled. "Oh, if only we had time." Jo sighed. "However, duty beckons. Belinda called; she said she has something we need to see. She's going to meet us back at her house in half an hour."

He toweled his hair and then wiped down his torso. "Did she find out what NC-15 is?"

Jo shook her head. "Didn't say. She said she was in a hurry, so I didn't get many details." She hesitated, and then bit her lower lip. "I can't help but worry about her. She sounded a bit odd, but at the time I thought it was just that she was crunched for time. You don't think Candleworth has discovered what she's up to, do you? I wonder if we made a mistake getting her involved."

John stood up, wrapped the towel around his waist and pulled her to him. He felt a need to reassure her. And to reassure himself. "I'm sure she's fine. We finally convinced her that Candleworth is up to no good. She's got a huge stake in this, even more than we do. Not only that, she's smart. She'll be careful."

"Just the same, I'm going to have Frisco meet us at her place. I know it's out of his jurisdiction, but he said to call him if I got in a bind. I'd feel better having some back-up." She shrugged. "Call me paranoid."

"I'd never call you paranoid. Just prepared. So, no word then from your guys in Minneapolis?"

"They planned on heading up first thing this morning, but a whopper of a snowstorm hit the Cities last night. They might be here later today, but I'm not holding my breath. Gotta love Minnesota winters."

He released her and bent down to pick up his clothes from one of the deck chairs. He pulled on his shirt and jeans, and tugged on his fur-lined boots. Giving his hair one last rub with the towel, he put on his coat and followed her out into the cold.

▬ ▬ ▬ ▬ ▬ ▬

FRISCO WAS LEANING AGAINST HIS CAR, smoking a cigarette when they pulled over several yards from the entrance to the CFO's winding driveway. He tossed the butt to the road and ground it out with his toe. He walked to Jo's open window and greeted them. "I see the two of you more than I see my wife and kids these days. So, are you thinking this might be a double-cross?"

Jo shook her head. "Not necessarily. Yesterday, Ms. Peterson seemed fully convinced that she's been a victim of NeuroDynamics. She sounded a little strange when she called. It's probably just me being overly cautious."

"Nothing wrong with listening to your gut. Never doubt it, myself. Maybe that's what's kept me alive for twenty years on the force."

"I don't want Belinda to know you are backing us up. Do you mind waiting here? Just before I enter her house, I'll call you and leave the phone on, in my pocket. That way, you will be able to hear if anything is amiss. That work for you?"

"Sounds like a plan."

Jo closed the car window and drove forward, turning into the entrance. The driveway was icy. The trees lining the drive prevented the sun from melting the snow. As they neared the house, she attached a small microphone to her cell phone. She then hit the speed dial for Frisco's cell and slipped her phone into her jacket's inner pocket. Jo threaded the microphone's wire through a tiny hole just beneath the stitching at the collar.

They carefully walked up the slick steps to the front door and rang the doorbell. Today, Belinda answered immediately.

It was obvious to John that the CFO was in a great deal of pain and any concerns he had about her being a threat to them vanished. Her face was pinched and there was very little color in her face. He reached out and touched her shoulder. "Ms. Peterson, how are you feeling? You look like you have a terrible headache."

She rubbed her forehead. "It'll pass. These headaches seem to come and go. I was fine this morning and then it came back with a vengeance. I took some more ibuprofen before you arrived. It'll be better soon."

John had his doubts. "I can write a prescription for something stronger, if that would help. I hate to see you suffer like this."

Belinda waved her hand, as if swatting a pesky fly. "Maybe I'll take you up on that later." She led them to the fireplace, once more. "I didn't sleep too well last night, trying to figure out where I could find the data on NC-15. I finally got up and went into the office around six this morning."

Jo cleared her throat and said, "I didn't think to ask yesterday. I noticed your husband and kids aren't around . . ."

Belinda's eyes filled with tears and she said, "Michael thought it best to take the kids and visit his mother. We've been arguing a lot lately and well, as you know, I haven't exactly been myself." She shrugged. "He needed a break, but I miss them so much. They are my whole world."

John felt the sadness roll off of the woman like lake fog. He was more determined than ever to do what he could to restore this woman's life to her before it was too late. *If it wasn't already too late.*

Jo said, "You said you found something we should see . . ."

"Yes." Some of the color returned to Belinda's face as she spoke. "I went to the labs. A few of the researchers were in already, and I told them I was there to conduct a surprise audit."

John said, "Do you normally audit the labs?"

Belinda smiled briefly. "No. No need to. The financial records of the labs are handled by my department. Of course, the scientists don't know that. I told them Candleworth was concerned with their record keeping and that there were discrepancies. I threw in a few financial terms for good measure, like return on investment and unit cost analysis schedule." She let out a dry chuckle. "Those lab geeks never knew what hit them. They couldn't give me access to their files fast enough."

John smiled. Belinda's plan had been simple, but bold, no doubt about it. "So, what did you find? Anything to explain what they are injecting into people?"

Belinda pulled out a thick, blue binder. "I compiled this. It's filled with all the paperwork I could find with reference to NC-15. Even with my experience with this company, it didn't make much sense to me. Maybe you can decipher the medical mumbo-jumbo."

John took the binder from her hands and paged through, reading here and there as particular phrases would catch his eye. He devoured the pages, anticipation spurring him on to read faster. The answer was here, he knew it in his soul.

Belinda spoke up, "Did you find anything?"

John did not respond for quite some time. He was sickened by what he had found. When he looked up, he stared off into the darkened fireplace. *This is even worse than I could have imagined. I can't tell her about this, at least, not yet.* He cut his eyes toward Jo and then towards Belinda, hoping Jo would understand that he would explain everything later, when they were alone.

Jo's eyes widened slightly and she gave him a barely perceptible nod. *Good; she understands.* Her eyes strayed away from the CFO's face when she spoke up for John, "I think we should take the information back to the condo for further analysis, don't you think, Dr. Goodman?"

Before John could respond, Belinda looked at him and said, "Oh, no. You're not going to keep this from me. I saw it in your eyes. It's bad, isn't it? You know what's in the injections." When John didn't say anything, Belinda turned to Jo. "You two are trying to protect me. I need to hear this." Her eyes pleaded with them both. "Please."

John decided that she was right. Waiting to tell her wasn't going to make it any easier. "Very well. Yes, I found something and it's . . . well, it's not good. Didn't think it was possible. I've read about this, but I thought it was several more years away . . ."

Jo gently touched his thigh, startling him out of his thoughts. "Are you going to let us in on that brain wave of yours?"

John could no longer contain the rage he felt. He spat out the words, "A huge piece of the puzzle just fell into place. NC-15 is a serum containing nanochips, which are injected to flow into the . . ."

Jo held up her hand. "Whoa. Nanochips? I thought we were talking about microchips here."

He took a deep breath and forced himself to speak slower, calmer. He had to make it clear to them both, especially Belinda. "We are, sort of. Think of them as a much smaller cousin of the microchip. They're invisible to the naked eye, minute as a speck of dust. There have been studies to determine their use in surgical instrumentation, diagnosis, and drug delivery. Scientists in London have been working on nanochips to act as 'micro-shuttles' to deliver specific doses of medicine to the correct location. Afterwards, they can be used to monitor the patient's recovery."

"So, you're saying they inject these nanochips to flow into the . . . ?

"The locus ceruleus."

Jo massaged her temples. "God, this stuff is giving *me* a migraine. Locust what?"

"Locus ceruleus, or LC for short. It's a nucleus in the brain stem involved with physiological responses to stress and panic. For such a small part of the brain, it is very important. It is the origin of Post Traumatic Stress Disorder, or PTSD for short. Also, in Alzheimer's patients, there can be a loss of up to seventy percent of neurons in the LC."

He tapped his forehead. "You've heard of research showing that brain injuries to the frontal lobe can cause criminal behavior, right?"

"Yes. In a college psych class, I wrote a term paper on a guy that was perfectly normal until he suffered a brain injury and then he murdered seventeen women."

John nodded. "That's right. But what's not as widely known is that increased aggressiveness and lack of impulse control can sometimes be traced to increased levels of norepinephrine levels in the LC."

Belinda spoke up. "Okay, so how does that relate to mind control?"

He could feel his heart racing as the anger filled him once more. "What if the injected nanochips shuttle through the blood stream to the LC? Once it arrives at its destination, it increases the norepinephrine and decreases the neurons, thereby shutting down the ability of the person to choose between right and wrong."

Jo's face flushed. John could tell she had caught on to the importance —and horror—of what he was saying. "So, you're thinking that these mad scientists told Belinda and the others that they were going to have a microchip implanted to control their migraines, or depression, or what have you. They receive a microchip, but also an injection of nanochips— the NC-15—that flows into the, what did you call it? Oh, yeah. The LC."

"Makes sense so far."

John saw that Belinda had gone pale again. She was silent, seeming to absorb their discovery. He was concerned more than ever about her health. He reached out to her once more and placed a hand over hers. "Ms. Peterson, are you alright?"

Her eyes stared forward, focused on some distant point in the room. "I . . . I honestly don't know. How does the mind control . . . I can't believe I'm saying those words. How does the mind control work?"

Jo spoke. "Let's assume that John's right about the NC-15 destroying inhibitions. Moving forward, as you and the other patients recovered from the surgery, you had several post-surgery visits. Only instead of just monitoring your recovery, they are testing the effectiveness of the nanochips in destroying your ability to distinguish between right and wrong."

As if Jo couldn't sit still any longer, she stood up and walked to the fireplace. "They tested you with petty crimes, and then recorded the results in the files."

Belinda's face was scrunched in confusion. "But why bother with the microchip at all?"

"I think it has to do with the success rate of the NC-15. If the nanochips fail to reach the LC or if they don't fully alter the test subject's morals, then NeuroDynamics would need to have a way to destroy the test subject, no questions asked."

The CFO's hand flew to her mouth as she realized the enormity of what had happened to her. "My God. What have I done?"

John knelt by her side. "You can't blame yourself; you couldn't have known what they were doing to you. You were looking for a way to end your headaches . . ."

Belinda turned to him. It was as if the life had already left her eyes. "No, you don't understand. I didn't know . . . I thought you were mistaken. I wanted to prove you wrong. I confronted Charles this morning with what you told me."

Jo sat up straight, her eyes wide. "Belinda, why would you do that? I thought we made it clear that we needed to keep this quiet. Don't you realize you've jeopardized this whole investigation?"

Belinda's face flushed crimson and she stared at her hands in her lap. "I know, I screwed up." She looked up into Jo's face once more, her eyes pleading for understanding. "But you've got to realize that I've worked for Charles for fifteen years. He gave me a job right out of college. I didn't want to believe he was capable of doing this . . . doing this to *me.*"

Just then there was a loud crash from the other side of the house. Jo leaped up and shouted into the microphone, "Frisco! They know . . . we've been set up!" She yanked out her Glock from its hiding spot at the small of her back and raised it in front of her. Her eyes darted around, searching for any danger. John felt the panic radiate off of her.

The door leading to the kitchen flew open, banging into the wall behind it. Jo and John whirled around to face Charles Candleworth. Belinda yelled, "Charles! What are you doing? How did you get in here?"

"After our little chat, I decided it would be prudent to keep an eye on you and find out just what the good doctor has discovered. By the way, you are going to need a new lock on that back door." Holding up a cell phone, he turned to Jo and said, "You just couldn't stay out of my business, could you?" John inhaled sharply when he saw that Charles had a gun in his other hand and it was pointed directly at his heart.

Without taking his eyes off of his old classmate, John caught Jo's movement out of the corner of his eye. She pointed her gun at Charles Candleworth's head. Jo barked, "FBI! Put the gun down."

It was at that moment that John realized that Jo's voice was emitting from the phone Candleworth held in front of him. He felt nauseous as he realized that it was the detective's phone. *Where's Frisco?*

NeuroDynamics's CEO appeared unfazed. "I don't think you want to be waving that pistol at me. You see, I don't take kindly to threats." Candleworth's voice was calm and almost pleasant. *He's enjoying this, the bastard.*

Jo let out a puff of air. "I really don't give a damn what you take kindly to. I said drop the gun or I'll shoot."

He ignored her as if she were a toddler throwing a temper tantrum and turned his attention to John. "Nice of you to join us, Dr. Goodman. Been a long time." Without changing the aim of his gun away from John, he called over his shoulder, in the direction of the kitchen. "Thompson. Wilson. Bring in our other guest, will you?"

Belinda let out a yelp when two large men dressed in black dragged a body into the room, their arms hooked under each arm of the man between them. When they dropped him with a loud *thunk* on the hardwood floor of Belinda's family room, John realized that the bloodied body in front of him was Frisco. He could not detect a rise and fall of the detective's chest.

Preoccupied with trying to determine if Frisco was still alive, John lurched up and reached for Frisco's neck, wanting to check for a pulse.

John felt the whack at the base of his skull. He pitched forward and fell to his knees, his eyesight fading to black.

CHAPTER THIRTY-FOUR

"HEY, OUT AGAIN ALL NIGHT? You've been making a habit of this. What kind of a woman are you, Honey? Today is your big day at the vet's. Do you want to go in the car and see Jane?" When Honey heard the word "car," she ran to the Volvo and sat by the back door thumping her tail.

Between Honey and Runt the back seat of the Volvo had been ruined. It was covered with muddy paw prints and snotty nose smears. Plus, Runt had managed to rip the leather upholstery and pull out a wad of the padding. At one time Chip used to spazz over so much as a gum wrapper in the ashtray of this car, now he had capitulated to his dogs, and the car had "gone to the dogs." He started to refer to it as "Katrina," the car with hurricane destruction, and to joke that he might apply for a FEMA car.

As they drove into town, Chip marveled at the perfect rows of tender corn stalks lining acre after acre. It hadn't occurred to him until then, why tiny braids of hair were called cornrows.

In the past few weeks he had been tutored about pre-emergent herbicides, genetically resistant corn seed and GPS-plotted applications of fertilizer and pesticides. At the Bun he overheard discussions between the Pioneer farmers and the Northrup King farmers as to which seed was superior. When Oscar Nelson asked his opinion on RoundUp Powermax, he had to defer by saying, "I'll have to get back to you on that one, Oscar."

Honey seemed to sense what was in store for her. She stiffened her legs and refused to move. Chip had to carry her into the clinic exam room.

"She's pregnant again, Chip," reported Jane after her pre-op exam.

"How can that be?"

"I hardly think I need to give you a lesson on the birds and the bees. She must have been in heat a couple of weeks ago. Looks like you are going to be a puppy daddy again."

"She has been restless and roaming a lot and her butt did look sore, I just didn't know that all that meant she was in heat. Guess I better start lining up potential owners. Hope she doesn't have eight again."

Mabel popped her head into the exam room.

"Mabel, Honey is going to have another litter," Chip announced. He marveled at the pride and excitement he heard in his own voice. *More puppies, how awful! How wonderful!*

"Lovely, dear. Chief Fredrickson is here to see you, Jane. Should I show him in?"

"Sure," said Jane.

The chief had his official TV cop face on and was in full uniform, including his hat. His pants were hanging at half-mast and his sizable beer belly was draped over his belt, which was further weighted down with his service revolver and holster.

"Good, you're here too, Chip. I have a lead on your stolen property. I wonder if both of you would come over to Flora's office with me. She has something to show us on her computer."

━━ ━━ ━━ ━━ ━━

JANE AND CHIP FOLLOWED THE CHIEF AND Flora to a small conference room in Town Hall. Pastor and Christine Henderson were seated in two of the chairs, worried looks on their faces. On the table was Flora's newest purchase, a laptop projector.

"Just for the record, folks, I tried to locate Hal, but no one seems to be able to find him. I think you'll see why. Flora, please show us what you found," said the chief.

Flora stood, as if to give a formal presentation. "I received a call yesterday from Sylvia Hubbard over at the high school. We've been friends for years. Even though she's near retirement, she's still the dance line coach. With her gout, I really don't know how she manages it . . ."

"Flora, could you get to the stolen property," interrupted the chief.

"I feel some background is needed here, Walter. Now where was I? Sylvia is not computer literate, so she called me. She overheard the dance line girls talking about something on YouTube. They clammed up when she questioned them about it, so she thought that maybe someone should look into it, especially since it had to do with beer. Syliva does not approve of drinking or smoking. She's a fine Christian woman, even if she is Catholic, Pastor Henderson, and . . ."

"Flora, move it along. Get to the bottom line here," interrupted the chief again. His "just the facts, ma'am" tone did not faze Flora. She gave him her poisonous smile, the one laced with arsenic.

"Hush, Walter, I won't be rushed." She paused, straightened her suit jacket and began her recital again. "So I began an exhaustive search for anything in the social networks that may lead me to the YouTube posting the girls were talking about, and bingo, I found it."

With a flourish she turned on the power and an image appeared on the pull-down projector screen in the corner of the room. She clicked PLAY and a jerky video recording started to roll.

A tall slim figure dressed in black jeans and a black turtleneck appeared. He was wearing a ski mask. He had a tire iron in his hand and smashed a window in a door. Chip immediately recognized it as his farmhouse door. Christine Henderson put her hand over her mouth to cover her low moan. Pastor Henderson put his arm around her shoulders. Chip looked over at Jane. The color had drained from her face, and she sat very still, her eyes fixed on the screen. A silent vacuum cleaner was sucking the air out of the room.

"Even with the mask, we can see that's our son," Christine said with a whisper. No one in the room responded as they watched the drama unfold.

Leif Henderson moved to the kitchen table and unplugged Chip's laptop. His voice had a hollow sound. "God, it's right in plain sight. This is too easy." The camera followed him into Chip's living room.

"Sweet. Look at these speakers. Let's take these, too." Leif unplugged the Bose speakers and picked them up. Returning to the kitchen, he opened the refrigerator door and removed the six-pack of beer and set it on the floor along with the rest of his loot. He opened the freezer and took out a plastic bucket of ice cream.

From off camera an adolescent voice cracked. "What the fuck are you doing? Dad said to just snatch the computer and get back to Grandma's party before anyone notices we're gone." Jane didn't make a sound, but Chip could see her chest pulsate with short, rapid breaths.

"Well, then put down that friggin' video camera and help me carry this stuff."

The screen went blank. All eyes turned to Chief Fredrickson. He pushed himself out of his chair, as if he had anvils on his shoulders. "I'm sorry folks. I'm going to have to haul the boys in for questioning. I want to talk to each of them separately before I talk with Hal. Pastor, I'll have to ask you to go over to the school and get Leif and bring him over to the station. This is his second offense, so you might warn him that I expect his full cooperation. When I'm finished with Leif, Jane, I'll give you a call to bring Sven on over. For now, let's keep this as quiet as possible, okay?" The heads of three heavy-hearted parents nodded in agreement.

"What about Hal?" asked Jane.

"When we find him, you can be assured I'll be talking to him. He's got a lot of explaining to do," said the chief. "And not just about this robbery."

Chip had a fleeting memory of another teenage boy in trouble. His parents sitting in the schoolmaster's office, the Mount Rushmore of his father's face, his mother wringing a lace-trimmed handkerchief. All these years later, he now understood his parents' anguish.

BACK AT THE CLINIC, CHIP ASKED MABEL to get them three coffees to go at the Bun.

"We didn't see it on the tape, but they must have taken Runt out of the playpen where I left him."

"What would make Sven do this, Chip? And, why would he tape it and post the tape for everyone to see? It doesn't make sense."

"It's the teenage mind, Jane. It doesn't think. It seeks pleasure and adventure. Hormones control it. What worries me more is Hal's involvement. If he wanted my computer, he somehow knows that I'm the one that put you on to his shenanigans. He now has our best evidence of what he's doing. It sure as hell complicates Plan B. I've got to confess to you, Jane, I'm a wimp when it comes to defending myself. If he sends his thugs after me, I'll be mincemeat."

"First let me deal with Sven. Then I'll put a stop to Hal. You need to keep out of this, Chip. Trust me, I won't show Hal any mercy."

▬ ▬ ▬ ▬ ▬ ▬

"WELL GIRL, YOU EVADED THE SCALPEL FOR NOW, but this is the last litter, hear me?" Honey put her head in Chip's lap and looked up at him with brown dewy eyes. "I hope you at least were carousing with a man of good breeding and not some farmyard mutt." Honey licked Chip's hand with her velvety tongue.

"Lucinda told me to write and stay away from the dames, but don't worry, I don't think that includes you, sweetie." Chip powered up his new laptop and switched his own mind to minds controlled by microchips and the insidious NC-15. Lucinda's deadline was looking impossible at this point. Writing on a timetable was not to his liking. He wondered how some authors could churn out one or two of these novels every year, year after year.

CHAPTER THIRTY-FIVE

Brain Freeze
Two Harbors, Minnesota

JOHN HEARD A VOICE SAYING HIS NAME as he struggled to the surface of consciousness. His head pounded and waves of nausea rose up into his throat.

"John, wake up. John?" The voice was demanding, persistent, but all he wanted to do was sleep.

When he tried to reach up and hold his aching skull, his realized his hands were tied behind him. His feet were likewise restrained. The area beneath his stretched out body was hard and dug into his back. He felt his body jerk to one side and then the other. *Where am I?* The scent of gasoline and the tang of blood filled his nostrils.

"John!" The voice had become panicky and shrill.

His eyes flew open and he saw Jo sitting on the floor next to him. She looked down at him, her face pinched with concern. She blew out a puff of air. "Oh, thank God! You scared me."

Clouds of confusion finally began to lift and he looked around. He was lying on the floor of a van. The only windows were in the back doors. They were covered in stained, gauzy fabric, letting in a muddy-colored light. Swaying to one side when the vehicle made a sharp turn, his head bounced painfully off the floor of the van.

"Where . . . where are we? What happened?"

Her reply was bitter. "Candleworth got the jump on me. I acted like a first-day rookie." She shook her head. "The little bastard. Should have shot him in the kneecap the minute he pointed that gun at you. Thought I had it all under control."

He realized for the first time that they were alone in the back of the van. "Where is he now?"

Jerking her chin toward the front of the van, she said, "Up there. They threw us in here and made sure we were locked up tight." She twisted her back so that he could see her hands were tied up, along with her legs. Jo was wearing her boots, but their coats had been left behind at Ms. Peterson's house. John heard Jo's teeth chatter in the chilly, dank air of the vehicle.

"What are they going to do with us?"

"Hell if I know. Candleworth said he's taking us back to NeuroDynamics. Said he has big plans for us."

"That doesn't sound good."

"You're right about that. By the way, how's the head?"

John tried to sit upright, but winced as the pain came roaring back. He squeezed his eyes shut, waiting for the throbbing to subside. "Not so good. A few cobwebs need to be cleared out. Are you okay?"

Her tongue probed a cut in the corner of her mouth, where there was a small trickle of dried blood. "Nothing that won't heal in a couple of days." Her lips twisted into a wry smile. "My wounded pride might take a little longer, though."

"What happened? I'm still a little fuzzy. Last thing I remember, you were pointing a gun at Candleworth and he had one pointed at me."

"You don't remember Frisco then?"

With a shock, he recalled seeing the body of Detective Frisco at his feet in the family room at Belinda Peterson's house. He sucked in a breath. With a growing sense of dread, he asked, "He wasn't moving. How is he? Don't tell me he's dead."

A shadow crossed Jo's features. "I don't know for sure. I could have sworn I saw his finger move as we left. But Wilson stayed behind with Frisco. Candleworth told him to kill Frisco and get rid of the body. Do you recognize Wilson's name?"

"No, should I?"

"He was another one of the test subjects in the files."

"Oh, no. No telling what he's capable of doing."

Jo nodded. "Exactly."

John briefly forgot his aching head and felt a hard lump in his chest. "My God." For a moment, he couldn't say anything else. His mind whirled with thoughts of all the damaged lives. Finally, he said, "I vaguely remember reaching out for Frisco, to check his pulse . . ."

"Yeah, well, that's when I lost my focus and Candleworth's goons made their move."

John had a sour taste in his mouth. *I acted without thinking, just like Candleworth wanted. Jo would never have lost her concentration if I hadn't reacted.* "You mean you were distracted because of me. You mean it was my fault . . ."

Jo interrupted. "No. It was *my* error. For God's sake, I've been trained to keep an eye on the bad guy. Been taught that from day one. All I could think about was you and the weapon coming down on your head."

John didn't agree with Jo's assessment that it was her fault. *This was exactly the type of situation that makes our relationship a bad idea. Jo can't do her job if she is worried about me.*

He was quiet for a moment, and then he realized that Jo hadn't mentioned Belinda Peterson. "What's happened to Ms. Peterson? What did they do to her?"

"They loaded her into the front of the van. She put up a pretty good fight. Candleworth pulled out some kind of gadget—it looked like a primitive remote control. He pushed a button and then she went into a seizure." Jo's voice grew brittle. "It was horrible to watch. He was controlling the microchip. The pain she must have been in . . ."

John clenched his jaw. "This ends now. I'm not watching that son-of-a-bitch get away with killing and torturing people anymore." He rocked to one side. "Can you help me sit up? I'm tired of feeling like a victim lying on the floor of this van."

Jo maneuvered herself around and helped him get some leverage. After several false starts, John sat upright and he leaned against the wall of the van. His body was drenched in sweat from the exertion, and his head felt like it was exploding, but he felt more in control.

He gave Jo a small triumphant smile, and then said, "So, any brilliant plans to get us out of this mess?"

"I think we'd better do as they say until we get inside. Thompson is in the front of the van with Candleworth and Belinda. I doubt Belinda will be very helpful to us in her condition. That basically leaves two bad guys against the two of us. Not bad odds, but we're a little hobbled with these damn restraints. Before you came to, I tried to get myself loose, but they used plastic cuff-ties. The more I struggled, the tighter they got. Once we're inside, maybe we can distract them."

The brakes of the van screeched as it slowed and then came to a stop. John said, "Here we go."

The door of the van creaked open a moment later. A blast of frigid air rushed into the vehicle and he saw that Jo's lips had turned blue with the cold. John squinted, letting his eyes adjust to the sunlight bouncing off the snow outside. When he could see clearly, he saw that Candleworth stood in the open doorway.

"So glad you decided to join us, Dr. Goodman. You've missed quite a bit of the excitement while you were resting."

John flexed his fists behind his back. *Just you wait.* "What do you want?"

"Oh, you'll find out soon enough."

When one of the guys from Belinda's house came around to the back of the van, the CEO spoke to him, never taking his eyes off of Jo and John. "Thompson, please show Special Agent Schwann our accommodations. Keep a close eye on her. We wouldn't want any nasty surprises."

Thompson pulled a knife out of his jacket pocket and flicked open the blade. John sucked in a breath, wondering what Candleworth's man would do to her. Thompson reached into the van and sliced through the ties that bound Jo's feet together and then unceremoniously hauled her out of the van by her arms.

Jo's green eyes blazed, but she said nothing. Seeing Jo's anger calmed him. *If she can tuck away her fear, then so can I.* Panic and guilt would not fix this problem. He had to have a clear head.

He watched as Jo was marched toward the headquarters building, walking carefully on the frozen ground. A gun to her back. A part of him willed her to make a run for it, but he realized that it would be too dangerous. Assuming she somehow managed to avoid being shot in the back, in her current state of dress, hypothermia would rapidly set in and she would die in the secluded woods.

John studied the CEO. He hadn't seen Charles Candleworth for over a decade. In other circumstances, he would have almost felt sorry for the guy.

The years had not been kind. He had to be in his mid-thirties, like John, but he looked to be in his late fifties. His carefully sculpted blonde hair blew up in the wind, showing the shiny scalp beneath. A paunch pushed at the buttons of his jacket. His nose was red and bulbous, with spider veins creeping across his considerable cheeks. The man clearly enjoyed more than just a social drink or two in his evenings.

Candleworth reached in and sliced off the plastic ties at John's ankles. Fishing a gun out of his jacket pocket, he pointed it at John's head and said, "Just keep this gun in mind in case you decide to be a hero."

John stumbled out of the vehicle, his feet burning with the sudden release of blood flow. Candleworth pushed him forward, towards the building. The gun dug into his back.

The sharp wind bit into John's face and cut through his sweater. As they walked, John decided to keep Candleworth talking, to find out what he could. "Where is Ms. Peterson?"

"She's already inside. Cooperative as a little lamb, now." John heard the CEO chuckle behind him, "I have to say, after you told her our little secret, she was not too happy with me. However, in the end, my methods were quite convincing."

John spat out, "I'll bet. Hard to disagree when someone is threatening to blow an artery in your head." He briefly lost his balance on a patch of ice, but caught himself just in time. "What are you going to do with us?"

"You'll know soon enough. Wouldn't want to spoil the surprise." He cleared his throat. "I have to say, I'm really quite honored that a highly esteemed specialist such as yourself has taken an interest in the goings on of my humble little company."

John forced his voice to be steady when he responded. "Charles, false modesty from you? What you've done is hardly humble. Tell me, are you doing it for the money? Or is living out your God complex reason enough?"

Wheezy laughter came from the CEO. "John, John. Always a bit of a wise-ass. I'm glad you've joined us. Very few people could truly appreciate what we've achieved. Look at Ms. Peterson, for example. I took a perfectly normal, ambitious mother of two and made her into a criminal. Her money-laundering talents are elegant in their complexity. Even you have to admit that's quite a feat."

John gritted his teeth and said, "You think it takes talent to destroy people's lives? All it takes is a psychopathic mind like yours. What kind of monster are you?"

He felt the muzzle of the gun dig into his back. "Name calling won't get you anywhere. Not very polite."

They had reached the building. Candleworth stepped to the side of John and yanked open the door. Heat enveloped them and for a moment John was relieved to be inside. The polished floors squeaked beneath their wet boots as the CEO led John down one hallway, then another.

Finally, they stopped when they came to a set of locked double doors. Candleworth reached around John and touched a pad with his palm. There was an audible *click* and then the doors swung open. They walked down another hallway, this one more brightly lit and sterile-looking than the others. Charles stopped him at the last door on the left. John felt his arms being tugged as Charles spoke. "I'm going to untie you now. I've got something in mind for you, but don't forget for one second that I have a gun centered on your back."

John turned toward the CEO. He was sorely tempted to take a swing at Candleworth. He would take great pleasure in beating him, not stopping until the breath left his body. John could picture landing the first punch in the man's mouth and he would savor the welcome pain to his knuckles. However, he knew that Candleworth would probably shoot him before he had a chance to move.

Candleworth studied him. "You know, for such a civilized man, you enjoy this violence. I can see it in your eyes." He tilted his head to the side. "You want to kill me, don't you?" He looked down at John's clenched hands.

John rubbed the back of his hand in the palm of the other. "The thought crossed my mind." Pointing to the gun, he said, "Call off your thugs and maybe I'll leave you for the courts."

Candleworth's burst of laughter was loud in the hallway. "Where would be the fun in that?"

John's tone was dry. "Forgive me if I don't find this amusing."

"Ah, but you may be interested to know that Belinda is under my full control now. Does that bother you?"

Cocking his head, John said, "I'm curious. How can you be so sure that Ms. Peterson will do anything you tell her? She clearly knows what you've done to her."

Charles pulled an item out of his pocket, about the size of a small cell phone and held it up. It had a large, green button in the middle, with three smaller red buttons below. His grin was devilish. "My little insurance policy. This remote sends out waves to the microchip in Belinda's head. If she disobeys, she gets a zap. One jolt will cause excruciating pain. Several will cause an aneurysm and certain death."

John felt dread course through his body. "What are you going to do with Agent Schwann?"

"It'll be much more thrilling to show you. Patience, Dr. Goodman, patience."

Feeling like he didn't have much choice but to humor the CEO, John tried another tactic. "We found the financial files, you know. They show all your contracts with known terrorists and drug lords all over the world. You're building an army of people who can't think for themselves, who will do what they are programmed to do. It must be quite a lucrative business for you."

Candleworth's eyes sparkled. "Yes, very. You know, I'm really quite pleased that you and Agent Schwann nosed around. Half the fun is having friends to share it with, wouldn't you agree?"

John crinkled his nose, as if he had smelled something particularly offensive. "You really are a slimy bastard, aren't you? You think that everyone thinks the way you do, crawls in the same sewers as you do."

He was rewarded when Candleworth's face turned a deep burgundy. "Enough. Time to teach you some manners." He looked down at his watch. "They should be just about ready for us now."

John sucked in a breath. "What do you mean, 'just about ready for us'?"

"I don't want to spoil the surprise."

Moments later, Thompson stepped through the doorway. "They're waiting for you, Dr. Candleworth. Do you need me for anything else?"

"Make sure that all the other employees have gone for the day. We don't want anyone to distract us. Once you are sure the building is empty, you may wait in your office in case I require any further assistance."

"Yes, sir." He walked down the hallway and disappeared around the corner.

Candleworth stepped aside, allowing John to walk in front of him.

His thoughts raced as they walked through the doorway. For the first time, he noticed a sign to the right of the door that simply said "PROCEDURES." A chill swept up John's spine. *Surely they didn't mean to operate on Jo?*

As if he'd heard John's silent question, Charles spoke again. "Don't you think that a special agent of the FBI would make a superb assassin? The U.S. government has already spent so much money on her training. Would be a shame to waste that talent." He smiled. "I know a very wealthy man down in South America who'd be willing to pay top dollar for her."

John's stomach lurched. The chilly air circulating through the room cooled the sweat clinging to John's body, making him shiver. Across the way Belinda Peterson stood next to an operating table. He roared when he saw Jo on the table. Running towards her, he thought of nothing but setting her free. Candleworth tossed his gun to Belinda. Catching it, she stepped in front of John, and rammed the barrel into his ribs. John came to an abrupt halt.

Charles chuckled. "I don't think I'd try anything, if I were you. Belinda would not hesitate to shoot you in her current state of mind."

John studied her carefully. She no longer resembled the woman they had seen a short time ago. There were deep, dark circles under eyes that held no spark of life. She resembled a robot, without compassion, without remorse. He wondered just how much longer she would live with the damage to her brain. There was nothing left of her but a shell.

Looking over the woman's shoulder, he stared at Jo. She was stretched out on her stomach on a padded operating table, with her face jammed into a hole at one end. Straps around her waist, arms and legs restrained her. She was dressed in a surgical gown with the tie strings loosened around her upper back. An IV snaked from her arm to a bag of fluids next to the table.

Her head was also tied down. Jo's hair was pulled up in a knot at the top of her head and covered with a cap. The lower half at the base of her neck had been shaved. Lovely red curls lay in a puddle at the base of the table leg. Jo was tacked in place like a specimen.

She grunted once and wriggled to no avail. The restraints were cinched tight. Bile rose in John's throat. He twisted away from the gun in his side, only to feel it jammed in the small of his back. He looked back at Candleworth and spat out, "You son-of-a-bitch!"

From the website photos, John recognized the man standing next to the table as Malcolm Steward, NeuroDynamics's chief surgeon. He was dressed in scrubs and a surgical mask, administering a local anesthesia at the base of Jo's skull. John noticed that the surgeon's hands shook as he worked.

A nervous smile appeared on his face when he saw John. "Pleasure to meet you, Dr. Goodman. I'm a huge fan. I attended the symposium on cerebrovascular diseases in Boston last October and heard you speak." His eyes slid to Candleworth, his face crimson.

Candleworth grunted, "Get on with it, Malcolm."

The surgeon shifted on his feet and lowered his eyes. "Um, sir, I don't feel right about this." His eyes cut over to Belinda and the gun. "I didn't sign on for this."

Charles clenched his teeth. "You'll do what you are told. I didn't hear any complaints when you received your bonus. I've made you a rich man." He grinned again. "I *own* you."

John watched the interplay between the surgeon and the CEO and hope rose in his chest. He glanced at Belinda, who stared blankly at Candleworth, as if awaiting further instructions. *Maybe if I can distract them . . .*

John forced his voice to be calm. "Dr. Steward, you're right. You don't want to do this. The other patients signed release forms. I saw them. This is something different. This will destroy your life when it gets out."

Candleworth screamed, "Shut up! Steward, do as I say or you won't have a life worth saving."

John saw the indecision in the surgeon's eyes. Malcolm took a deep breath and reached for a scalpel. Unsteady hands grasped the instrument, but it fell and clattered to the floor.

Candleworth shook his head. "Steward, you've always been a disappointment to me. You see, Dr. Goodman here really should be our chief surgeon. Fortunately, that's easy enough to remedy." Candleworth turned to Belinda. "Kill Malcolm."

The surgeon's eyes flew open and he turned to run. A loud *boom* filled the room, echoing off the walls. The bullet struck the man in the back. A straight shot to the heart. He slid down the wall, leaving a wide smear of blood on the spotless tiles that lined the perimeter of the operating room.

John spun around and tried to seize the gun away from Belinda, but she was too quick for him. She smacked the gun across his chin, catching him off-guard. He fell to the floor. He was getting to his feet again when he heard Candleworth.

"Now that we've lost Malcolm, you'll take his place. I suggest you prep for surgery. Your girlfriend is lucky you're such a brilliant surgeon. Wouldn't want to accidentally kill her, now would we?"

CHAPTER THIRTY-SIX

Turners Bend
May

THE TURNERS BEND POLICE DEPARTMENT was located on the ground
level of Town Hall with its entrance at the back of the building. The
TBPD's two squad cars were parked in the back parking lot. One was
eight years old, the other fifteen years old. Both were in mint condition
and had relatively low mileage considering their ages. The department
consisted of Chief Walter Fredrickson, Deputy Jim Anderson, and
dispatcher/receptionist/administrative assistant Sharon Smith. Sharon
ran into a spot of trouble with the law twenty years ago, and the chief
gave her the job as "rehabilitation." She was a tough cookie, and it
turned out she was ideal for the job.

Other than the fax machine, phone system and radio dispatch
system, the TBPD was low tech. Both the chief and Jim carried service
revolvers. The only time Jim had fired his was at the practice range.
The "jail" consisted of a room with a large window facing the office
area. It was equipped with a push-button code lock and two cots for
the local drunks and bad boys to sleep it off or contemplate an attitude
adjustment.

"When Leif gets here can we do good cop-bad cop?" asked Jim.

"For Pete's sake, Jim, we aren't some stupid TV cops and robbers
show. The kid is under eighteen, so his parents will be here with him.
He's a preacher's kid. Do you think we're going to rough him up for
a confession in front of his Lutheran pastor father?"

"From what I've seen of him, he's going to be a hard one to
crack."

"Jim, you go patrol the parking lot at the high school and let me
handle this case. I guarantee the kid is going to come clean pretty darn
quick when we tell him we've seen the tape."

"What if I see trouble in the parking lot?"

"Radio Sharon, and she'll let me know."

After Jim left the office, the chief muttered to Sharon. "Lord help me from fool deputies. If it weren't for you, we'd be the sorriest police department in the state."

Leif and his parents sat in three chairs in front of the chief's desk. Christine's eyes were puffy and she held a wadded up tissue. Pastor Henderson's hands were folded as if in prayer. Leif slouched in his chair. His long blond hair hung over one eye. He was dressed all in black, a black T-shirt with a picture of Lady Gaga on the front and black jeans that rode low on his hips.

"Leif you want to tell me about the robbery?" started the chief.

"What robbery? I don't know what you're talking about?"

"Let's cut to the chase here. We saw the videotape that Sven made of you robbing Mr. Collingsworth's house, so tell us how that all came down."

"That was some other dude in the ski mask. It wasn't me."

"How do you know the robber was wearing a ski mask then?"

"Like everyone at school has seen it, that's how. I plead the fifth. I ain't saying anymore without my lawyer present. Nobody even read me my Miranda rights."

"You haven't been charged with anything, at least not yet. Go home with your parents and think about this long and hard. If you don't cooperate, you won't just be picking up trash along the highway this time, Leif."

An hour later Jane and Sven sat in front of the chief's desk. Sven fidgeted in his chair. A light film of sweat was on his face and his eyes darted around the office.

"Why don't you just tell us all about it, Sven?"

Sven began to cry. He looked like a little boy in a teenager's body. He wiped his nose on the sleeve of his shirt.

"Dad said Chip was plotting against AgriDynamics and had something on his computer that he needed to take to the feds. He told me I could have a new car this summer, if I snatched the computer. I got Leif to come along so I could videotape it. It was Leif's idea to take the other stuff."

"Why did you put that tape on YouTube?"

"I didn't think anyone would know it was us. Leif had on a ski mask. It's just cool to have all those hits. We've had over 1,500 hits already. I'm not going to go to jail, am I?"

He turned to his mother and laid his head on her shoulder. "Mom, I'm sorry. I was trying to help Dad, but it was stupid. It got out of hand. I didn't know how to stop it. I'm scared. I don't want to go to the pen with a bunch of criminals."

"It's okay, son, you cooperated with me," said the chief. "You told the truth. I'm not going to send you to jail. You go home with your mother now and do your homework. I may have to talk with you again, but Mr. Collingsworth just wants his stuff back. Where is it?"

"I gave the laptop to Dad. The other stuff is in the trunk of the Henderson's Chevy. Except we ate the ice cream and drank two of the beers."

The chief smiled. "Well, I think you'll have to pay Mr. Collingsworth for a six-pack and a gallon of ice cream. Jane, after you take Sven home, would you and Chip mind meeting me here again?"

"Sure, give us an hour, and we'll come back. Come on, Sven, let's go home."

JIM RETURNED FROM PATROLLING THE SCHOOL PARKING LOT.

"I take it there wasn't any trouble over at the school today," said the chief.

"I gave the Johnson kid a warning ticket because his right turn-signal light wasn't working on his pickup. Told him he had a week to get it fixed. He gave me the finger, so I gave him a citation for insulting an officer of the law."

"Insulting an officer, huh? That's a new one on me."

Sharon stuck her head into his office. "Jane and Chip are here to see you, Chief."

Jane and Chip sat down. "I'm spending far too much time in your office, Chief," said Jane. "Thanks for being so considerate to Sven. Poor kid, got himself into more than he bargained for it seems."

"I'm trying to put this together, and there's seems to be some missing pieces. Would you two care to fill me in?"

Jane and Chip told him about the source of the poisonings and what they had found out about the hazardous conditions and waste disposal at the plant. They aired their suspicions about the assault on Owen Hansen and about the state of Hal's business.

"On my laptop I have photos I took at AgriDynamics. Hal must have seen me or somehow found out what I was doing. That's why he wanted Sven to steal it. We've been hesitant to rat on him."

"Until now," said Jane. "He lured Sven into a crime with a bribe of a new car. He's gone too far. I want him prosecuted up one side and down the other. If you don't call in the FBI and the EPA, Walter, I will."

"For your own safety, you two need to stay out of this. I'm not at liberty to say, but I can tell you the authorities have been working on this for some time. This could get very ugly, very fast. In the meantime, Chip, Hal has your computer, but you can go over to the Hendersons and get your other stuff out of the trunk of their Chevy. I'll give the pastor a call and give him a heads up. Oh, and Sven will be paying for your lost beer and ice cream."

"Seems you're awfully light on juvenile crimes, Chief," said Chip.

"Oh, I'll send them to juvenile court. That should put the fear of God into them. But it's Hal's whereabouts that's the bigger problem right now and things are about to move in that area."

Tuesday, May 10, 1:30 p.m.
Lucinda,
Here's another chapter. Brain Freeze *is heading into its final chapters. It looks like I'll make that deadline. By the way, a big sting is about to go down here in TB. You, in fact, supplied key information when you told me about the conversation you had with Hal Swanson in the Bend. Chip AKA The Crimebuster*

CHAPTER THIRTY-SEVEN

Brain Freeze
Two Harbors, Minnesota

Wₕᵢₗₑ Bₑₗᵢₙdₐ ₗₒₒₖₑd ₒₙ ᵥᵢₜₕ ₜₕₑ Gₗₒ꜀ₖ firmly in her grasp, Dr. John Goodman prepped for surgery. He slipped booties over his shoes and donned a face mask, covering his nose and mouth. He placed a surgical cap on his head, making sure all his hair was tucked inside. Moving to the sink, he scrubbed with an antibacterial skin cleanser, using the brush and nail-pick to thoroughly clean his hands.

He didn't think about each step. After hundreds of surgery preps, the motions came as naturally as breathing air. The familiar routine calmed his galloping heartbeat. He thought about Jo and what he was going to have to do to save them both. *This is all on me.* His nimble mind sifted through plan after plan. By the time he slipped on a surgical gown and pulled on the latex gloves, his mind was settled.

John turned toward Belinda. He raised his eyebrow and tilted his head toward the gun, "Belinda, is this what you want? I know you are still in there somewhere and that you know this is wrong. Please don't do this." Not expecting a response, he wasn't surprised when the gun stayed on the imaginary target he felt on his chest. He felt sweat gathering under his arms despite the coolness of the room.

He walked over to the operating table, his slippers a susurrus on the tile floor. The blinding lights above the table illuminated Jo. She was completely immobilized, yet he could see her trembling. He saw her back rise and fall with rapid breaths. *I don't blame her for being terrified.* He wished he could see her eyes, to reassure her—to reassure them both— that everything would turn out all right. *Trust me, Jo.*

His fingers grazed her lower back, knowing she would not feel his touch at the base of her skull. The full effects of the local anesthesia would have kicked in by now. She let out a startled squeak and tugged at her restraints.

John could see the abraded skin around the straps at her wrists. He bent to whisper in her ear. "It's me. I've got an idea." Beneath his hand, he felt her body relax a fraction.

His idea was a gamble, of course. It depended upon finding a speck of humanity left in Belinda Peterson.

The NeuroDynamics's CEO spoke. "That's enough chit-chat with your girlfriend, Dr. Goodman." John turned towards him.

Candleworth chuckled. "I'm going to enjoy watching you slice into her. You two have been troublesome." Stepping closer, he pointed at Jo with a stubby index finger. "She will be a worthy asset."

Jo screamed into the padding of the table. Anger rose up in John once again. His gloved hands clenched at his sides. *Wait for it, you bastard. Just wait.*

Candleworth looked at John, and must have seen the hatred in his eyes. He flapped a hand in the direction of Belinda. "Make sure you watch the doctor carefully. He's crafty, that one."

Belinda spoke for the first time. Her voice was raspy as she said, "It's time, Doctor. Get to work."

John stared at her for a moment, gauging her. He was ready to begin. There was a *clink* of metal as he picked up the scalpel on the tray. He was grateful that Candleworth and Belinda stood behind him. John surreptitiously sliced through the band at Jo's waist, covering his movements with his body.

He gazed over his shoulder at the CEO. "You do realize that I've never done this before? I get the general idea, but microchip implants and nanochips are a bit out of my field of study."

Candleworth's hoarse laughter bounced off the tiled walls. "Oh, but you underestimate yourself. It was you I had in mind when I first conceived my little cottage industry. Do you remember when I tried to hire you a few years back?"

"All I recall about that conversation was when I told you to go fuck yourself."

Candleworth clicked his tongue. "Tsk, tsk. And after I provided you another chance to work for me." He sighed. "I guess I'll have to help you out, now won't I?"

The CEO moved closer. John could feel his heart pound in his chest; adrenalin rushed through him. *A little bit closer.* He felt like a spider waiting for a fat, tasty fly to land on his web. John kept his eye on the remote in the man's hand, knowing that things would go terribly wrong for Belinda if he activated the microchip.

"The incision should be . . . awk!" Candleworth's voice was pinched off. The remote clattered to the floor and slid under the operating table. John had deftly stepped behind the CEO and wrapped an arm around his chest. He held the scalpel to the man's meaty throat, pinning him to the edge of the table. John could smell the aftershave and underlying sweat on the man's skin.

John's voice was deep as he said, "Charles, listen to me very carefully. You utter a sound and this blade will remove your vocal cords. Understood?" The CEO nodded.

Belinda strode to the opposite side of the operating table to face the two men. She raised the Glock, pointing it at Jo's head. Fury washed over John.

His voice was firm and clear. "Belinda. Remember what we talked about? You don't want to do this. Think of your children. They shouldn't grow up with a mother in prison for murder."

The gun wavered, but it was still a menace to Jo. John tried again. "You told us that your family is your whole world. They *need* your love, every bit as much as you need theirs. Don't destroy their lives."

The transformation on Belinda's face was remarkable. The blank look had been replaced with one of confusion, like a child lost in the woods. She lowered the gun a few inches. "What will happen to my children?" Belinda looked over to where the surgeon lay in a heap on the floor. She sucked in sharply.

John let loose the breath he had been holding. "Jo and I will help you. We'll convince the jury that you were under duress. They'll go easy on you. But you have to put the gun down."

She began to shake. She wiped her brow with the back of her hand that still held the gun. "What have I done?" She peered at John, who held the scalpel to her boss's neck. She appeared to be trying to figure out where the puzzle pieces fit.

"It wasn't your fault. Charles tricked you. He . . ."

John was jolted when Candleworth shot out an elbow that landed in his mid-section. He released a string of curses. The CEO wormed his way out of John's grasp and reached down under the table, hands frantically searching for the remote. When he had it in his grasp, he darted around the table and pointed it at Belinda, pressing the large, green button in the center. The wireless activated the microchip in her head.

She let out a screech of pain, her free hand reaching up to hold her head. Candleworth screamed in the woman's face. "Finish them both!" She braced herself against the table, keeping her fist around the grip of the weapon. Her eyes closed and she moaned in agony.

The CEO yelled again, "Kill them, I said!"

John's heart hammered in his chest. He knew he had to keep talking to her in a calm voice. Had to reach her through the pain in her head, drowning out Candleworth's commands. "Belinda. Don't listen to him. Listen to *me*. Fight back, dammit!"

Horror dawned on Belinda's features. She raised the gun, this time pointing it at the CEO. Candleworth shouted, "I've done nothing but help you. You belong to me." His face was splotchy and his lip was swollen. A red stripe of blood oozed above his collar where the blade had left its mark. His finger depressed the key again.

Belinda wailed in her misery. She tottered, lowering both of her hands to the table to hold herself upright. Candleworth continued to yell at Belinda, spit flying from his lips. "Goddamn it, give me the gun!" When he grabbed at the Glock in her hand, it exploded. *Boom!*

Jo shrieked at the blast. Blood spatter sprayed the back of her surgical gown. The CEO stood wobbling for a moment, then collapsed to the floor.

John knew they had nothing to fear from Belinda Peterson now. He reached over and gently took the gun away from Belinda and shoved it into the waistband of his pants.

He unhooked the straps binding Jo to the table. Gently pulling out the IV needle in her arm, he held a piece of surgical gauze to the tiny wound. John helped her to sit up. She massaged her skin, as if to restore circulation in her hands. An involuntary shudder went through Jo's body as the overhead lights glinted off the stainless steel tray of instruments that were meant for her surgery.

She slid off the table and stood next to John, swaying a bit. He was overjoyed when he saw that she was getting her bearings.

Once he was certain that she was steady on her feet, he dashed over to the side of the table where Candleworth lay at Belinda's feet, a pool of blood spreading out from his body. John bent over, checking for a pulse at the man's throat. Straightening, he looked over at Jo and shook his head.

Jo walked over to Belinda. "Ms. Peterson, do you remember anything?"

The woman shook her head. "Not much. What did I do?" The sorrow on her face was a living thing.

Jo reached out and touched Belinda's shoulder. "This was not your doing. It's all over now."

Belinda nodded and stared at the body. A fat tear rolled down her cheek, and then her shoulders shook as she wept.

Jo said, "We need to find Thompson."

John pointed to Belinda, and then said, "Should we bring her along?"

"No, we aren't out of danger yet. Thompson might have heard the shots. We have no idea what we're getting into and she's unstable. She'll be safer here." John tenderly led the CFO to a chair in the corner.

He grabbed a long doctor's coat off one of the hooks by the door and wrapped it around Jo's body. She said, "Do you have any idea where Thompson went?"

"He said he was headed to his office. I'll go with you."

John followed Jo as she dashed down the hallway and then went down the stairwell. She paused before they entered the floor of offices. She whispered. "Still got that gun you took from Belinda?"

John pulled it out and handed it to Jo. She checked the clip for bullets, and then opened the stairwell door, peering around the corner. Cautiously, they crept down the hallway, their footsteps quiet on the carpet. Jo checked the name plaques outside each door and paused at the third one on the right. The name read "L. Thompson, Security." She whispered, "I can hear a radio inside. Stay behind me."

Jo slowly turned the handle of the office door. She shoved it open and stood in the threshold, a classic shooter's stance. "Thompson. You are under arrest."

Thompson stood up and lurched for the pistol on the desk in front of him. "STOP! Don't make me shoot you."

When he swung around with the gun, Jo pulled the trigger and a burst of blood spattered from his forearm. Thompson's weapon fell to the floor and he cradled his wounded arm to his chest. John retrieved the gun and pointed it at Thompson. "What now?"

Jo said, "I'm going to call the locals to take this idiot into custody. We need to find Frisco."

John fashioned a make-shift bandage for Thompson's arm while Jo kept the gun on him. She sent John in search of some rope and he came back minutes later with cording that he had found in a supply closet. While Jo tied Thompson securely to the chair, he let out a nasty chuckle. "That detective is long dead by now. Wilson's really good at killing."

Jo gave the rope around his chest a vicious tug, causing him to suck in a breath of pain. "There, that ought to hold you until the authorities get here." She turned to John. "Time to get Frisco."

John nodded and said, "Let's take Belinda with us. In her current state, she shouldn't be on her own."

ONCE THEY ENTERED THE OPERATING ROOM, they found Belinda right where they had left her. She was a lost soul. John pulled Jo aside and quietly asked, "What's going to happen to her now? Will she be sent to prison?"

Jo looked at the body of the dead surgeon against the wall. She shrugged. "I'm not sure." Sighing, she said, "It's not like any of this was her fault. Her only mistake was letting that maniac into her brain. I'm going to argue that she needs medical care and deprogramming. Maybe we can keep her out of prison."

John shook his head. "For the time she has left."

Jo grabbed his arm. "What do you mean?"

"The damage done to her brain is irreversible. The jolts that Candleworth gave her with that gadget have taken their toll. The nanochips will continue to eat away at the neurons, and I can't do anything to eliminate them. The best I can do is to remove the microchip to prevent a brain aneurysm. But it's only a matter of time."

CHAPTER THIRTY-EIGHT

Turners Bend
May

"Holy moley. Look at that." Bernice had just put glasses of ice tea with lemon in front of Flora and Sylvia and glanced out the front window of the Bun. "It's just like in the movies."

A black sedan with tinted windows had pulled up outside the café. A woman and two men got out of the car. The woman had short-cropped hair, black with a few strands of gray. Her ebony skin was in sharp contrast to her starched white shirt. She wore wraparound sunglasses, as did the two men. Both men had powerful looking chests and slim waists, one was short and had dark curly hair, the other was well over six feet and had a Marine-style crewcut. All three looked up and down the street, scanning the store fronts and roof tops as if looking for snipers, then entered the Bun and took a seat at a table near the door.

Bernice's voice trembled with excitement as she moved to wait on them. "What can I get for you folks?"

"Three Cokes to go, please." The woman ordered. "Say, we're looking for the police chief. The deputy said he might be here."

Bernice sensed that Flora and Sylvia hadn't missed a word or movement. Flora stood and bustled over to the table. "I'm Flora Fredrickson, the city clerk and the police chief's wife. May I ask who you are and what you want with my husband?"

The woman spoke with a broad Eastern accent. "We're federal agents, and we're here on official business."

"I'll have to see some identification prior to revealing any information to you," said Flora. The three looked at each other, then pulled out black leather folders which they flipped open to reveal shiny badges on one side and ID cards on the other.

Bernice was impressed by Flora's assertiveness. She watched on as Flora took her time to examine each ID card. "Well, Special Agent Masterson," said Flora "my husband is fly fishing out on the Raccoon River, west of town." The female agent nodded to one of the men, the one Bernice thought looked just like a tall version of Paul Newman. He took out his iPad, grabbed one of the Cokes and headed out the door.

"Thank you, Ms. Fredrickson. You wouldn't happen to know where we can find a man named Hal Swanson, would you?"

"You could try the bar down the street. He might be there, although no one has seen him for several days, I believe." Agent Masterson nodded to the other man, who left and headed down the street.

"Looks to me like you're the one in charge," Flora said to Agent Masterson. "I like that. Good for you."

Bernice, whose fantasy life had always including meeting movie stars, thought the shorter agent looked like Robert Downy, Jr. The whole scene left her breathless and left her food orders getting cold behind the counter. After the agents departed, she continued to ignore her customers until she had placed phone calls to Chip and Jane.

⸻

AN HOUR AFTER RECEIVING BERNICE'S CALL, Chip and Jane found the chief seated in his office with Agent Masterson. He was still wearing his lucky fishing hat, studded with brightly colored flies, and his multi-pocketed fishing vest. Chip guessed his waders and gear were in the back of the squad car.

Chip eyed two male agents questioning Dispatcher Sharon and Deputy Jim and briefly tuned into the conversation.

"Are you aquatinted with Hal Swanson, Ms. Smith?" asked the agent. Sharon gazed into his steel blue eyes. He seemed to be turning on his charm, and Chip could tell that Sharon was more than willing to cooperate.

"Everyone in Turners Bend knows that Hal Swanson is a no-good drunk. He's always trying to pick-up women. Once he tried to feel me up over at the Bend. Let's just say he never tried that again," said Sharon. When she fluffed her hair and gave the agent a big toothy smile, Chip fully expected her to hand over her phone number in hopes of snagging a date with him.

The other agent was taking a no-nonsense approach with Jim.

"What can you tell me about Hal Swanson, Deputy?" The agent's piercing gaze made Jim look like a frightened woodland animal.

He stuttered as he replied. "The chief and I have had him under surveillance. We suspect he is involved in a robbery and a cover-up. Sorry I can't stick around and help with the investigation, but someone has to be out on the streets protecting the people of Turners Bend." Jim put on his hat and caught the chief's eye. The chief gave him permission to leave with a nod. Chip almost laughed out loud at the deputy's attempt at a swagger as he exited the squad room.

Agent Masterson took charge of the inquiry, directing her questions at Chip and Jane. "The chief here gave us a call two weeks ago, and we opened an investigation into AgriDynamics. The EPA will be arriving tomorrow to check out the plant, and I'm following up on some other investigations, too. First, I understand you two have some information to share with me. I'm going to record this if you don't mind." She placed a tiny digital recorder on the desk. Chip sat back and listened as Jane launched into her statement.

"First Jethro died of a mysterious cause."

"Does this Jethro have a last name?"

"I don't think so. Jethro was Oscar Nelson's prize bull. Then Mabel got very sick also."

"I see, and is Mabel a cow?"

"Heavens no. Mabel is my assistant at the clinic. Here are the lab reports on the water from Beaver Creek. We determined the creek was highly polluted with toxic levels of nitrates and heavy metals." Jane handed over several lab reports. Masterson scanned them.

"And Mabel was the only person to get sick?"

"Yes, Mabel's well was an old driven one. It was on the property before her house was built, and she never replaced it with a deeper drilled one that taps into the aquifer. Hers was shallow and cracked, so the groundwater seeped into her well. She has a new one now. Also Mabel has an underlying medical condition that made her especially susceptible to the toxins."

Taking over from Jane, Chip stepped over to the county map on the office wall and followed the creek with his finger. "Beaver Creek flows behind Mabel's property and the affected farms and out past AgriDynamics. I got a hint that Hal might be up to some shady dealings."

"And that hint came from who, Mr. Collingsworth?"

"Hal was bragging to my literary agent about it one day when he had a little too much to drink. That and Owen Hansen's beating led us to suspect AgriDynamics as the source of the pollution."

"I don't suppose Owen Hansen is a bull," said Masterson.

She gave a quick smile.

"No, we think Owen Hansen may have threatened to blow the whistle on AgriDynamics," interrupted the chief.

"Where is this Owen Hansen now, Chief?"

"He moved his family to Des Moines. Think he's working at a Kum and Go there."

"So, you knew about the pollution?"

"Most of the details. We've been following up on this ever since the poisonings."

Masterson turned to Chip. "I understand you had a robbery and your computer is missing. How does your stolen computer play into this, Mr. Collingsworth?"

"I researched industrial chemicals and downloaded photos that I took when I was undercover at the plant. Someone must have observed me taking the photos on my cell phone. Then when Jane was on her stake out, she traced barrels of hazardous waste to the landfill by the creek."

"Wait a minute. You didn't call in the authorities? You went undercover and you staked out at the plant? I think you've been watching too much TV or reading too many crime novels."

The agent sighed and shook her head. "Wait, wait . . . you aren't the Collingsworth that wrote *The Cranium Killer*, are you?"

"One and the same," said Chip. "I'm surprised you heard of it."

"I get a kick out of crime stories where the FBI is involved because most writers don't have a clue as to how the bureau actually operates and what agents do. So, any idea who took the computer and where it is now?"

Chip glimpsed Jane as she gave the chief a furtive glance. The color drained from her face, and her son's words, "I don't want to go to jail," echoed in his mind. He looked at the wall map, avoiding eye contact with the agent, and silently prayed the chief would not directly mention the boys' part in the robbery, so that Jane's pain over Sven's involvement might be eased.

"We know that Hal Swanson was involved in the robbery. He had the computer, but we don't know if he still has it or if he ditched it someplace," replied the chief.

"Is there a woman named Brandy Wine that lives here in Turners Bend?" asked Masterson.

"Never heard that name before," said the chief.

"I didn't think so, the name is obvious an alias." The agent pulled a grainy photo out of her briefcase. It showed a young woman in a big sun hat and sunglasses. "Does she look familiar to any of you?" The photo was passed around.

"I can't be sure, but it could be Heather Steffenhauser, a girl I've seen with Hal a couple of times," said Jane. "She's about nineteen or twenty. Ingrid, my daughter, refers to her as 'Dad's most recent girlfriend'. Nice, huh?"

"This photo was taken from a hidden camera at a bank in the Cayman Islands. We don't have any jurisdiction over offshore island or Swiss banks, but the CIA lets us know when Americans make suspicious deposits. On this end, we like to trace where that money is coming from. Most of it is from drug cartels or illegal gain of various sorts. There's an account in the name of Brandy Wine from Iowa. We may be looking at something more than environment pollution here.

Mr. Swanson was possibly using his company to launder drug money. I know it's strange to think a wind turbine manufacturer would be involved in money laundering, but we recently had a similar case with a toy company in California."

The inspector then pulled out two more photos and showed them to Chip and Jane. They were mug shots of two tough-looking Hispanic men.

"Have you seen these guys around Turners Bend?"

Jane and Chip looked at the photos and shook their heads no.

"Well, if you do, stay clear of them and let Chief Fredrickson know. In the meantime, I'd appreciate it if you would stop your amateur sleuthing, Dr. Swanson and Mr. Collingsworth, and let us take over from here. Chief Fredrickson, of course I expect your cooperation."

JANE AND INGRID WERE STOCKING THE DRAWERS under the exam table when Agent Masterson knocked on the open office door. They knew that the chief and agents Masterson, Fuller, and Wagner had spent the last two days tracking Hal and Heather. Scuttlebutt moved through Turners Bend like wildfire. Through cell phone and credit card records the pair had been traced to the Cayman Islands. Financial records revealed that all the funds from AgriDynamics's accounts had been emptied. Hal, Heather, and the money were gone. Jane sensed that Ingrid's emotions swung between despising her father and anxiety and worry over his welfare.

"I'd like to ask you a few more questions about your husband, Dr. Swanson."

"My ex-husband. We've been divorced for many years."

"I stand corrected. Were you aware that he was defrauding the government and stashing funds offshore?"

"No. He paid his child support, and I kept out of his business."

"What about this Steffenhauser woman, did you know about her?"

"Like I said before, she's just one of a long line of Hal's girlfriends."

"She's a slut," interjected Ingrid. "She was always talking about how she and Dad were going to move to Miami and buy a yacht and sail around the world, and how Dad was going to hire a photographer to take her picture for the *Sports Illustrated* swimsuit edition. Dad was always drooling over her. It was disgusting."

"If he makes any attempt to contact you, let us know. There are more than a few federal agencies that would like to have a talk with him."

IVER AND MABEL WERE ENJOYING THE SUN on their patio, having a late afternoon Bud Light and pretzels. The old well had been sealed and a new one drilled. The days of pounding and clanking had just about driven Mabel to the edge. The well workers were gone and the yard had been destroyed in the process—patches of sod had been ripped up and the drilling equipment had left deep ruts in the ground—but the water was now safe to drink.

"I don't know, Iver, it just about broke my heart when they plowed through my lilac bushes. Here we are in May, and I should be enjoying their sweet smell. Instead I'm looking at Ground Zero. Where do we start to repair this mess?"

"Let's just pave it over and paint it green," said Iver.

"Not very funny, my dear."

A white van came up the driveway. "Oh, Iver, I bet those are the EPA guys that closed down the plant. I heard they spent all day today collecting samples of trash at the landfill. Goodness, they look like astronauts, don't they?"

Two men still in their neon yellow HAZMAT suits stepped out of the van and lumbered over to Mabel and Iver.

"You Mabel Ingebretson?" asked one of the men.

"Yes, I am, young man."

"We'd like to take a sample from the creek out back and take some soil samples from your yard. We'd also like your signed permission to look at your medical records at the Mayo Clinic."

"Certainly, you collect your samples. It's a good thing you arrived before my husband here poured concrete over the whole shebang. When you're done you come into the kitchen, I'll put on a pot of coffee and give you a nice piece of chocolate cake." When in a dubious situation, Mabel believed offering cake and coffee was always the proper thing to do.

━━ ━━ ━━ ━━ ━━

WITHIN THREE DAYS LIFE IN TURNERS BEND had been turned upside down, churned and spit out in pieces. Tongues wagged, heads shook, women cried, men swore, and pots boiled all over town. It gave Chip a lot to think about. It appeared that Hal was into a lot more than just dumping hazardous waste, just like in *Brain Freeze* where Candleworth was proving to be a complicated criminal, as well as a totally evil sleazebag.

CHAPTER THIRTY-NINE

Turners Bend
May

THE EPA VANS PULLED OUT OF TURNERS BEND followed by Agent Masterson and her two underlings. AgriDynamics was closed, and Hal and Heather had vanished into the Bermuda Triangle. The FBI, CIA, EPA and Treasury Department were all on the hunt. In the meantime, Chief Fredrickson was left to deal with local crimes, namely the robbery and its two perps, as Deputy Jim liked to call Sven and Leif.

On a fresh sunny morning in May, a small caravan left Turners Bend for Juvenile Court in the Boone County courthouse. Sven rode with Jane and Chip, Leif with his parents and the chief led the way in his squad car.

Sven sat in the back of Chip's Volvo. He was wearing his church clothes and his freshly cut hair was spiky from the gel he applied that morning. He hadn't been able to eat any breakfast, and it felt like worms were gnawing away on the lining of his stomach. "Mom, what's going to happen to me?" His voice cracked.

"I don't know, Sven. We can only hope the judge will be lenient, given this is your first offense." His mother's voice sounded more sad than hopeful.

"If they find Dad, will he go to jail?" He wasn't sure whether he wanted the answer to be yes or no. He hated his father for what he had done to their family, but he loved him, too. Love and hate were duking it out in his head and any way Sven looked at it, there wasn't going to be a winner.

"I don't know what's going to happen to your father, Sven. I imagine he'll have a lot of explaining to do to the authorities."

"He's not going to give me a car, is he?" Sven already knew the answer to his question. He wondered how he could have been so stupid, so naïve, so willing to be duped for the promise of a car.

"No, I expect not."

Looking out the car window was making Sven nauseous. He closed his eyes willing back the acid he felt rising from his stomach. He recalled driving down the dusty road to his dad's hunting shack. He had only been fourteen, but Hal let him drive. They turned up the radio full blast and sang "Country Roads" along with John Denver. Hal made him promise not to tell his mother. He never did, and he never would. That once wonderful memory was now painful. His mother would only see it as another example of Hal leading him astray.

— — — — —

LEIF SLUMPED IN THE BACKSEAT OF THE PASTOR'S Honda Civic. He was dressed all in black. Unbeknownst to his parents, the night before he had dyed his blond hair black with a red streak through it. He had done it purposely to upset them, to embarrass them. Being a preacher's kid sucked. He hated it, he hated them, he hated school, he hated his life, he hated himself. Vermin were eating away at his soul. He knew the Bible, and he was pretty sure he was destined for hell.

The tension in the car was thick, cloying, suffocating. The silence was deafening. It was periodically punctuated by whimpering sighs from his mother. Here he was on the road to perdition, and he didn't care. Or so he kept telling himself.

— — — — —

PRESIDING IN JUVENILE COURT WAS JUDGE HARRY WALLBERG, an old National Guard buddy of the chief's. Sitting on the bench had added considerable girth to the judge and his robe was more than a wee bit snug. He glasses were perched on the end of his nose, and he peered over the top of them, revealing eyebrows as bushy as caterpillars.

"Hi, Walter, nice to see you," said the judge. "See you've got two hoodlums for a closed juvenile hearing today." Aside from the judge and bailiff, the only other official present was the stone-faced court reporter.

"Well, Harry, I think you'll see by my report these two boys got in over their heads and made a couple of poor choices, but there were some extenuating circumstances."

"Okay, let's me see what they have to say for themselves." He called Sven to stand before him. He let the boy stand for a full minute, let him sweat a little, he thought.

"How'd you get involved in this robbery, son?"

"My dad asked me to get Chip's computer because he thought Chip was plotting against him. He said he'd buy me a car, if I did it for him. I recruited Leif to help me."

"For the record, your father's name is Harold Swanson III, and Chip is Charles Collingsworth III, correct?"

Sven cleared his throat. "Yes, sir."

The court reporter nodded in acknowledgement to the judge, and recorded the full names, never altering the neutrality of her face.

"The police report states you video taped the robbery and then posted it on YouTube. I'm curious as to why you would do such a thing."

"I want to be a filmmaker someday. I heard that posting your films on social networks is a good way of getting into the business. I didn't think anyone would be able to identify us from the tape."

"What do you think of your choices now?"

"They were pretty stupid, I guess, and I'm really sorry I did it."

"Okay, son, I'm going to give you 100 hours of community service under the supervision of Chief Fredrickson, and don't let me see you in this court again, you hear?" Harry remembered doing a few stupid things himself when he was Sven's age and an image of "Killroy Was Here" painted on the water tower came to mind. It looked to him like the kid was punishing himself enough.

"Yes, sir. Thank you, your honor."

Leif's answers to the judge's questions netted a series of yups, nopes and whatevers. The judge ended by asking, "Did you drink the beer you took from Mr. Collingsworth's refrigerator?"

"Like it was only a six-pack, no big deal," answered Leif.

"Well young man, let me see, you have one more year of high school. I'm giving you fourteen months of probation. You will have to report to a probation office once a month. You will finish high school and get yourself into college during that time. If I get any reports of underage drinking or drugs or any other brushes with the law, you will be doing some time. Do you understand me?"

"It's not fair that Sven got off so easy. He's the one who started this."

"Don't push it or I might change my mind. Court dismissed." He pounded his gavel and hoisted himself out of his chair. It saddened him to know this was probably not the last time he would see Leif Henderson in this courtroom.

BACK IN THE VOLVO THE ATMOSPHERE HAD LIGHTENED considerably, relief had lifted spirits and caused Sven's teenage hunger to kick in. "Mom, can we drive through Hardee's? I couldn't eat this morning, and now I'm starving. I'll buy."

Chip and Jane let him pay.

"Are you serious about this filmmaking?" asked Chip as they drove along the road back home.

"I know you want me to be a veterinarian, Mom, and it's not that I don't like animals, but I want to make films. I want to be a movie director some day. The school counselor is always saying we should follow our passion. I want to go to New York University and study film. That's what I'm passionate about. Ingrid's the one who wants to be a vet."

"I'm sorry, Sven, if I was forcing those expectations on you," said Jane. "I want both you and Ingrid to be happy with your career choices. Film is a tough way to make a living, but then so is being a vet. Maybe you can film something as part of your community service."

"Let me tell you a little story," said Chip. "My grandfather was a famous neurosurgeon, my father is a very prominent neurosurgeon and everyone, including myself, expected me to follow in their footsteps. I tried, but I was a miserable failure and became a huge disappointment to my family. My brother ended up being the neurosurgeon, and I became a bum, at least in their eyes. Only very recently have I discovered something I'm good at and some place I want to be. You're lucky to have discovered your passion so young. Maybe I can help you."

"Really, would you?" Sven was feeling like he had just been released from prison and won the lottery all in the same day.

"You finish high school and apply to NYU, then I may be able to pull some strings and get you an internship working on the filming of *The Cranium Killer*. Seems like my literary agent has some influence with Howard Glasser."

"Oh, that would be way cool, Chip."

Jane mouthed, "Thank you," to Chip.

Sven polished off two hamburgers, a large order of onion rings and a super-sized Dr. Pepper. "Mom, I'm still hungry. Can I go to the Bun, when we get back into town?"

"Speaking of my agent," interrupted Chip, "If I don't finish my second book by May 15, she'll have my head on a platter, plus I'll be financially penalized in a big way."

"Surely with all that's been happening here, she'll give you another extension," remarked Jane.

"You don't know Lucinda. She's a she-devil. If I don't have it done on time, she will chew me up and use her pitchfork to pick me out of her teeth. I'm going to go into isolation for the next few days and finish it off. I've solved the murders and the romance is a done deal, I've just got to re-write a few spots."

"A romance, huh," said Jane. "Am I in this story of yours?"

"Ah, you'll have to wait until it's published to find out, my curious friend."

Until the conversation in the car, Sven had not really paid much attention to Chip, much less noticed the relationship between Chip and his mother. Was this guy really an awesome dawg or was all the talk about helping him become a filmmaker just a way of getting at his mother? These thoughts drained some of the pleasure out of being saved from probation or worse, Juvenile Detention.

━━ ━━ ━━ ━━ ━━

CHIP STAYED HOME FOR THE NEXT TWO DAYS. He ate, drank and slept *Brain Freeze*. He read the whole book aloud to himself. He made corrections and edits. Finally on the afternoon of the ides of May, he saved it to a flash drive and was about to send it to Lucinda, when his phone rang. It was Jane.

"Chip, the tornado sirens are going off here in town. Get yourself and the dogs into your root cellar ASAP. I've got to go." She hung up.

Chip had been working so intently he failed to notice the eerie stillness that had crept into the air. He looked out the kitchen window and was transfixed by the green hue to the sky. Honey was agitated and whining. Runt was standing stiff-legged, his eyes glazed and his tongue sticking out. He peed on the floor. Chip picked him up and with Honey following, they ran outside and around the side of the house to the root cellar door. He opened the heavy slanted hatch and descended into the hole, closing the door behind him.

The root cellar was dark and dank. Cobwebs brushed his face. As he settled himself on the dirt floor, the thought of rodents crossed his mind. He shivered. Tornadoes were an unknown to him. On the East Coast he had experienced hurricanes and nor'easters, but the weather reports had always given residents several days' warning. This had come out of nowhere on a perfectly beautiful day. He waited with Runt on his lap and Honey nestled at his side.

Then he heard it. It sounded like a freight train rumbling through town. There was a loud crack followed by a thud on the cellar door. A few minutes passed . . . then silence.

At first the cellar door would not budge. He put his shoulder to it and pushed. It opened slightly, and he could see that a branch from his red maple tree had fallen across the door. He was able to squeeze out the crack and climb over the branch. His yard was full of shredded leaves. It looked like someone had taken a giant salad shooter to his trees. A few shingles from the roof were scattered around the yard. All the windows on the east side of the house had been blown out, but otherwise the house seemed to have sustained little damage. Out on the road he saw a downed telephone wire. He backed the Volvo up to the cellar door and with a towrope moved the branch and freed the dogs. He put them in the house.

He ran to the road and determined he would be able to drive around the live wire. He headed for town, figuring that help would be needed and wanting to make sure that Jane was okay.

Two tornadoes, one an F3, the other an F4, had hopped through the county. One came through Turners Bend. In its path it had chewed up hundreds of acres of corn, taken the roofs off of five houses in town, destroyed one barn and taken one precious life.

Within hours the residents of Turners Bend had mobilized into disaster teams. Temporary housing was located for the displaced families. Linemen went to work on downed power and telephone lines. A call was made to the governor for National Guard assistance and FEMA assessment.

Two days later there was a funeral at First Lutheran for the fallen farmer. The church was packed with mourners, and Chip was among them. He didn't cry until he came home, then he hummed a few bars of "For He's a Jolly Good Fellow" and added a dedication to *Brain Freeze*.

For Oscar Nelson,
A Yankee-Doodle Dandy,
Born on the Fourth of July

HE HAD MISSED HIS DEADLINE. The events surrounding the storm had taken over his time and his energy. Lucinda, who time and again had granted him leniency, had called the tornado "another trumped-up excuse." *Brain Freeze* would be published and the sale of the movie rights was pending, but Chip would lose the bulk of his earnings from the book. He began to wonder if other published authors were actually making any money on their books.

CHAPTER FORTY

Brain Freeze
Two Harbors & Duluth, Minnesota

Jo LED JOHN AND BELINDA TOWARDS THE FRONT of the building, walking down dim corridors. She had taken a few precious minutes to pull on her boots and her clothes, making her feel human again. The anesthesia had not worn off yet and the numbness in the back of her head felt strange. It made her jumpy. She peered around corners with the Glock in her hand. John said that Candleworth had cleared the building, but she wasn't taking any chances.

They were nearing the lobby when John called out. "Jo, wait up. I'm going to have to carry her. She can't keep up any longer." Belinda moaned as John whisked her up into his arms.

Jo turned around and was alarmed by the ashy hue of Belinda's face. "John, we can't take her with us when we go after Frisco. She'll never make it."

John looked down at the woman, who had passed out. "You're right. I'll call for an ambulance and stay with her. But you can't go alone . . ."

John was interrupted by a shout, "Stop right there!"

Jo whirled around and felt the weight of the last few hours lighten a bit. She came face to face with her co-workers from Minneapolis. "Took you guys long enough." They lowered their weapons.

John released a loud puff of air behind her and spoke up, "Friends of yours, I presume?"

Jo nodded. "These are special agents Michele Prentiss, Thomas Falcowski, and Jared Daniels."

She went into supervisory agent mode as she addressed her co-workers. "Don't get too comfortable, we've got things secured here, but there's still work to be done. One of the local detectives is being held hostage in a private home. It's possible that we are too late, but God, I hope not."

She pointed to the elevators. "Prentiss, there's a suspect tied up in the lower level of the building. Take him to the locals, and we'll sort out the jurisdiction details later. Falcowski and Daniels, follow me. We've lost a lot of valuable time."

She looked down at her clothing, thought about the temperatures outside and added, "Prentiss, hand me your jacket, will you?"

Special Agent Prentiss stripped off her parka and passed it to Jo. Agent Daniels watched her put on the jacket and said, "You'll need a Kevlar vest too. I've got an extra in the back of the SUV."

"Thanks." She turned to John, and pointed to Belinda. "Will they be able to remove the microchip and repair the damage to her brain?"

John frowned. "I'm not sure. We'll have to track down her husband to get permission to operate. We'll go from there."

"Good luck."

"You too. Let me know how it goes with Frisco." His blue eyes bore into hers. "Jo, be careful."

———   ———   ———   ———   ———

JO DROVE LIKE A WOMAN POSSESSED. The Highlander's all-weather tires crunched on the snow-packed roads. She knew that there was a good chance that she would not find the detective alive, but she couldn't give up. She had lost too many people she cared about on this case.

She spoke as she drove, "So briefly, here's the lay of the land. Detective Frisco of the Duluth PD is the local point person on this case." She couldn't bring herself to refer to Frisco in the past tense. *I have to believe he's still alive.*

She continued, "The detective was badly beaten and left behind with one of the perps. We're going back there now to rescue him." She glanced at Daniels, who sat in the passenger seat. "I can't stress enough about the need to use extreme caution; this is not your average bad guy." She went on to explain the microchips and mind control issues involved in the case.

Agent Falcowski leaned forward from the back seat. "What a mess. Never thought I'd be investigating microchips. It's like something right out of a science fiction movie."

"Just keep your eyes and mind open."

Jo pulled down the long driveway to Belinda's house. She parked the car in the driveway and pulled out her gun, checking the clip. Snapping it back into place, she said, "Ready?"

The other two agents checked their weapons. Daniels replied, "As we'll ever be."

They crept up the front steps, and Jo saw that the door was ajar. She called out, "FBI! Come out with your hands above your head!"

Silence, except for the creak of a branch rubbing against the house. She nodded to Agent Daniels, who shoved the door open. He repeated, "FBI!"

Jo heard it then, a low sound coming from the back of the house. She entered Belinda Peterson's house, Daniels and Falcowski one step behind her. They swept their guns from side to side, looking for a trap.

Jo moved toward the family room. There, in front of the stone fireplace, lay Detective Frisco. He was on his side, with his eyes closed. His right arm was raised above his head. She couldn't detect any movement.

Her stomach clenched. *We're too late . . .* She reached out to check his pulse and jumped when he let out a groan. Relief flooded through her. She knelt by his side. "Frisco, it's me, Agent Schwann. Frisco, can you hear me . . . do you know where Wilson is?"

"He went . . . that way." Frisco pointed towards the kitchen.

Jo patted Frisco's shoulder and said, "We'll be right back. Hang on."

She leapt up and dashed after Daniels and Falcowski, who had already moved to the kitchen entrance. The door was wide open, but she couldn't see past the kitchen island. Her heart thumped in her chest. This was the part of the job that felt like a roller coaster ride when the cart was at the edge of a precipice. She was plunging into fear and exhilaration all at the same time.

Falcowski called out. "Federal officers! Toss out your weapon."

Nothing. Jo nodded and counted silently with her fingers: One. Two. Three. When they entered the kitchen, Jo walked around to the other side of the island and saw the body of Wilson. He was sprawled out on the tiled floor, with a gun in his relaxed grip. With the agents covering her, she moved forward and kicked the gun out of his hand. When he didn't move, Jo crouched down and touched the artery on the side of his neck. Not even a thread of a pulse. Another one of Candleworth's assassins was dead.

They went back to Frisco, and as Agent Daniels called for an ambulance, Jo looked him over for bullet wounds. She released a sigh of relief when she found none. A quick check showed that he would need some stitches and when he inhaled sharply at her touch to his side, she determined he probably had some broken ribs as well. Assuming there was no internal bleeding, it looked like the detective had gotten off easy. She helped him to the couch, where he leaned into the cushions. "Frisco, you are one lucky bastard."

He chuckled in response, they sucked in a breath. "Don't make me laugh. My side hurts like I got kicked by a mule. Better get a medal for this one."

It was great to hear him joking again, even if he was in a lot of pain. "I'll see to it. So, what happened?"

Frisco's voice was wheezy as he spoke. "The guy . . . was pointing his gun at me, and . . . and then all of a sudden, he started screaming. Reached for his head, like it was going to come off or something. Wouldn't stop . . . stop yelling. He stumbled into the kitchen and I heard a crash. Didn't hear him anymore." Frisco paused for a moment, shifting his weight. His face grimaced in pain.

Jo tucked some pillows behind him. She looked over at Agent Daniels. "Any ETA on that ambulance?"

"Emergency dispatch said five minutes. They'll take him to a small hospital in Two Harbors. I'll wait at the top of the driveway and flag them in." He zipped up his parka and headed out the front door.

Jo turned her attention once again to the detective. "You scared us Frisco. Thought you were a goner."

"Would take more than a . . . a beating to put me in the grave." He smirked, and then winced as he sat up straighter on the couch. "Besides, couldn't let you have all the fun."

— — — — —

A WEEK LATER, JOHN AND JO STOOD TOGETHER on the snow-covered hill. The temperature was above average for this time of winter, but the wind off Lake Superior was sharp, and it whipped Jo's red curls around her face. Her feet were numb. She had worn a dress for this solemn occasion and her pumps provided little protection from the cold.

As Father Mike spoke, his vestments billowed beneath his parka. "We, therefore, commit the body of Belinda Carver Peterson to the ground. Earth to earth, ashes to ashes, dust to dust, in the sure and certain hope of the resurrection to eternal life."

Jo wiped the tear that slid down her cheek. It felt right that she mourn this woman whose quest to be migraine-free led her down a horrific path. Belinda's children stood on either side of their father, clutching his hands tightly. The girl, who appeared to be about ten, flinched when the first handful of cold dirt was thrown on the casket. Her younger brother buried his tear-stained face in his father's wool coat.

John gripped her gloved hand tightly in his own. She looked up to see him staring at the girl, his face drawn. Jo gave his hand an answering squeeze. *This is a good man.* She refused to think about the plane that was taking him back to Baltimore tomorrow. Jo refused to think about a lot of things when it came to John. *He has his life and I have mine.* She sighed.

Jo smiled as Father Mike pulled on his gold and green stocking cap with the large "G" and walked toward his Ford Focus. *All these years of living in Minnesota and he hasn't given up his love of the Green Bay Packers.*

After the family climbed into the waiting limo, John and Jo headed towards the Highlander. Hearing a shout, they turned to see Detective Frisco. They waited as he moved stiffly towards them. The bruises on his face had taken on a green and yellow hue, and pink skin puckered where the stitches in his chin had recently been removed. "Hey. Tough funeral, huh?" He faced John. "Peterson's husband wanted me to tell you thanks for trying to save her. You did the best you could."

John cleared his throat and looked towards the gaping hole in the ground created by the back hoe. "It wasn't enough, though, was it?"

Jo thought about that last day at NeuroDynamics. Hard to believe that only a week had passed. It seemed like months ago. John had received approval to operate on Belinda, and he removed the microchip from her head within hours of the shootings. However, it was clear the damage was beyond even his skills, and she slipped into a coma during the procedure.

On the evening following the surgery, neither he nor Jo slept, though they were both exhausted. They lay wrapped together on the bed, not moving, not talking, each lost in their own replay of the day's events. When they got the call a few days later that Belinda Peterson had passed away, Jo had wept bitterly in John's arms.

Jo snapped back to the present when Frisco turned to her and spoke. He jerked his chin at the departing limo. "Good of you to keep Belinda Peterson's name out of the papers. Not right to leave that shame to her kids."

When she thought of her own sorrow after her father's death, it was an easy decision to go light on the reputation of the former CFO of NeuroDynamics. Her family deserved the small amount of comfort Jo could provide. Michael Peterson was in shock and didn't fully comprehend. His understanding of what happened to his wife ended with the microchip causing an aneurysm. Perhaps that was best, although it would be pretty hard to keep all the details from him in the days to come. News media from all over the country were already starting to swarm.

John spoke up. "So the ME reported that Wilson died of an aneurysm?" Frisco nodded.

Jo said, "Any word yet on the location of the last test subject, Dennis Farley?"

The detective shook his head. "Nah. Gotta APB out on him. He'll turn up one of these days. 'Sides, if he's anything like the others, he won't be breathing air much longer." He looked at Jo. "How's your investigation coming along at NeuroDynamics?"

"We've got about twenty agents from the Minneapolis office going through Candleworth's offices and multiple businesses with a fine-tooth comb. We've found several additional victims from earlier tests of NC-15. Candleworth's wife is claiming she didn't know anything, but I'd bet my paycheck that she's in on it all. We'll see." That was one person Jo did not intend to go light on.

Frisco spat on the ground. "Pisses me off that bastard Candleworth got off easy. Dying was too quick for him. Would've loved to see *him* suffer from an aneurysm first."

John said, "I'm with you on that one." He reached out a hand to the detective. "Detective Frisco, it's been a pleasure."

Frisco pumped John's hand. "You too, Doc. Sure you can't stick 'round? I'm sure Agent Schwann can always find stuff for you to do." He winked at Jo.

Jo paid close attention to John's reaction. He cleared his throat. Looking at Frisco, he quietly responded, "I've got responsibilities back East." His eyes shifted to the view of Lake Superior.

The detective nodded and walked towards his car, waving over his shoulder without a glance back. He stopped when John called out, "Hey, Frisco! Can you point me in the direction of Sid's gravesite? I'd like to pay my respects."

Frisco motioned him over. John turned to Jo. "Want to join us?"

Jo shook her head. "There's someone else here I need to see. I'm overdue."

John's brows came together. He spoke quietly. "Would you like some company?"

"No, I need to do this on my own. You go on with Frisco to see Sid. I'll meet you there in a minute."

John reached over and gave her a light kiss on the cheek. "Give your dad my best." She watched him jog over to the detective.

She was shivering by the time she located her father's grave. She hadn't been to visit. The last time she was here, they were lowering his casket into the ground. Jo closed her eyes at the memory.

When she opened them again, she studied his gravestone. It was a joint marker with her mother, and it pierced her heart to look at them together. She didn't remember much about her mother, because she died when Jo was very young. For some reason, the smell of Prell shampoo always reminded her of her mother.

She swiped the snow from the arched top of the stone. "Hi, Daddy. I'm sorry I haven't come to visit sooner. It was just too hard."

Jo shifted from one foot to the other. "At first I was too angry to visit. It felt like you abandoned me. I buried my anger in books and then work."

She looked across the hill toward Lake Superior. The lift bridge and the light house could be seen in the distance. Her eyes shifted back to her father's gravestone. "Maybe it's this case and all the senseless loss of life, but I think I finally understand. The betrayal, the isolation you felt. I wish I could have taken some of that away for you."

Jo swiped at a tear that had slipped down her cold cheek. "I need some advice. I'm involved with someone. You'd like him; he's a doctor, like you.

He cares deeply for people. He makes me . . . .happy." She took a deep breath and looked across the cemetery to see John and Frisco standing together in front of Sid's grave.

"The thing is, I don't know what to do. He has a life back East and maybe I don't belong there. If I talk him into staying here, he might end up hating me for it."

Jo smiled to herself. "I'm probably getting ahead of myself. I'm not even sure if he *wants* me in his life. How do I tell him how I feel? I wish you were here to give me some advice. God, I miss you."

━━ ━━ ━━ ━━ ━━

NEITHER OF THEM SPOKE MUCH ON THE RIDE BACK to the condo. John kept thinking about Frisco's departing words at Sid's grave. "Minneapolis isn't as nice as Duluth, but hell, you'd find plenty of brain work to do there. Baltimore may have the ocean, but I bet it doesn't have another Agent Schwann." *Good point, Detective.* Frisco didn't miss a trick.

Caddy danced circles of joy when they walked through the door. John got down on one knee and scratched her behind the ears. "How are you, old girl? We've been neglecting you lately, haven't we?" He looked up at Jo. "I've made the arrangements to take her home on the plane. Hope she travels all right. She's not a young pup anymore."

John felt odd talking about home as his house back in Baltimore. For the last couple of weeks, home was this condo, here with Jo and Caddy. For the first time in his life, he realized that home was not a place, but a person. He was filled with dread every time he thought about leaving, but Jo had given no indication that she felt the same way. *She's probably ready to get back to her life.*

John didn't even know if she had a boyfriend. She was very guarded about her life in the Twin Cities. He tamped down the jealousy that filled him when he thought about Jo with another man.

They had been busy with the case all week and had avoided discussing the future. John had lent his technical expertise, and the FBI was grateful for his help. Jo spent most of her time at NeuroDynamics, directing the other agents as they dug deeper. They both were drained at the end of the day and usually fell asleep right after a quick dinner.

Last night, though, Jo had padded into his room and climbed naked into his bed. Even now, he could feel his body reacting to the memory of their passion. Her abandon. It felt like saying goodbye.

His voice was hoarse when he spoke again. "Jo, I . . ." *How do I tell her I can't leave her?*

She turned to him, tears filling her eyes. "Don't leave."

Her words shook him because they mimicked what he was thinking. "What are you saying?"

She spoke in a rush. "I know you've got responsibilities out East and that you have a life there. But . . . do you think maybe we could spend some time together after I wrap up this case?" Need and fear warred in her green eyes when she looked at him.

John reached out and pulled her to him, kissing her hard. She melted against him, and he thought he might never let go. His heart pounded so quickly. Surely she could feel it.

When he finally leaned away, he looked down at her. "I think we can work something out." He brushed a loose curl from her eyes. "I'm in love with you, Jo. I think I've been in love with you ever since you sassed me in the car on the way to Duluth."

Her smile was dazzling.

CHAPTER FORTY-ONE

Turners Bend
June

BRAIN FREEZE WAS IN THE POSSESSION OF CHIP'S new editor, Clive Edmington, a name Lucinda thought more fitting for an editor than the ill-fated Sha'desha. With time on his hands, he decided to paint his farmhouse. He enlisted Iver to help. The color he chose was a bright yellow, Jonquil.

Iver objected. "In my opinion a farmhouse should be white, just like a barn's gotta be red. Mabel thinks yellow is a 'lovely' color for your house; but Christ, do you want a 'lovely' house, Chip? Folks are going to think you're a fruitcake."

"I have to keep up my image of being Turners Bend's oddball, Iver. A writer should have a house of a different color. Plus, yellow is a happy color, and for the first time in a long time, I'm happy."

The phone rang, and Chip put down his brush and went into the house. He reached the phone on the fourth ring.

"Hello."

"Hello, is this Charles Collingsworth?"

"Sure is, and who is this?"

"This is your father's office calling. Please hold. He wishes to speak to you."

Acids immediately started to churn in his stomach. If his father was calling him, it had to be bad news. He tried to remember the last time his father had called him or if he ever had called him. It had to be something about his mother or maybe his brother. He steeled himself for the conversation.

"Chip, this is your father."

"What's happened Dad? Is it mother?"

"No, for heaven's sake, your mother's fine. She's off having lunch with the Daisies and Daffies." That's how his father always

233

referred to his mother's garden club. "We read about the tornado in Ohio and wanted to make sure you were okay."

"Iowa, Dad. I'm in Iowa. We had a couple of tornadoes rip through here, but I'm fine." This was surreal, his father calling about his welfare.

"Stewart Cushmore over in Gastrointestinal showed me the article in *Variety*. He's into community theater and fancies himself an actor. I don't normally read *Variety*, of course."

"What article? I'm not in the habit of reading *Variety* either, Dad."

"The article about Howard Glasser making your book into a movie. Says he is signing on that fellow who won all those Oscars. Also says he wants the option on your next book."

"Yes, Dad, that's true." Chip was baffled. Where was his father going with this phone call?

Dr. Collingsworth hesitated and cleared his throat. "Your mother and I wanted to let you know we're happy that you've turned your life around and finally made something of yourself."

"That hardly sounds like a compliment, Dad."

A pause. "I know I've been hard on you in the past. I realize you never would have made a decent physician. Your brother's much better suited for the profession."

"Yes, well at least Parker hasn't been a disappointment."

"I can't image why, but your mother wants to come this summer and visit you in that place."

"Turners Bend, Iowa, Dad, and that would be fine. Mother would be welcome." Chip paused; then he said something he never thought he would say. "You, too, Dad. You could come along with her if you wanted to."

"Well, we might just do that. Iowa, you say. Isn't there a famous writer's workshop at some university in Iowa? Lots of Pulitzer Prize winners from there, I believe."

"Medical crime writers don't get Pulitzers, Dad."

"Got to go, son. I've got to scrub for a neuroblastoma resection. Bye, Chip."

Chip sat in the kitchen for a few minutes trying to process the conversation with his father. He grabbed two beers from the refrigerator and went outdoors.

"Here, Iver. Let's take a break."

"Seems to me you've been taking a break, and I'm the one who's been painting."

They sat under the maple. The tree now had a weird shape after having one of its main branches amputated after the storm. The cold beer bottles sweated in their hands. The malty brew slaked their thirst and lulled them into silent companionship. Chip envisioned his mother and father in Turners Bend, maybe having dinner with Mabel and Iver. He laughed out loud.

"What's so dang funny?" asked Iver.

"Nothing much."

"Well, I'll tell you what's funny. A yellow farmhouse, that's what's funny."

AFTER PAINTING FOR MOST OF THE DAY, Chip showered, changed his clothes and headed for the town meeting at Sacred Heart Catholic Church. The parish hall was the largest meeting room in Turners Bend, and a large crowd was expected.

"Better bring in some more folding chairs from the Youth Room and unlock the Nursery. Looks like we might have some crying wee ones tonight," said Father Kelly to the church custodian. Father Kelly was only Irish on his father's side, but ever since he made a pilgrimage to Ireland a few years ago, he spoke with an Irish brogue. He was addicted to old movies with an Irish priest played by Bing Crosby or Barry Fitzgerald or best of all, Spencer Tracy. He'd watched *Boy's Town* so many times that he wore out the tape.

"*Ni neart go cur le cheile* . . . there is no strength without unity," he said in Gaelic as the townspeople entered the church.

Mayor Johnson let Flora take charge of the meeting. From experience he knew she would whether or not she had been asked. Flora was in her element.

"May I have your attention, please? The purpose of tonight's meeting is to discuss the closing of AgriDynamics and to provide the city council with ideas for future planning for our citizens. Please take note of the agenda that Mayor Johnson is passing out. We will follow strict Robert's Rules of Order. This meeting is now called to order." She pounded a gavel on the podium and the PA system screeched.

The meeting proceeded according to the agenda. A representative from the EPA explained their findings and reasons for the plant's closure. The bank president gave a brief rundown on the company's financial situation. Chief Fredrickson was called upon to present an update on the federal and local criminal investigations. Aside from a few groans, the displaced workers were polite and attentive. Restless and crying children were escorted from the room.

Flora explained how the open mike session would be controlled. "A speaker must state his or her name and then limit their comments to three minutes. Father Kelly will manage the stopwatch."

Hank was the first of many speakers. "How are we going to feed our kids and pay our mortgages? That rat Hal Swanson breaks the law, endangers us workers and takes off with all the money to bask on some yacht somewhere. Isn't fair. Seems to me the government should be giving us some aid."

The next seven speakers gave similar rants. Flora interjected, "Does anyone have a solution or constructive comment?"

Iver lumbered to the mike. He took off his cap to reveal his shaggy hat-hair. "I've got an idea, Flora. I heard that employees can buy a company and run it themselves without some fat cat taking all the profits. That's my constructive idea."

Iver's idea triggered an hour of excited discussion. Could they do it? How would it work? Who would head it up? Where would they get the money? Iver took another stroll to the mike.

"Sounds to me like Herman, being a real engineer and all, would be a damn good president. And about the start-up money, most of you know my brother Knute. When Pa died, Knute and I sold the farm, and he hoodwinked me into buying a bunch of stock in that company that's run by the young geeky guy with the glasses. Something to do with computers. If three million is enough, I reckon Knute and I can bankroll this operation."

The crowd was stunned. Then one by one the workers stood and started clapping. The clapping led to whooping, high-fiving and backslapping. Flora whacked the gavel. "Meeting adjourned."

For many, the meeting was reconvened at the Bend and continued until Joe closed it down.

CHAPTER FORTY-TWO

The Bun
June

"HOLY COW, WHAT A MORNING. We ran out of cinnamon rolls and bacon. Sorry, Chip." Bernice's hair was frizzed from the heat and humidity in the kitchen, and her white apron was splotched with grease spots and coffee stains. Today she had a pencil behind each ear. "We've been slammed with business ever since that town meeting last week. Sausage okay today?"

"Sure, Bernice. What'll you have, Herman?"

"Just coffee, Bernice, with lots of sugar and cream. I'll tell you, Chip, this has been a frigging carnival since last week. Things are happening so fast my head is spinning like a turbine. And, can you believe that Iver? Three million bucks."

"I must admit that was a shocker. The guy has a heart of gold. I just didn't know he had a stock portfolio to match."

"We've formed a steering committee and named a board of directors. The first thing we did was change the company name. AgriDynamics had too narrow a focus. We named it after Iver . . . IWP, Ingebretson Wind Power. We asked him to be on the board, but he said if it meant going to any meetings then he wasn't interested."

"I remember Hank telling me that you thought the company was behind the times and not keeping up with the industry. Have you got big plans for revamping the company?"

"China was outpacing us in new technology and innovation. There's no way we can compete with them in most areas. They're into offshore floating turbines and undersea cable installations. Plus they have developed free-flying kite turbines, which don't require a tower, and magnetic levitation systems. Awesome stuff. You've got to give them credit for advancing the industry by leaps and bounds in the past five years."

"So, what direction is IWP going to go?"

"We're going small, concentrating on portable turbines for charging batteries in remote homes, sailboats, telecom transmitters. The UK has a rooftop turbine about the size of a satellite dish for home use. We're already talking with them about the American market for that product. I'm so damn excited that I can't sleep or eat. This is going to put Turners Bend on the map."

Chief Fredrickson pulled up a chair and joined them at the table. He was shaking his head. "That deputy is going to be the death of me yet. He wants a Taser gun. I can just see it now. He'd be stunning everything that moves."

"What do you hear about Hal?" asked Herman.

"Got a call from Agent Masterson yesterday. Heather dumped him and took up with a porn photographer in Miami. She's still calling herself Brandy Wine. They picked her up, questioned her and took away her passport."

"What about Hal?" asked Chip.

"Heather spilled the beans about him. He's on his way to Colombia. The Coast Guard is tracking him through international waters right now. The CIA has alerted Colombian officials. Seems President Uribe down there is more than willing to extradite criminals back to the U.S. Unless Hal's able to disappear into the jungle first, they'll nab him. He's going to be one sorry bastard."

───── ───── ───── ───── ───── ─────

AS HE DROVE UP HIS DRIVEWAY, Chip viewed his yellow house. It did look a bit strange, but he liked it. So did Jane. They had been spending part of every day with each other and an occasional night. Flora and Mabel were both giving him some pressure about his relationship with Jane. He sometimes found himself wanting more, but a fourth marriage seemed too risky. He did make one momentous decision. Turners Bend was no longer a pit stop along the road, a place to hide out from his failures. Like the corn, he had taken root and was growing into the ripeness of life, to full maturity. Turners Bend was home, and the people of the town were his new family.

Getting started on his third novel was difficult. He had given himself direction for the story at the end of *Brain Freeze*. There was an assassin on the loose, and Dr. Goodman and Jo would be drawn into an international escapade this time around. If it weren't for Lucinda though, he would be visiting with farmers and driving around the countryside with Runt and Honey in the backseat. Lucinda, however, never tired of alternating her prodding with her threats.

Monday, June 25, 5:00 p.m.
Chip,
I'm getting damn fed up with having to remind you of your contractual agreement. Howard just signed the movie rights for Brain Freeze *based on the pre-print. Trilogies are a must these days, so get your head out of the cabbage patch and bring Mama another little story. BTW, Clive wants you to write an Epilogue for* Brain Freeze *. . . one that has your readers clamoring for the next installment. While you're working away (hint, hint) Clive and I are off to Paris for a week or two.*
Au revoir,
Lucinda

CHIP SAT DOWN AT HIS COMPUTER TO BEGIN SKETCHING out a plot for *Mind Game*. He decided to draw on the events of the past year in Turners Bend. Since Hal was rumored to be on his way to Colombia, he thought that might be the ideal location for an assassination of a crooked US businessman. Ideas began to form just as Honey began to whine.

"Hush, girl, Lucinda will chop me into dog kibble if I don't make some headway on this book."

The whining continued. Chip looked over to see Honey lying on her rug panting. "Oh, Lord, is it time for more puppies already?"

Chip called Jane, and she said it would be easier if he just brought Honey to the clinic. He loaded both dogs in the backseat of the Volvo,

240

which by now reeked of wet dog and was covered with dog hair and littered with half-chewed rawhide and leathery pig's ears.

— — — — — —

WITH HONEY SETTLED IN A WHELPING BOX, they watched and waited for the puppies to arrive.

"Chip, I can never thank you enough for what you've done for Sven. He's a different kid. Walter gave him the job of filming the Fourth of July parade coming up and the town's anniversary picnic in August. The women of the Historical Society are thrilled with the project, and they also asked him to put old photographs into a video presentation. He's thinking documentaries may be his calling.

"Leif, on the other hand, got caught smoking pot last week. Poor Christine. I think she might be headed for a nervous breakdown."

"How's Ingrid doing?"

"She spends a lot of time with her horse. I think this thing with Hal has been hard on both of the kids, but they'll work through it. They're strong."

"Like their mother." Chip held her hand as they witnessed the birth of Honey's litter of four male and two female puppies.

"French names this round, I think. How about Pierre, Claude, Jacques, and Henri for the boys and Mimi and Colette for the girls?" said Chip.

The laughed and kissed . . . and kissed some more.

EPILOGUE

Brain Freeze
Two Harbors, Minnesota and Cartegena, Columbia

JO SAT BACK IN BELINDA'S CHAIR, taking a short break from the grueling hours she had been putting in on the investigation of NeuroDynamics. They had set up shop in the former headquarters and a team of fifteen junior agents, technicians, and lab experts were turning over every bit of the place.

She munched on a sandwich that John had packed for her, before he left for Baltimore. His patients needed him back home and his expertise was no longer required on the NeuroDynamics case. Any medical loose ends for the case could be handled remotely.

Jo was glad to be busy with the case. John's absence already felt like gaping hole in her life. John had promised he'd be back in a few weeks, and she made plans for a quiet, romantic weekend upon his return.

Before climbing into his rental car this morning, John had given Jo a long, lingering kiss. She was lost in thought about that kiss when Kevin Parker, one of the technicians, rapped on the doorframe, startling her.

"Got a sec?"

Jo set the sandwich down on the desk and wiped her fingers on a napkin. She swallowed and said, "Sure, whatcha got?" She could see that Kevin was fairly dancing with excitement.

"Remember when you told us to let you know immediately if we found out anything about the missing test victim, Dennis Farley?"

She sat up straight, curiosity getting the better of her. "Oh, yeah. Frisco's still looking for him. So, what did you discover?"

"Looks like we may have found him . . . well, at least the file on the guy. We were searching Candleworth's office and came across this." He tossed a thick manila folder on the desk, next to Jo's sandwich. It landed with a heavy *thunk*.

"Why don't you give me the condensed version?"

"Um, sure. The notes indicate that Mr. Farley responded above expectations in the clinical studies, not only showing a decrease in migraine pain, but also an increased willingness to engage in criminal behavior. No stimulus of the microchip to control behavior was necessary."

Jo rubbed her temple. "So, it would appear they developed the perfect psychopath in Dennis Farley." She thought for a moment. "Does the file indicate where this lab-created monster currently resides?"

Kevin shifted on his feet at Jo's intense green stare. "Well, no. But there was a reference to his contract being activated, whatever that means."

"I'll bet they sold his services to the highest bidder. Looks like Detective Frisco was wrong when he thought this guy would wander off quietly and die." She looked up at Kevin. "Good work, Parker. Keep digging. We gotta find this guy."

— — — — —

THE ASSASSIN SAT DOWN AT THE TABLE on the cobblestone patio of the café on the Plaza Santo Domingo. He shaded his gray eyes from the glaring, tropical sun. His vision was drawn to the hot pink hibiscus flowers filling the enormous cobalt blue pots lining the café entrance. The old colonial buildings across the street were brightly painted in bold reds, blues and yellows. He watched a giggling group of tourists snapping photos standing next to a policeman.

He pulled the damp shirt away from his body; only 10:00 a.m. and already it felt like a sauna. Having arrived in Cartagena, Colombia, four days ago, he had yet to adapt to the climate. Minnesota boys were not raised at a constant ninety percent humidity level.

Juan bustled over to his table, sweaty water pitcher in hand. A large grin revealed white, even teeth against a deep tan. Dennis had the fair skin of his English ancestors, and only managed to acquire a peeling, sun-burnt nose during his stay. "Señor Olson. So wonderful to see you again! Will Mr. Nash be joining you again this morning?" Juan's English was excellent, even if his accent was strong. He poured a glass of still water and set it down in front of "Mr. Olson," the name on the passport Dennis had used to leave the United States.

Mr. Nash was an alias, too, for that matter. The one his target, Michael Turnbolt Swenson III, had used to slip out of the United States.

"Yes. He should be here shortly. We'll have *dos cervezas, por favor.*" Juan did not act as if he thought it odd to take beer orders in the morning. *I'm sure I'm not the first tourist to order alcohol before noon.* Juan ducked through the doorway, leaving Dennis alone with his thoughts.

The time was finally here. He had received a call on his international cell phone late last night. "Export likely. Proceed. Funds will be transferred upon completion."

Everything's in code with these Department of Defense guys; nothing is what it seems. No wonder I don't trust them. In this case, "export" meant extradition. As in the extradition of Michael Swenson back to the States. Dennis wasn't quite sure what the DOD guys were afraid of, but whatever it was, they wanted Swenson eliminated. He intended to find out their reasons before he completed his mission. That kind of information might be valuable.

Dennis had spent days cultivating Swenson's trust. He arranged to "bump into" Swenson in this very café upon arrival. The man was jumpy and constantly looking over his shoulder. Several cervezas, numerous shots of tequila and two whores later and they were the best of friends.

Michael Swenson was a lonely, frightened man. He was a shadow of the person in the photo Dennis carried in his bag. In the picture, Swenson was slim and handsome, just a touch of gray at the temples. Every inch the successful CEO of a Fortune 500 company. Now he looked bloated and disheveled. His former strong jaw line was fleshy and his eyes were constantly bloodshot with alcohol.

Today would be the end for Swenson. Dennis had rented a car and would suggest that the two of them do a little sightseeing. Once away from prying eyes, the assassin would dispose of his new friend. Dennis possessed the calm of a man with well thought-out plans. And one without a conscience. It had been destroyed by nanochips several weeks ago.

He found that he was good at this new career. His first two kills were with that idiot, Kurt Manning, when they were sent to retrieve the microchip from the ME's office in Duluth. *Murder had not been in the plans.* Dennis shrugged his shoulders in a philosophical way. *Messy, but in the end, necessary.* He had learned a lot that day.

And the money was great. From this job alone, he was looking at a payoff of a quarter of a million dollars. He had no idea how much NeuroDyamics had received for their part in his contract, but he really didn't care. *Just as long as I get my fair share.*

The whine of an approaching moped distracted Dennis. A pretty brunette was expertly weaving the scooter around stopped cars, her skirt hiked up to reveal toned, bronzed legs. He was instantly aroused. Before the microchip implant, he had been shy around women. As a teen, constant migraines had forced him to spend hours, even days alone in his darkened room. He had no opportunities to develop social skills. Now that the headaches were gone, he felt powerful. Like he could *take* any woman he chose. He would satisfy his lust soon.

After his job was completed, of course.

He snapped open the morning's issue of *USA Today.* He flipped through the pages until he got to the section for the individual states. Under the Minnesota heading, a small article caught his eye:

CEO wanted for questioning in Department of Defense scandal, involving SolarSource, a highly profitable alternative fuel source company based in Minneapolis. Authorities have tracked Michael Turnbolt Swenson III, to an unnamed country in South America. Sources close to the case have indicated that extradition is imminent.

Dennis whistled softly. *No wonder they're getting antsy.* SolarSource had been in the news frequently in recent years, because it had been awarded defense contracts worth billions over the last couple of years. The military wanted lightweight, portable energy sources for their vehicles and camps in Afghanistan and Iraq. Everyone was happy until the solar panels proved faulty and overpriced. There were rumors of bribery at the highest levels of the Pentagon.

Most outrageous of all, there were reports that the DOD was fully aware of the defective solar panels when they signed the purchase orders. Several documented cases had surfaced of soldiers dying as a result of the flawed panels. The case receiving the greatest share of attention occurred at a Marine outpost in the northeastern part of Afghanistan. Eighty-six

Marines were killed when their communication links were lost due to failed solar panels. Unable to call for air support, they were overrun by Taliban forces and massacred.

An ambitious Congress woman from Iowa was leading the crusade to investigate the improprieties. *Swanson's testimony would bring down a shitstorm on the heads of the DOD.*

Dennis turned back to the front page and scanned the headlines. Beneath the fold, the name "NeuroDynamics" was in bold print. He sat up straight and read quickly, horrified to discover that the man responsible for his release from a lifetime of pain had been killed. Dennis read about the FBI's investigation into "dangerous neurological experiments." Special Agent Schwann and the famous neurosurgeon, Dr. John Goodman were featured as heroes that broke the case.

For a moment, Dennis couldn't breathe. His anger was so intense that his vision dimmed. *How dare they interfere with the genius of Charles Candleworth?* Not only was the man responsible for curing him, he also provided a new, lucrative career for Dennis.

He closed his eyes and took a deep breath. Calm settled in once again. He would deal with Special Agent Schwann and Dr. Goodman personally when he returned to the States. He owed it to Candleworth.

Dennis looked up in time to see the approach of Swenson. His mind was clear and so was his mission. His work day had begun.

AFTERWORD

Fourth of July

"Knee high by the Fourth of July" is the standard measurement of corn growth, but in Turners Bend the corn was shoulder high this Fourth, making local farmers shamelessly proud. Bingo tables were set under awnings on the lawn of Sacred Heart Church, while the aroma of grilled meat wafted over from the lawn of First Lutheran. Volunteer firemen were busy setting up for the evening's firework display. Children ran around town with sparklers and squirt guns, shrieking and howling like banshees. Parade units lined up in the park. Flag bearers squeezed their bellies into musty old military uniforms. Teenage baton twirlers with ample bosoms strutted in their sequined costumes. Sven, sporting a beret, was everywhere with his video camera, yelling "Action" and "Cut."

Iver Ingebretson was the parade's Grand Marshal. Chip put down the top of his Volvo, and Iver and Mabel perched on the top of the backseat. Mabel wore her wedding suit but traded the pillbox hat for a sun visor. Iver, at Mabel's urging, had consented to wear a wild Hawaiian shirt with palm leaves and a straw hat with miniature beer cans around the brim. They had a bucket of Tootsie Pops and Jolly Ranchers to toss to the children along the parade route. Runt sat in the passenger seat, his head held high as if he were royalty. Chip slowly motored down Main Street, honking the horn and waving to friends. All of Honey's first litter and their owners were along the route, even Petunia who had traveled from Des Moines for the event. They barked their greetings to Runt, and he woofed in return.

On the sidewalk in front of the Bun stood Maribelle Collingsworth and Dr. Charles Jr., Chip's mother and father. Maribelle was dressed in a Donna Karan sundress and a huge floppy-brimmed hat with a gigantic chiffon bow. She was further decked out in three-inch high heels with peek-a-bow toes and a dozen gold bracelets. She was perfectly dressed for the Kentucky Derby or Ascot. The doctor wore white pants and a navy blazer, very nautical. They were quite an attraction. His mother waved a little American flag as Chip passed by. His father, looking uncomfortable and totally out of his element, saluted.

Jane and Ingrid were in front of the veterinary clinic with Honey. The new puppies were in a pen. Ingrid had made a sign, which read "Puppies Free to Good Homes." By the end of the day all the puppies were spoken for. Chip's mother had fallen in love with little Colette, who would soon be traveling to her new home in Baltimore.

As he drove along with the sun beating down on his bare head, Chip marveled at his happiness and his deepening sense of belonging to a place. He briefly turned to the backseat and said, "Hey, Iver, this is the good life, isn't it?"

"God's in his heaven, and all is right with the world," replied Iver.

The man never ceased to amaze Chip. *Who would have thought Iver could quote Robert Browning?*

Chip scanned the crowd on the left side of the street and spotted two men. They looked like migrant workers. Something was vaguely familiar and strangely unsettling about them, but he couldn't recall where he had seen them before. He gave them a friendly wave. Neither acknowledged his gesture, but as one of the men reached in his jeans pocket to retrieve a pair of sunglasses, Chip glimpsed a gun holster under his arm.

Book Group Discussion Guide

1. Chip Collingsworth has been married and divorced three times. With a track record like his, do you think it is possible for a person to achieve a healthy, lasting fourth marriage? What are your experiences with multiple marriages?

2. For decades Americans have sheltered money offshore in Swiss and Cayman Island banks, just as Hal Swanson does in this story. Given sufficient funds, would you consider this tax strategy? What are your reasons? Do you know of anyone who is doing this now?

3. The state of Iowa has invested heavily in alternative power with wind farms and corn ethanol. What do you see as the pros and cons of alternative energy efforts? What sacrifices would you be willing to make to reduce America's reliance on fossil fuels?

4. In *Headaches Can Be Murder*, Mabel and livestock have been victims of polluted water. How comfortable are you with drinking the water from your household tap? What are the pros and cons of switching to filtered water? Bottled water?

5. Mind control is the theme of *Brain Freeze*. Behavior can be controlled by conditioning and hypnosis, among other ways. Do you believe a person can be forced to act in a way against his or her moral values? If so, what are some examples? If not, why not?

6. Often there is a fine line between victim and abettor. In *Brain Freeze*, is Belinda a victim or did she contribute to her own downfall?

7. Cinnamon rolls are so popular in Iowa that there is an annual Cinnamon Roll Contest at the Iowa State Fair. Share with each other where you can find the best cinnamon rolls in your city or state. (Then run right out and treat yourself to one!)